All the Sad Young Men

All the Sad Young Men

F. Scott Fitzgerald

ALMA CLASSICS

ALMA CLASSICS LTD
London House
243-253 Lower Mortlake Road
Richmond
Surrey TW9 2LL
United Kingdom
www.almaclassics.com

All the Sad Young Men first published in 1926
This edition first published by Alma Books Ltd in 2013
Reprinted July 2013

Cover image © Bridgeman Art Library

Extra material © Richard Parker
Notes © Alma Classics Ltd

Printed and bound by CPI Group (UK) Ltd, Croydon, CR0 4YY

ISBN: 978-1-84749-304-0

Contents

F. Scott Fitzgerald (1896–1940)

Edward Fitzgerald,
Fitzgerald's father

Mary McQuillan Fitzgerald,
Fitzgerald's mother

Ginevra King

Zelda Fitzgerald

The Fitzgeralds' house in Montgomery, Alabama

The Fitzgeralds' grave in Rockville, Maryland,
inscribed with the closing line from *The Great Gatsby*

The original cover illustration for
All the Sad Young Men

All the Sad Young Men

The Rich Boy

B EGIN WITH AN INDIVIDUAL and before you know it you find that you have created a type; begin with a type, and you find that you have created – nothing. That is because we are all queer fish, queerer behind our faces and voices than we want anyone to know or than we know ourselves. When I hear a man proclaiming himself an "average, honest, open fellow" I feel pretty sure that he has some definite and perhaps terrible abnormality which he has agreed to conceal – and his protestation of being average and honest and open is his way of reminding himself of his misprision.

There are no types, no plurals. There is a rich boy, and this is his and not his brothers' story. All my life I have lived among his brothers, but this one has been my friend. Besides, if I wrote about his brothers I should have to begin by attacking all the lies that the poor have told about the rich and the rich have told about themselves – such a wild structure they have erected that when we pick up a book about the rich, some instinct prepares us for unreality. Even the intelligent and impassioned reporters of life have made the country of the rich as unreal as fairyland.

Let me tell you about the very rich. They are different from you and me. They possess and enjoy early, and it does something to them, makes them soft where we are hard and cynical where we are trustful, in a way that, unless you were born rich, it is very difficult to understand. They think, deep in their hearts, that they are better than we are, because we had to discover the compensations and refuges of life for ourselves. Even when they enter deep into our world or sink below us, they still think that they are better than we are. They are different. The only way I can describe young Anson Hunter is to approach him as if he were a foreigner and cling stubbornly to my point of view. If I accept his for a moment I am lost – I have nothing to show but a preposterous movie.

II

ANSON WAS THE ELDEST of six children who would some day divide a fortune of fifteen million dollars, and he reached the age of reason – is it seven? – at the beginning of the century when daring young women were already gliding along Fifth Avenue in electric "mobiles". In those days he and his brother had an English governess who spoke the language very clearly and crisply and well, so that the two boys grew to speak as she did – their words and sentences were all crisp and clear and not run together as ours are. They didn't talk exactly like English children, but acquired an accent that is peculiar to fashionable people in the city of New York.

In the summer the six children were moved from the house on 71st Street to a big estate in northern Connecticut. It was not a fashionable locality – Anson's father wanted to delay as long as possible his children's knowledge of that side of life. He was a man somewhat superior to his class, which composed New York society, and to his period, which was the snobbish and formalized vulgarity of the Gilded Age, and he wanted his sons to learn habits of concentration and have sound constitutions and grow up into right-living and successful men. He and his wife kept an eye on them as well as they were able until the two older boys went away to school, but in huge establishments this is difficult – it was much simpler in the series of small- and medium-sized houses in which my own youth was spent – I was never far out of the reach of my mother's voice, of the sense of her presence, her approval or disapproval.

Anson's first sense of his superiority came to him when he realized the half-grudging American deference that was paid to him in the Connecticut village. The parents of the boys he played with always enquired after his father and mother, and were vaguely

4

excited when their own children were asked to the Hunters' house. He accepted this as the natural state of things, and a sort of impatience with all groups of which he was not the centre – in money, in position, in authority – remained with him for the rest of his life. He disdained to struggle with other boys for precedence – he expected it to be given him freely, and when it wasn't he withdrew into his family. His family was sufficient, for in the East money is still a somewhat feudal thing, a clan-forming thing. In the snobbish West, money separates families to form "sets".

At eighteen, when he went to New Haven, Anson was tall and thick-set, with a clear complexion and a healthy colour from the ordered life he had led in school. His hair was yellow and grew in a funny way on his head, his nose was beaked – these two things kept him from being handsome – but he had a confident charm and a certain brusque style, and the upper-class men who passed him on the street knew without being told that he was a rich boy and had gone to one of the best schools. Nevertheless his very superiority kept him from being a success in college – the independence was mistaken for egotism, and the refusal to accept Yale standards with the proper awe seemed to belittle all those who had. So, long before he graduated, he began to shift the centre of his life to New York.

He was at home in New York – there was his own house with "the kind of servants you can't get any more" – and his own family, of which, because of his good humour and a certain ability to make things go, he was rapidly becoming the centre, and the debutante parties, and the correct manly world of the men's clubs, and the occasional wild spree with the gallant girls whom New Haven only knew from the fifth row. His aspirations were conventional enough – they included even the irreproachable shadow he would some day marry, but they differed from the aspirations of the majority of young men in that there was no mist over them, none of that quality which is variously known as "idealism" or "illusion". Anson accepted without reservation the world of high finance and high extravagance, of divorce and dissipation, of snobbery and of privilege. Most of our lives end as a compromise – it was as a compromise that his life began.

He and I first met in the late summer of 1917 when he was just out of Yale and, like the rest of us, was swept up into the systematized hysteria of the war. In the blue-green uniform of the naval aviation he came down to Pensacola, where the hotel orchestras played 'I'm Sorry, Dear'* and we young officers danced with the girls. Everyone liked him, and though he ran with the drinkers and wasn't an especially good pilot, even the instructors treated him with a certain respect. He was always having long talks with them in his confident, logical voice – talks which ended by his getting himself, or more frequently another officer, out of some impending trouble. He was convivial, bawdy, robustly avid for pleasure, and we were all surprised when he fell in love with a conservative and rather proper girl.

Her name was Paula Legendre, a dark, serious beauty from somewhere in California. Her family kept a winter residence just outside of town, and in spite of her primness she was enormously popular; there is a large class of men whose egotism can't endure humour in a woman. But Anson wasn't that sort, and I couldn't understand the attraction of her "sincerity" – that was the thing to say about her – for his keen and somewhat sardonic mind.

Nevertheless, they fell in love – and on her terms. He no longer joined the twilight gathering at the De Soto bar, and whenever they were seen together they were engaged in a long, serious dialogue, which must have gone on several weeks. Long afterwards he told me that it was not about anything in particular, but was composed on both sides of immature and even meaningless statements – the emotional content that gradually came to fill it grew up not out of the words but out of its enormous seriousness. It was a sort of hypnosis. Often it was interrupted, giving way to that emasculated humour we call fun; when they were alone it was resumed again – solemn, low-keyed and pitched so as to give each other a sense of unity in feeling and thought. They came to resent any interruptions of it, to be unresponsive to facetiousness about life, even to the mild cynicism of their contemporaries. They were only happy when the dialogue was going on and its seriousness bathed them like the amber glow of an open fire. Towards the end there came an interruption they did not resent – it began to be interrupted by passion.

Oddly enough Anson was as engrossed in the dialogue as she was and as profoundly affected by it, yet at the same time aware that on his side much was insincere and on hers much was merely simple. At first too, he despised her emotional simplicity as well, but with his love her nature deepened and blossomed, and he could despise it no longer. He felt that if he could enter into Paula's warm safe life he would be happy. The long preparation of the dialogue removed any constraint – he taught her some of what he had learnt from more adventurous women and she responded with a rapt holy intensity. One evening after a dance they agreed to marry and he wrote a long letter about her to his mother. The next day Paula told him that she was rich, that she had a personal fortune of nearly a million dollars.

III

IT WAS EXACTLY AS IF THEY COULD SAY "Neither of us has anything: we shall be poor together" – just as delightful that they should be rich instead. It gave them the same communion of adventure. Yet when Anson got leave in April and Paula and her mother accompanied him north, she was impressed with the standing of his family in New York and with the scale on which they lived. Alone with Anson for the first time in the rooms where he had played as a boy, she was filled with a comfortable emotion, as though she were pre-eminently safe and taken care of. The pictures of Anson in a skullcap at his first school, of Anson on horseback with the sweetheart of a mysterious forgotten summer, of Anson in a gay group of ushers and bridesmaids at a wedding, made her jealous of his life apart from her in the past, and so completely did his authoritative person seem to sum up and typify these possessions of his that she was inspired with the idea of being married immediately and returning to Pensacola as his wife.

But an immediate marriage wasn't discussed – even the engagement was to be secret until after the war. When she realized that only two days of his leave remained, her dissatisfaction crystallized in the intention of making him as unwilling to wait as she was. They were driving to the country for dinner and she determined to force the issue that night.

Now a cousin of Paula's was staying with them at the Ritz, a severe bitter girl who loved Paula but was somewhat jealous of her impressive engagement, and as Paula was late in dressing, the cousin, who wasn't going to the party, received Anson in the parlour of the suite.

Anson had met friends at five o'clock and drunk freely and indiscreetly with them for an hour. He left the Yale Club at a proper time, and his mother's chauffeur drove him to the Ritz, but his usual capacity was not in evidence, and the impact of the steam-heated sitting room made him suddenly dizzy. He knew it, and he was both amused and sorry.

Paula's cousin was twenty-five, but she was exceptionally naive, and at first failed to realize what was up. She had never met Anson before, and she was surprised when he mumbled strange information and nearly fell off his chair, but until Paula appeared it didn't occur to her that what she had taken for the odour of a dry-cleaned uniform was really whiskey. But Paula understood as soon as she appeared; her only thought was to get Anson away before her mother saw him, and at the look in her eyes the cousin understood too.

When Paula and Anson descended to the limousine they found two men inside, both asleep; they were the men with whom he had been drinking at the Yale Club, and they were also going to the party. He had entirely forgotten their presence in the car. On the way to Hempstead they awoke and sang. Some of the songs were rough, and though Paula tried to reconcile herself to the fact that Anson had few verbal inhibitions, her lips tightened with shame and distaste.

Back at the hotel the cousin, confused and agitated, considered the incident, and then walked into Mrs Legendre's bedroom saying: "Isn't he funny?"

"Who is funny?"

"Why – Mr Hunter. He seemed so funny."

Mrs Legendre looked at her sharply.

"How is he funny?"

"Why, he said he was French. I didn't know he was French."

"That's absurd. You must have misunderstood." She smiled. "It was a joke."

The cousin shook her head stubbornly.

"No. He said he was brought up in France. He said he couldn't speak any English and that's why he couldn't talk to me. And he couldn't!"

Mrs Legendre looked away with impatience just as the cousin added thoughtfully, "Perhaps it was because he was so drunk," and walked out of the room.

This curious report was true. Anson, finding his voice thick and uncontrollable, had taken the unusual refuge of announcing that he spoke no English. Years afterwards he used to tell that part of the story, and he invariably communicated the uproarious laughter which the memory aroused in him.

Five times in the next hour Mrs Legendre tried to get Hempstead on the phone. When she succeeded there was a ten-minute delay before she heard Paula's voice on the wire.

"Cousin Jo told me Anson was intoxicated."

"Oh, no…"

"Oh, yes. Cousin Jo says he was intoxicated. He told her he was French and fell off his chair and behaved as if he was very intoxicated. I don't want you to come home with him."

"Mother, he's all right! Please don't worry about—"

"But I do worry. I think it's dreadful. I want you to promise me not to come home with him."

"I'll take care of it, Mother…"

"I don't want you to come home with him."

"All right, Mother. Goodbye."

"Be sure now, Paula. Ask someone to bring you."

Deliberately Paula took the receiver from her ear and hung it up. Her face was flushed with helpless annoyance. Anson was stretched asleep out in a bedroom upstairs, while the dinner party below was proceeding lamely towards conclusion.

The hour's drive had sobered him somewhat – his arrival was merely hilarious – and Paula hoped that the evening was not spoilt after all, but two imprudent cocktails before dinner completed the disaster. He talked boisterously and somewhat offensively to the party at large for fifteen minutes and then slid silently under the table, like a man in an old print – but, unlike an old print, it was rather horrible without being at all quaint. None of the young girls present remarked upon the incident – it seemed to merit only silence. His uncle and two other men carried him upstairs, and it was just after this that Paula was called to the phone.

An hour later Anson awoke in a fog of nervous agony, through which he perceived after a moment the figure of his Uncle Robert standing by the door.

"…I said are you better?"

"What?"

"Do you feel better, old man?"

"Terrible," said Anson.

"I'm going to try you on another bromo-seltzer. If you can hold it down, it'll do you good to sleep."

With an effort, Anson slid his legs from the bed and stood up.

"I'm all right," he said dully.

"Take it easy."

"I thin' if you gave me a glassbrandy I could go downstairs."

"Oh, no—"

"Yes, that's the only thin'. I'm all right now… I suppose I'm in dutch dow' there."

"They know you're a little under the weather," said his uncle deprecatingly. "But don't worry about it. Schuyler didn't even get here. He passed away in the locker room over at the Links."

Indifferent to any opinion, except Paula's, Anson was nevertheless determined to save the debris of the evening, but when after a cold bath he made his appearance most of the party had already left. Paula got up immediately to go home.

In the limousine the old serious dialogue began. She had known that he drank, she admitted, but she had never expected anything like this – it seemed to her that perhaps they were not suited to each other after all. Their ideas about life were too different, and so forth. When she finished speaking, Anson spoke in turn, very soberly. Then Paula said she'd have to think it over; she wouldn't decide tonight; she was not angry but she was terribly sorry. Nor would she let him come into the hotel with her, but just before she got out of the car she leant and kissed him unhappily on the cheek.

The next afternoon Anson had a long talk with Mrs Legendre while Paula sat listening in silence. It was agreed that Paula was to brood over the incident for a proper period and then, if mother and daughter thought it best, they would follow Anson to Pensacola. On his part he apologized with sincerity and dignity – that was all; with every card in her hand Mrs Legendre was unable to establish any advantage over him. He made no promises, showed no humility, only delivered a few serious comments on life which brought him off with rather a moral superiority at the end. When they came south three weeks later, neither Anson in his satisfaction nor Paula in her relief at the reunion realized that the psychological moment had passed for ever.

IV

H E DOMINATED AND ATTRACTED HER and at the same time filled her with anxiety. Confused by his mixture of solidity and self-indulgence, of sentiment and cynicism – incongruities which her gentle mind was unable to resolve – Paula grew to think of him as two alternating personalities. When she saw him alone, or at a formal party, or with his casual inferiors, she felt a tremendous pride in his strong attractive presence, the paternal, understanding stature of his mind. In other company she became uneasy when what had been a fine imperviousness to mere gentility showed its other face. The other face was gross, humorous, reckless of everything but pleasure. It startled her mind temporarily away from him, even led her into a short covert experiment with an old beau, but it was no use – after four months of Anson's enveloping vitality there was an anaemic pallor in all other men.

In July he was ordered abroad, and their tenderness and desire reached a crescendo. Paula considered a last-minute marriage – decided against it only because there were always cocktails on his breath now, but the parting itself made her physically ill with grief. After his departure she wrote him long letters of regret for the days of love they had missed by waiting. In August Anson's plane slipped down into the North Sea. He was pulled onto a destroyer after a night in the water and sent to hospital with pneumonia; the armistice was signed before he was finally sent home.

Then, with every opportunity given back to them, with no material obstacle to overcome, the secret weavings of their temperaments came between them, drying up their kisses and their tears, making their voices less loud to one another, muffling the intimate chatter of their hearts until the old communication was only possible by letters from far away. One afternoon a society reporter waited for two hours in the Hunters' house for a confirmation of their engagement. Anson denied it; nevertheless an early issue carried the report as a leading paragraph – they were "constantly seen together at Southampton, Hot Springs and Tuxedo Park". But the serious dialogue had turned a corner into a long, sustained quarrel, and the affair was almost played out. Anson got drunk flagrantly and missed an engagement with her, whereupon Paula made certain behaviouristic demands. His despair was helpless before his pride and his knowledge of himself: the engagement was definitely broken.

"Dearest," said their letters now, "Dearest, Dearest, when I wake up in the middle of the night and realize that after all it was not to be, I feel that I want to die. I can't go on living any more. Perhaps when we meet this summer we may talk things over and decide differently – we were so excited and sad that day and I don't feel that I can live all my life without you. You speak of other people. Don't you know there are no other people for me but only you…"

But as Paula drifted here and there around the East she would sometimes mention her gaieties to make him wonder. Anson was too acute to wonder. When he saw a man's name in her letters he felt more sure of her and a little disdainful – he was always superior to such things. But he still hoped that they would some day marry.

Meanwhile he plunged vigorously into all the movement and glitter of post-bellum New York, entering a brokerage house, joining half a dozen clubs, dancing late, and moving in three worlds – his own world, the world of young Yale graduates and that section of the half-world which rests one end on Broadway. But there was always a thorough and infractible eight hours devoted to his work in Wall Street, where the combination of his influential family connection, his sharp intelligence and his abundance of sheer physical energy brought him almost immediately forward. He had one of those invaluable minds with partitions in it; sometimes he appeared at his office refreshed by less than an hour's sleep, but such occurrences were rare. So early as 1920 his income in salary and commissions exceeded twelve thousand dollars.

As the Yale tradition slipped into the past, he became more and more of a popular figure among his classmates in New York, more popular than he had ever been in college. He lived in a great house and had the means of introducing young men into other great houses. Moreover, his life already seemed secure, while theirs, for the most part, had arrived again at precarious beginnings. They commenced to turn to him for amusement and escape, and Anson responded readily, taking pleasure in helping people and arranging their affairs.

There were no men in Paula's letters now, but a note of tenderness ran through them that had not been there before. From several sources he heard that she had "a heavy beau", Lowell Thayer, a Bostonian of wealth and position, and though he was sure she still loved him, it made him uneasy to think that he might lose her after all. Save for one unsatisfactory day she had not been in New York for almost five months, and as the rumours multiplied he became increasingly anxious to see her. In February he took his vacation and went down to Florida.

Palm Beach sprawled plump and opulent between the sparkling sapphire of Lake Worth, flawed here and there by houseboats at anchor and the great turquoise bar of the Atlantic Ocean. The huge bulks of the Breakers and the Royal Poinciana rose as twin paunches from the bright level of the sand and around them clustered the Dancing Glade, Bradley's House of Chance and a dozen modistes and milliners with goods at triple prices from New York. Upon the trellised veranda of the Breakers two hundred women stepped right, stepped left, wheeled and slid in that then celebrated callisthenic known as the double shuffle, while in half-time to the music two thousand bracelets clicked up and down on two hundred arms.

At the Everglades Club after dark, Paula and Lowell Thayer and Anson and a casual fourth played bridge with hot cards. It seemed to Anson that her kind serious face was wan and tired – she had been around now for four, five years. He had known her for three.

"Two spades."

"Cigarette?... Oh, I beg your pardon. By me."

"By."

"I'll double three spades."

There were a dozen tables of bridge in the room, which was filling up with smoke. Anson's eyes met Paula's, held them persistently, even when Thayer's glance fell between them...

"What was bid?" he asked abstractedly.

"Rose of Washington Square,"

sang the young people in the corners:

"I'm withering there
In basement air..."*

The smoke banked like fog, and the opening of a door filled the room with blown swirls of ectoplasm. Little Bright Eyes streaked past the tables seeking Mr Conan Doyle among the Englishmen who were posing as Englishmen about the lobby.

"You could cut it with a knife."

"...cut it with a knife."

"...a knife."

At the end of the rubber Paula suddenly got up and spoke to Anson in a tense, low voice. With scarcely a glance at Lowell Thayer, they walked out the door and descended a long flight of stone steps – in a moment they were walking hand in hand along the moonlit beach.

"Darling, darling..." They embraced recklessly, passionately, in a shadow... Then Paula drew back her face to let his lips say what she wanted to hear – she could feel the words forming as they kissed again... Again she broke away, listening, but as he pulled her close once more she realized that he had said nothing – only "*Darling! Darling!*" in that deep, sad whisper that always made her cry. Humbly, obediently, her emotions yielded to him and the tears streamed down her face, but her heart kept on crying: "Ask me – oh, Anson, dearest, ask me!"

"Paula... *Paula!*"

The words wrung her heart like hands, and Anson feeling her tremble knew that emotion was enough. He need say no more, commit their destinies to no practical enigma. Why should he, when he might hold her so, biding his own time, for another year – for ever? He was considering them both, her more than himself. For a moment, when she said suddenly that she must go back to her hotel, he hesitated, thinking first, "This is the moment after all," and then: "No, let it wait – she is mine..."

He had forgotten that Paula too was worn away inside with the strain of three years. Her mood passed for ever in the night.

He went back to New York next morning filled with a certain restless dissatisfaction. Late in April, without warning, he received a telegram from Bar Harbor in which Paula told him that she was engaged to Lowell Thayer and that they would be married immediately in Boston. What he never really believed could happen had happened at last.

Anson filled himself with whiskey that morning and, going to the office, carried on his work without a break – rather with a fear of what would happen if he stopped. In the evening he went out as usual, saying nothing of what had occurred; he was cordial, humorous, unabstracted. But one thing he could not help – for three days, in any place, in any company, he would suddenly bend his head into his hands and cry like a child.

V

IN 1922 WHEN ANSON WENT ABROAD with the junior partner to investigate some London loans, the journey intimated that he was to be taken into the firm. He was twenty-seven now, a little heavy without being definitely stout, and with a manner older than his years. Old people and young people liked him and trusted him, and mothers felt safe when their daughters were in his charge, for he had a way, when he came into a room, of putting himself on a footing with the oldest and most conservative people there. "You and I," he seemed to say, "we're solid. We understand."

He had an instinctive and rather charitable knowledge of the weaknesses of men and women, and, like a priest, it made him the more concerned for the maintenance of outward forms. It was typical of him that every Sunday morning he taught in a fashionable Episcopal Sunday school – even though a cold shower and a quick change into a cutaway coat were all that separated him from the wild night before.

After his father's death he was the practical head of his family and, in effect, guided the destinies of the younger children. Through a complication his authority did not extend to his father's estate, which was administrated by his Uncle Robert, who was the horsey member of the family, a good-natured, hard-drinking member of that set which centres about Wheatley Hills.

Uncle Robert and his wife, Edna, had been great friends of Anson's youth, and the former was disappointed when his nephew's superiority failed to take a horsey form. He backed him for a city club which was the most difficult in America to enter – one could only join if one's family had "helped to build up New York" (or, in other words, were rich before 1880) – and when Anson, after his election, neglected it for the Yale Club, Uncle Robert gave him a little talk on the subject. But when on top of that Anson declined to enter Robert Hunter's own conservative and somewhat neglected brokerage house, his manner grew cooler. Like a primary teacher who has taught all he knew, he slipped out of Anson's life.

There were so many friends in Anson's life – scarcely one for whom he had not done some unusual kindness and scarcely one whom he did not occasionally embarrass by his bursts of rough conversation or his habit of getting drunk whenever and however he liked. It annoyed him when anyone else blundered in that regard – about his own lapses he was always humorous. Odd things happened to him, and he told them with infectious laughter.

I was working in New York that spring, and I used to lunch with him at the Yale Club, which my university was sharing until the completion of our own. I had read of Paula's marriage, and one afternoon, when I asked him about her, something moved him to tell me the story. After that he frequently invited me to family dinners at his house and behaved as though there was a special relation between us, as though with his confidence a little of that consuming memory had passed into me.

I found that despite the trusting mothers, his attitude towards girls was not indiscriminately protective. It was up to the girl – if she showed an inclination towards looseness, she must take care of herself, even with him.

"Life," he would explain sometimes, "has made a cynic of me."

By life he meant Paula. Sometimes, especially when he was drinking, it became a little twisted in his mind, and he thought that she had callously thrown him over.

This "cynicism", or rather his realization that naturally fast girls were not worth sparing, led to his affair with Dolly Karger. It wasn't his only affair in those years, but it came nearest to touching him deeply, and it had a profound effect upon his attitude towards life.

Dolly was the daughter of a notorious "publicist" who had married into society. She herself grew up into the Junior League, came out at the Plaza, and went to the Assembly;* and only a few old families like the Hunters could question whether or not she "belonged", for her picture was often in the papers, and she had more enviable attention than many girls who undoubtedly did. She was dark-haired with carmine lips and a high lovely colour which she concealed under pinkish-grey powder all through the first year out, because high colour was unfashionable – Victorian pale was the thing to be. She wore black, severe suits and stood with her hands in her pockets, leaning a little forward, with a humorous restraint on her face. She danced exquisitely – better than anything she liked to dance – better than anything except making love. Since she was ten she had always been in love, and usually with some boy who didn't respond to her. Those who did – and there were many – bored her after a brief encounter, but for her failures she reserved the warmest spot in her heart. When she met them she would always try once more – sometimes she succeeded, more often she failed.

It never occurred to this gypsy of the unattainable that there was a certain resemblance in those who refused to love her – they shared a hard intuition that saw through to her weakness, not a weakness of emotion but a weakness of rudder. Anson perceived this when he first met her, less than a month after Paula's marriage. He was drinking rather heavily, and he pretended for a week that he was falling in love with her. Then he dropped her abruptly and forgot – immediately he took up the commanding position in her heart.

Like so many girls of that day Dolly was slackly and indiscreetly wild. The unconventionality of a slightly older generation had been simply one facet of a post-war movement to discredit obsolete manners – Dolly's was both older and shabbier, and she saw in Anson the two extremes which the emotionally shiftless woman seeks, an abandon to indulgence alternating with a protective strength. In his character she felt both the sybarite and the solid rock, and these two satisfied every need of her nature.

She felt that it was going to be difficult, but she mistook the reason – she thought that Anson and his family expected a more spectacular marriage, but she guessed immediately that her advantage lay in his tendency to drink.

They met at the large debutante dances, but as her infatuation increased they managed to be more and more together. Like most mothers Mrs Karger believed that Anson was exceptionally reliable, so she allowed Dolly to go with him to distant country clubs and suburban houses without enquiring closely into their activities or questioning her explanations when they came in late. At first these explanations might have been accurate, but Dolly's worldly ideas of capturing Anson were soon engulfed in the rising sweep of her emotion. Kisses in the back of taxis and motor cars were no longer enough; they did a curious thing:

They dropped out of their world for a while and made another world just beneath it where Anson's tippling and Dolly's irregular hours would be less noticed and commented on. It was composed, this world, of varying elements – several of Anson's Yale friends and their wives, two or three young brokers and bond salesmen and a handful of unattached men, fresh from college, with money and a propensity to dissipation. What this world lacked in spaciousness and scale it made up for by allowing them a liberty that it scarcely permitted itself. Moreover it centred around them and permitted Dolly the pleasure of a faint condescension – a pleasure which Anson, whose whole life was a condescension from the certitudes of his childhood, was unable to share.

He was not in love with her, and in the long feverish winter of their affair he frequently told her so. In the spring he was weary – he wanted to renew his life at some other source – moreover, he saw that either he must break with her now or accept the responsibility of a definite seduction. Her family's encouraging attitude precipitated his decision – one evening when Mr Karger knocked discreetly at the library door to announce that he had left a bottle of old brandy in the dining room, Anson felt that life was hemming him in. That night he wrote her a short letter in which he told her that he was going on his vacation and that in view of all the circumstances they had better meet no more.

It was June. His family had closed up the house and gone to the country, so he was living temporarily at the Yale Club. I had heard about his affair with Dolly as it developed – accounts salted with humour, for he despised unstable women, and granted them no place in the social edifice in which he believed – and when he told me that night that he was definitely breaking with her I was glad. I had seen Dolly here and there and each time with a feeling of pity at the hopelessness of her struggle, and of shame at knowing so much about her that I had no right to know. She was what is known as "a pretty little thing", but there was a certain reckless-ness which rather fascinated me. Her dedication to the goddess of waste would have been less obvious had she been less spirited – she would most certainly throw herself away, but I was glad when I heard that the sacrifice would not be consummated in my sight.

Anson was going to leave the letter of farewell at her house next morning. It was one of the few houses left open in the Fifth Avenue district, and he knew that the Kargers, acting upon erroneous information from Dolly, had forgone a trip abroad to give their daughter her chance. As he stepped out the door of the Yale Club into Vanderbilt Avenue the postman passed him, and he followed back inside. The first letter that caught his eye was in Dolly's hand.

He knew what it would be – a lonely and tragic monologue, full of the reproaches he knew, the invoked memories, the "I wonder ifs" – all the immemorial intimacies that he had communicated to Paula Legendre in what seemed another age. Thumbing over some bills, he brought it on top again and opened it. To his surprise it was a short, somewhat formal note, which said that Dolly would be unable to go to the country with him for the weekend, because Perry Hull from Chicago had unexpectedly come to town. It added that Anson had brought this on himself: "…if I felt that you loved me as I love you I would go with you at any time any place, but Perry is *so* nice, and he so much wants me to marry him…"

Anson smiled contemptuously – he had had experience with such decoy epistles. Moreover, he knew how Dolly had laboured over this plan, probably sent for the faithful Perry and calculated the time of his arrival – even laboured over the note so that it would make him jealous without driving him away. Like most compromises it had neither force nor vitality, but only a timorous despair.

Suddenly he was angry. He sat down in the lobby and read it again. Then he went to the phone, called Dolly and told her in his clear, compelling voice that he had received her note and would call for her at five o'clock as they had previously planned. Scarcely waiting for the pretended uncertainty of her "Perhaps I can see you for an hour", he hung up the receiver and went down to his office. On the way he tore his own letter into bits and dropped it in the street.

He was not jealous – she meant nothing to him – but at her pathetic ruse everything stubborn and self-indulgent in him came to the surface. It was a presumption from a mental inferior and it could not be overlooked. If she wanted to know to whom she belonged she would see.

He was on the doorstep at quarter-past five. Dolly was dressed for the street, and he listened in silence to the paragraph of "I can only see you for an hour", which she had begun on the phone.

"Put on your hat, Dolly," he said, "we'll take a walk."

They strolled up Madison Avenue and over to Fifth, while Anson's shirt dampened upon his portly body in the deep heat. He talked little, scolding her, making no love to her, but before they had walked six blocks she was his again, apologizing for the note, offering not to see Perry at all as an atonement, offering anything. She thought that he had come because he was beginning to love her.

"I'm hot," he said when they reached 71st Street. "This is a winter suit. If I stop by the house and change, would you mind waiting for me downstairs? I'll only be a minute."

She was happy; the intimacy of his being hot, of any physical fact about him, thrilled her. When they came to the iron-grated door and Anson took out his key she experienced a sort of delight.

Downstairs it was dark, and after he ascended in the lift Dolly raised a curtain and looked out through opaque lace at the houses over the way. She heard the lift machinery stop and, with the notion of teasing him, pressed the button that brought it down. Then on what was more than an impulse she got into it and sent it up to what she guessed was his floor.

"Anson," she called, laughing a little.

"Just a minute," he answered from his bedroom... then after a brief delay: "Now you can come in."

He had changed and was buttoning his vest.

"This is my room," he said lightly. "How do you like it?"

She caught sight of Paula's picture on the wall and stared at it in fascination, just as Paula had stared at the pictures of Anson's childish sweethearts five years before. She knew something about Paula – sometimes she tortured herself with fragments of the story.

Suddenly she came close to Anson, raising her arms. They embraced. Outside the area window a soft artificial twilight already hovered, though the sun was still bright on a back roof across the way. In half an hour the room would be quite dark. The uncalculated opportunity overwhelmed them, made them both breathless, and they clung more closely. It was imminent, inevitable. Still holding one another, they raised their heads – their eyes fell together upon Paula's picture, staring down at them from the wall.

Suddenly Anson dropped his arms and, sitting down at his desk, tried the drawer with a bunch of keys.

"Like a drink?" he asked in a gruff voice.

"No, Anson."

He poured himself half a tumbler of whiskey, swallowed it and then opened the door into the hall.

"Come on," he said.

Dolly hesitated.

"Anson – I'm going to the country with you tonight, after all. You understand that, don't you?"

"Of course," he answered brusquely.

In Dolly's car they rode out to Long Island, closer in their emotions than they had ever been before. They knew what would happen – not with Paula's face to remind them that something was lacking, but when they were alone in the still-hot Long Island night that did not care.

The estate in Port Washington where they were to spend the weekend belonged to a cousin of Anson's who had married a Montana copper operator. An interminable drive began at the lodge and twisted under imported poplar saplings towards a huge, pink, Spanish house. Anson had often visited there before.

After dinner they danced at the Linx Club. About midnight Anson assured himself that his cousins would not leave before two – then he explained that Dolly was tired; he would take her home and return to the dance later. Trembling a little with excitement they got into a borrowed car together and drove to Port Washington. As they reached the lodge he stopped and spoke to the nightwatchman.

"When are you making a round, Carl?"

"Right away."

"Then you'll be here till everybody's in?"

"Yes, sir."

"All right. Listen: if any automobile, no matter whose it is, turns in at this gate, I want you to phone the house immediately." He put a five-dollar bill into Carl's hand. "Is that clear?"

"Yes, Mr Anson." Being of the Old World, he neither winked nor smiled. Yet Dolly sat with her face turned slightly away.

Anson had a key. Once inside he poured a drink for both of them – Dolly left hers untouched – then he ascertained definitely the location of the phone, and found that it was within easy hearing distance of their rooms, both of which were on the first floor.

Five minutes later he knocked at the door of Dolly's room.

"Anson?" He went in, closing the door behind him. She was in bed, leaning up anxiously with elbows on the pillow; sitting beside her he took her in his arms.

"Anson, darling."

He didn't answer.

"Anson... Anson! I love you... Say you love me. Say it now – can't you say it now? Even if you don't mean it?"

He did not listen. Over her head he perceived that the picture of Paula was hanging here upon this wall.

He got up and went close to it. The frame gleamed faintly with thrice-reflected moonlight – within was a blurred shadow of a face that he saw he did not know. Almost sobbing, he turned around and stared with abomination at the little figure on the bed.

"This is all foolishness," he said thickly. "I don't know what I was thinking about. I don't love you and you'd better wait for somebody that loves you. I don't love you a bit, can't you understand?"

His voice broke and he went hurriedly out. Back in the salon he was pouring himself a drink with uneasy fingers, when the front door opened suddenly, and his cousin came in.

"Why, Anson, I hear Dolly's sick," she began solicitously. "I hear she's sick..."

"It was nothing," he interrupted, raising his voice so that it would carry into Dolly's room. "She was a little tired. She went to bed."

For a long time afterwards Anson believed that a protective God sometimes interfered in human affairs. But Dolly Karger, lying awake and staring at the ceiling, never again believed in anything at all.

VI

WHEN DOLLY MARRIED during the following autumn, Anson was in London on business. Like Paula's marriage, it was sudden, but it affected him in a different way. At first he felt that it was funny and had an inclination to laugh when he thought of it. Later it depressed him – it made him feel old.

There was something repetitive about it – why, Paula and Dolly had belonged to different generations. He had a foretaste of the sensation of a man of forty who hears that the daughter of an old flame has married. He wired congratulations and, as was not the case with Paula, they were sincere – he had never really hoped that Paula would be happy.

When he returned to New York, he was made a partner in the firm, and as his responsibilities increased he had less time on his hands. The refusal of a life-insurance company to issue him a policy made such an impression on him that he stopped drinking for a year and claimed that he felt better physically, though I think he missed the convivial recounting of those Celliniesque* adventures which, in his early twenties, had played such a part in his life. But he never abandoned the Yale Club. He was a figure there, a personality, and the tendency of his class, who were now seven years out of college, to drift away to more sober haunts was checked by his presence.

His day was never too full nor his mind too weary to give any sort of aid to anyone who asked it. What had been done at first through pride and superiority had become a habit and a passion. And there was always something – a younger brother in trouble at New Haven, a quarrel to be patched up between a friend and his wife, a position to be found for this man, an investment for that. But his specialty was the solving of problems for young married people. Young married people fascinated him and their apartments were almost sacred to him – he knew the story of their love affair, advised them where to live and how, and remembered their babies' names. Towards young wives his attitude was circumspect: he never abused the trust which their husbands – strangely enough in view of his unconcealed irregularities – invariably reposed in him.

He came to take a vicarious pleasure in happy marriages and to be inspired to an almost equally pleasant melancholy by those that went astray. Not a season passed that he did not witness the collapse of an affair that perhaps he himself had fathered. When Paula was divorced and almost immediately remarried to another Bostonian, he talked about her to me all one afternoon. He would never love anyone as he had loved Paula, but he insisted that he no longer cared.

"I'll never marry," he came to say. "I've seen too much of it, and I know a happy marriage is a very rare thing. Besides, I'm too old."

But he did believe in marriage. Like all men who spring from a happy and successful marriage, he believed in it passionately – nothing he had seen would change his belief, his cynicism dissolved upon it like air. But he did really believe he was too old. At twenty-eight he began to accept with equanimity the prospect of marrying without romantic love; he resolutely chose a New York girl of his own class, pretty, intelligent, congenial, above reproach – and set about falling in love with her. The things he had said to Paula with sincerity, to other girls with grace, he could no longer say at all without smiling, or with the force necessary to convince.

"When I'm forty," he told his friends, "I'll be ripe. I'll fall for some chorus girl like the rest."

Nevertheless he persisted in his attempt. His mother wanted to see him married, and he could now well afford it – he had a seat on the stock exchange, and his earned income came to twenty-five thousand a year. The idea was agreeable: when his friends – he spent most of his time with the set he and Dolly had evolved – closed themselves in behind domestic doors at night, he no longer rejoiced in his freedom. He even wondered if he should have married Dolly. Not even Paula had loved him more, and he was learning the rarity, in a single life, of encountering true emotion.

Just as this mood began to creep over him a disquieting story reached his ear. His Aunt Edna, a woman just this side of forty, was carrying on an open intrigue with a dissolute, hard-drinking young man named Cary Sloane. Everyone knew of it except Anson's uncle Robert, who for fifteen years had talked long in clubs and taken his wife for granted.

Anson heard the story again and again with increasing annoyance. Something of his old feeling for his uncle came back to him, a feeling that was more than personal, a reversion towards that family solidarity on which he had based his pride. His intuition singled out the essential point of the affair, which was that his uncle shouldn't be hurt. It was his first experiment in unsolicited meddling, but with his knowledge of Edna's character he felt that he could handle the matter better than a district judge, or his uncle.

His uncle was in Hot Springs. Anson traced down the sources of the scandal so that there should be no possibility of mistake, and then he called Edna and asked her to lunch with him at the Plaza next day. Something in his tone must have frightened her, for she was reluctant, but he insisted, putting off the date until she had no excuse for refusing.

She met him at the appointed time in the Plaza lobby, a lovely, faded, grey-eyed blonde in a coat of Russian sable. Five great rings, cold with diamonds and emeralds, sparkled on her slender hands. It occurred to Anson that it was his father's intelligence and not his uncle's that had earned the fur and the stones, the rich brilliance that buoyed up her passing beauty.

Though Edna scented his hostility, she was unprepared for the directness of his approach.

"Edna, I'm astonished at the way you've been acting," he said in a strong, frank voice. "At first I couldn't believe it."

"Believe what?" she demanded sharply.

"You needn't pretend with me, Edna. I'm talking about Cary Sloane. Aside from any other consideration, I didn't think you could treat Uncle Robert—"

"Now look here, Anson—" she began angrily, but his peremptory voice broke through hers:

"—and your children in such a way. You've been married eighteen years, and you're old enough to know better."

"You can't talk to me like that! You—"

"Yes I can. Uncle Robert has always been my best friend." He was tremendously moved. He felt a real distress about his uncle, about his three young cousins.

Edna stood up, leaving her crab-flake cocktail untasted.

"This is the silliest thing—"

"Very well, if you won't listen to me I'll go to Uncle Robert and tell him the whole story – he's bound to hear it sooner or later. And afterwards I'll go to old Moses Sloane."

Edna faltered back into her chair.

"Don't talk so loud," she begged him. Her eyes blurred with tears. "You have no idea how your voice carries. You might have chosen a less public place to make all these crazy accusations."

He didn't answer.

"Oh, you never liked me, I know," she went on. "You're just taking advantage of some silly gossip to try and break up the only interesting friendship I've ever had. What did I ever do to make you hate me so?"

Still Anson waited. There would be the appeal to his chivalry, then to his pity, finally to his superior sophistication – when he had shouldered his way through all these there would be admissions, and he could come to grips with her. By being silent, by being impervious, by returning constantly to his main weapon, which was his own true emotion, he bullied her into frantic despair as the luncheon hour slipped away. At two o'clock she took out a mirror and a handkerchief, shined away the marks of her tears and powdered the slight hollows where they had lain. She had agreed to meet him at her own house at five.

When he arrived she was stretched on a chaise longue which was covered with cretonne for the summer, and the tears he had called up at luncheon seemed still to be standing in her eyes. Then he was aware of Cary Sloane's dark anxious presence upon the cold hearth.

"What's this idea of yours?" broke out Sloane immediately. "I understand you invited Edna to lunch and then threatened her on the basis of some cheap scandal."

Anson sat down.

"I have no reason to think it's only scandal."

"I hear you're going to take it to Robert Hunter and to my father."

Anson nodded.

"Either you break it off – or I will," he said.

"What God-damned business is it of yours, Hunter?"

"Don't lose your temper, Cary," said Edna nervously. "It's only a question of showing him how absurd—"

"For one thing, it's my name that's being handed around," interrupted Anson. "That's all that concerns you, Cary."

"Edna isn't a member of your family."

"She most certainly is!" His anger mounted. "Why – she owes this house and the rings on her fingers to my father's brains. When Uncle Robert married her she didn't have a penny."

They all looked at the rings as if they had a significant bearing on the situation. Edna made a gesture to take them from her hand.

"I guess they're not the only rings in the world," said Sloane.

"Oh, this is absurd," cried Edna. "Anson, will you listen to me? I've found out how the silly story started. It was a maid I discharged who went right to the Chilicheffs – all these Russians pump things out of their servants and then put a false meaning on them." She brought down her fist angrily on the table. "And after Tom lent them the limousine for a whole month when we were south last winter—"

"Do you see?" demanded Sloane eagerly. "This maid got hold of the wrong end of the thing. She knew that Edna and I were friends, and she carried it to the Chilicheffs. In Russia they assume that if a man and a woman—"

He enlarged the theme to a disquisition upon social relations in the Caucasus.

"If that's the case it better be explained to Uncle Robert," said Anson drily, "so that when the rumours do reach him he'll know they're not true."

Adopting the method he had followed with Edna at luncheon he let them explain it all away. He knew that they were guilty and that presently they would cross the line from explanation into justification and convict themselves more definitely than he could ever do. By seven they had taken the desperate step of telling him the truth – Robert Hunter's neglect, Edna's empty life, the casual dalliance that had flamed up into passion – but like so many true stories it had the misfortune of being old, and its enfeebled body beat helplessly against the armour of Anson's will. The threat to go to Sloane's father sealed their helplessness, for the latter, a retired cotton broker out of Alabama, was a notorious fundamentalist who controlled his son by a rigid allowance and the promise that at his next vagary the allowance would stop for ever.

They dined at a small French restaurant and the discussion continued – at one time Sloane resorted to physical threats, a little later they were both imploring him to give them time. But Anson was obdurate. He saw that Edna was breaking up and that her spirit must not be refreshed by any renewal of their passion.

At two o'clock in a small nightclub on 53d Street, Edna's nerves suddenly collapsed and she cried to go home. Sloane had been drinking heavily all evening, and he was faintly maudlin, leaning on the table and weeping a little with his face in his hands. Quickly Anson gave them his terms. Sloane was to leave town for six months, and he must be gone within forty-eight hours. When he returned there was to be no resumption of the affair, but at the end of a year Edna might, if she wished, tell Robert Hunter that she wanted a divorce and go about it in the usual way.

He paused, gaining confidence from their faces for his final word.

"Or there's another thing you can do," he said slowly. "If Edna wants to leave her children, there's nothing I can do to prevent your running off together."

"I want to go home!" cried Edna again. "Oh, haven't you done enough to us for one day?"

Outside it was dark, save for a blurred glow from Sixth Avenue down the street. In that light those two who had been lovers looked for the last time into each other's tragic faces, realizing that between them there was not enough youth and strength to avert their eternal parting. Sloane walked suddenly off down the street and Anson tapped a dozing taxi driver on the arm.

It was almost four: there was a patient flow of cleaning water along the ghostly pavement of Fifth Avenue, and the shadows of two night women flitted over the dark façade of St Thomas's Church. Then the desolate shrubbery of Central Park, where Anson had often played as a child, and the mounting numbers, significant as names, of the marching streets. This was his city, he thought, where his name had flourished through five generations. No change could alter the permanence of its place here, for change itself was the essential substratum by which he and those of his name identified themselves with the spirit of New York. Resourcefulness and a powerful will – for his threats in weaker hands would have been less than nothing – had beaten the gathering dust from his uncle's name, from the name of his family, from even this shivering figure that sat beside him in the car.

Cary Sloane's body was found next morning on the lower shelf of a pillar of Queensboro Bridge. In the darkness and in his excitement he had thought that it was the water flowing black beneath him, but in less than a second it made no possible difference – unless he had planned to think one last thought of Edna, and call out her name as he struggled feebly in the water.

VII

A NSON NEVER BLAMED HIMSELF for his part in this affair – the situation which brought it about had not been of his making. But the just suffer with the unjust, and he found that his oldest and somehow his most precious friendship was over. He never knew what distorted story Edna told, but he was welcome in his uncle's house no longer.

Just before Christmas Mrs Hunter retired to a select Episcopal heaven, and Anson became the responsible head of his family. An unmarried aunt who had lived with them for years ran the house and attempted with helpless inefficiency to chaperone the younger girls. All the children were less self-reliant than Anson, more conventional both in their virtues and in their shortcomings. Mrs Hunter's death had postponed the debut of one daughter and the wedding of another. Also it had taken something deeply material from all of them, for with her passing the quiet, expensive superiority of the Hunters came to an end.

For one thing, the estate, considerably diminished by two inheritance taxes and soon to be divided among six children, was not a notable fortune any more. Anson saw a tendency in his youngest sisters to speak rather respectfully of families that hadn't "existed" twenty years ago. His own feeling of precedence was not echoed in them – sometimes they were conventionally snobbish, that was all. For another thing, this was the last summer they would spend on the Connecticut estate; the clamour against it was too loud: "Who wants to waste the best months of the year shut up in that dead old town?" Reluctantly he yielded – the house would go into the market in the fall, and next summer they would rent a smaller place in Westchester County. It was a step down from the expensive simplicity of his father's idea, and while he sympathized with the revolt it also annoyed him; during his mother's lifetime he had gone up there at least every other weekend – even in the gayest summers.

Yet he himself was part of this change, and his strong instinct for life had turned him in his twenties from the hollow obsequies of that abortive leisure class. He did not see this clearly – he still felt that there was a norm, a standard of society. But there was no norm, it was doubtful if there had ever been a true norm in New York. The few who still paid and fought to enter a particular set succeeded only to find that as a society it scarcely functioned – or, what was more alarming, that the Bohemia from which they fled sat above them at table.

At twenty-nine Anson's chief concern was his own growing loneliness. He was sure now that he would never marry. The number of weddings at which he had officiated as best man or usher was past all counting – there was a drawer at home that bulged with the official neckties of this or that wedding party, neckties standing for romances that had not endured a year, for couples who had passed completely from his life. Scarf pins, gold pencils, cuff buttons, presents from a generation of grooms had passed through his jewel box and been lost – and with every ceremony he was less and less able to imagine himself in the groom's place. Under his hearty goodwill towards all those marriages there was despair about his own.

And as he neared thirty he became not a little depressed at the inroads that marriage, especially lately, had made upon his friendships. Groups of people had a disconcerting tendency to dissolve and disappear. The men from his own college – and it was upon them he had expended the most time and affection – were the most elusive of all. Most of them were drawn deep into domesticity, two were dead, one lived abroad, one was in Hollywood writing continuities for pictures that Anson went faithfully to see.

Most of them, however, were permanent commuters with an intricate family life centring around some suburban country club, and it was from these that he felt his estrangement most keenly.

In the early days of their married life they had all needed him; he gave them advice about their slim finances, he exorcised their doubts about the advisability of bringing a baby into two rooms and a bath, especially he stood for the great world outside. But now their financial troubles were in the past and the fearfully expected child had evolved into an absorbing family. They were always glad to see old Anson, but they dressed up for him and tried to impress him with their present importance, and kept their troubles to themselves. They needed him no longer.

A few weeks before his thirtieth birthday the last of his early and intimate friends was married. Anson acted in his usual role of best man, gave his usual silver tea service, and went down to the usual Homeric to say goodbye. It was a hot Friday afternoon in May, and as he walked from the pier he realized that Saturday closing had begun and he was free until Monday morning.

"Go where?" he asked himself.

The Yale Club, of course: bridge until dinner, then four or five raw cocktails in somebody's room and a pleasant confused evening. He regretted that this afternoon's groom wouldn't be along – they had always been able to cram so much into such nights: they knew how to attach women and how to get rid of them, how much consideration any girl deserved from their intelligent hedonism. A party was an adjusted thing – you took certain girls to certain places and spent just so much on their amusement; you drank a little, not much more than you ought to drink, and at a certain time in the morning you stood up and said you were going home. You avoided college boys, sponges, future engagements, fights, sentiment and indiscretions. That was the way it was done. All the rest was dissipation.

In the morning you were never violently sorry – you made no resolutions, but if you had overdone it and your heart was slightly out of order, you went on the wagon for a few days without saying anything about it, and waited until an accumulation of nervous boredom projected you into another party.

The lobby of the Yale Club was unpopulated. In the bar three very young alumni looked up at him, momentarily and without curiosity.

"Hello there, Oscar," he said to the bartender. "Mr Cahill been around this afternoon?"

"Mr Cahill's gone to New Haven."

"Oh... that so?"

"Gone to the ball game. Lot of men gone up."

Anson looked once again into the lobby, considered for a moment and then walked out and over to Fifth Avenue. From the broad window of one of his clubs – one that he had scarcely visited in five years – a grey man with watery eyes stared down at him. Anson looked quickly away – that figure sitting in vacant resignation, in supercilious solitude, depressed him. He stopped and, retracing his steps, started over 47th Street towards Teak Warden's apartment. Teak and his wife had once been his most familiar friends – it was a household where he and Dolly Karger had been used to go in the days of their affair. But Teak had taken to drink, and his wife had remarked publicly that Anson was a bad influence on him. The remark reached Anson in an exaggerated form – when it was finally cleared up, the delicate spell of intimacy was broken, never to be renewed.

"Is Mr Warden at home?" he enquired.

"They've gone to the country."

The fact unexpectedly cut at him. They were gone to the country and he hadn't known. Two years before he would have known the date, the hour, come up at the last moment for a final drink and planned his first visit to them. Now they had gone without a word.

Anson looked at his watch and considered a weekend with his family, but the only train was a local that would jolt through the aggressive heat for three hours. And tomorrow in the country, and Sunday – he was in no mood for porch bridge with polite undergraduates, and dancing after dinner at a rural roadhouse, a diminutive of gaiety which his father had estimated too well.

"Oh no," he said to himself... "No."

He was a dignified, impressive young man, rather stout now, but otherwise unmarked by dissipation. He could have been cast for a pillar of something – at times you were sure it was not society, at others nothing else – for the law, for the Church. He stood for a few minutes motionless on the sidewalk in front of a 47th Street apartment house; for almost the first time in his life he had nothing whatever to do.

Then he began to walk briskly up Fifth Avenue, as if he had just been reminded of an important engagement there. The necessity of dissimulation is one of the few characteristics that we share with dogs, and I think of Anson on that day as some well-bred specimen who had been disappointed at a familiar back door. He was going to see Nick, once a fashionable bartender in demand at all private dances, and now employed in cooling non-alcoholic champagne among the labyrinthine cellars of the Plaza Hotel.

"Nick," he said, "what's happened to everything?"

"Dead," Nick said.

"Make me a whiskey sour." Anson handed a pint bottle over the counter. "Nick, the girls are different; I had a little girl in Brooklyn and she got married last week without letting me know."

"That a fact? Ha-ha-ha," responded Nick diplomatically. "Slipped it over on you."

"Absolutely," said Anson. "And I was out with her the night before."

"Ha-ha-ha," said Nick, "ha-ha-ha!"

"Do you remember the wedding, Nick, in Hot Springs where I had the waiters and the musicians singing 'God Save the King'?"

"Now where was that, Mr Hunter?" Nick concentrated doubtfully. "Seems to me that was—"

"Next time they were back for more, and I began to wonder how much I'd paid them," continued Anson.

"—seems to me that was at Mr Trenholm's wedding."

"Don't know him," said Anson decisively. He was offended that a strange name should intrude upon his reminiscences; Nick perceived this.

"Naw – aw..." he admitted. "I ought to know that. It was one of *your* crowd – Brakins... Baker—"

"Bicker Baker," said Anson responsively. "They put me in a hearse after it was over and covered me up with flowers and drove me away."

"Ha-ha-ha," said Nick. "Ha-ha-ha."

Nick's simulation of the old family servant paled presently and Anson went upstairs to the lobby. He looked around – his eyes met the glance of an unfamiliar clerk at the desk, then fell upon a flower from the morning's marriage hesitating in the mouth of a brass cuspidor. He went out and walked slowly towards the blood-red sun over Columbus Circle. Suddenly he turned around and, retracing his steps to the Plaza, immured himself in a telephone booth.

Later he said that he tried to get me three times that afternoon, that he tried everyone who might be in New York – men and girls he had not seen for years, an artist's model of his college days whose faded number was still in his address book – Central told him that even the exchange existed no longer. At length his quest roved into the country, and he held brief disappointing conversations with emphatic butlers and maids. So-and-so was out, riding, swimming, playing golf, sailed to Europe last week. Who shall I say phoned?

It was intolerable that he should pass the evening alone – the private reckonings, which one plans for a moment of leisure, lose every charm when the solitude is enforced. There were always women of a sort, but the ones he knew had temporarily vanished, and to pass a New York evening in the hired company of a stranger never occurred to him – he would have considered that that was something shameful and secret, the diversion of a travelling salesman in a strange town.

Anson paid the telephone bill – the girl tried unsuccessfully to joke with him about its size – and for the second time that afternoon started to leave the Plaza and go he knew not where. Near the revolving door the figure of a woman, obviously with child, stood sideways to the light – a sheer beige cape fluttered at her shoulders when the door turned and, each time, she looked impatiently towards it as if she were weary of waiting. At the first sight of her a strong nervous thrill of familiarity went over him, but not until he was within five feet of her did he realize that it was Paula.

"Why, Anson Hunter!"

His heart turned over.

"Why, Paula—"

"Why, this is wonderful. I can't believe it, *Anson*!"

She took both his hands and he saw in the freedom of the gesture that the memory of him had lost poignancy to her. But not to him – he felt that old mood that she evoked in him stealing over his brain, that gentleness with which he had always met her optimism as if afraid to mar its surface.

"We're at Rye for the summer. Pete had to come east on business – you know of course I'm Mrs Peter Hagerty now – so we brought the children and took a house. You've got to come out and see us."

"Can I?" he asked directly. "When?"

"When you like. Here's Pete." The revolving door functioned, giving up a fine tall man of thirty with a tanned face and a trim moustache. His immaculate fitness made a sharp contrast with Anson's increasing bulk, which was obvious under the faintly tight cutaway coat.

"You oughtn't to be standing," said Hagerty to his wife. "Let's sit down here." He indicated lobby chairs, but Paula hesitated.

"I've got to go right home," she said. "Anson, why don't you – why don't you come out and have dinner with us tonight? We're just getting settled, but if you can stand that—"

Hagerty confirmed the invitation cordially. "Come out for the night."

Their car waited in front of the hotel, and Paula with a tired gesture sank back against silk cushions in the corner.

"There's so much I want to talk to you about," she said. "It seems hopeless."

"I want to hear about you."

"Well" – she smiled at Hagerty – "that would take a long time too. I have three children – by my first marriage. The oldest is five, then four, then three." She smiled again. "I didn't waste much time having them, did I?"

"Boys?"

"A boy and two girls. Then – oh, a lot of things happened, and I got a divorce in Paris a year ago and married Pete. That's all – except that I'm awfully happy."

In Rye they drove up to a large house near the beach club, from which there issued presently three dark slim children who broke from an English governess and approached them with an esoteric cry. Abstractedly and with difficulty Paula took each one into her arms, a caress which they accepted stiffly, as they had evidently been told not to bump into Mummy. Even against their fresh faces Paula's skin showed scarcely any weariness – for all her physical languor she seemed younger than when he had last seen her at Palm Beach seven years ago.

At dinner she was preoccupied, and afterwards, during the homage to the radio, she lay with closed eyes on the sofa, until Anson wondered if his presence at this time were not an intrusion. But at nine o'clock, when Hagerty rose and said pleasantly that he was going to leave them by themselves for a while, she began to talk slowly about herself and the past.

"My first baby," she said, "the one we call Darling, the biggest little girl – I wanted to die when I knew I was going to have her, because Lowell was like a stranger to me. It didn't seem as though she could be my own. I wrote you a letter and tore it up. Oh, you were *so* bad to me, Anson."

It was the dialogue again, rising and falling. Anson felt a sudden quickening of memory.

"Weren't you engaged once?" she asked. "A girl named Dolly something?"

"I wasn't ever engaged. I tried to be engaged, but I never loved anybody but you, Paula."

"Oh," she said. Then after a moment: "This baby is the first one I ever really wanted. You see, I'm in love now – at last."

He didn't answer, shocked at the treachery of her remembrance. She must have seen that the "at last" bruised him, for she continued:

"I was infatuated with you, Anson – you could make me do anything you liked. But we wouldn't have been happy. I'm not smart enough for you. I don't like things to be complicated like you do." She paused. "You'll never settle down," she said.

The phrase struck at him from behind – it was an accusation that of all accusations he had never merited.

"I could settle down if women were different," he said. "If I didn't understand so much about them, if women didn't spoil you for other women, if they had only a little pride. If I could go to sleep for a while and wake up into a home that was really mine – why, that's what I'm made for, Paula, that's what women have seen in me and liked in me. It's only that I can't get through the preliminaries any more."

Hagerty came in a little before eleven; after a whiskey Paula stood up and announced that she was going to bed. She went over and stood by her husband.

"Where did you go, dearest?" she demanded.

"I had a drink with Ed Saunders."

"I was worried. I thought maybe you'd run away."

She rested her head against his coat.

"He's sweet, isn't he, Anson?" she demanded.

"Absolutely," said Anson, laughing.

She raised her face to her husband.

"Well, I'm ready," she said. She turned to Anson: "Do you want to see our family gymnastic stunt?"

"Yes," he said in an interested voice.

"All right. Here we go!"

Hagerty picked her up easily in his arms.

"This is called the family acrobatic stunt," said Paula. "He carries me upstairs. Isn't it sweet of him?"

"Yes," said Anson.

Hagerty bent his head slightly until his face touched Paula's.

"And I love him," she said. "I've just been telling you, haven't I, Anson?"

"Yes," he said.

"He's the dearest thing that ever lived in this world, aren't you, darling?… Well, goodnight. Here we go. Isn't he strong?"

"Yes," Anson said.

"You'll find a pair of Pete's pyjamas laid out for you. Sweet dreams – see you at breakfast."

"Yes," Anson said.

VIII

THE OLDER MEMBERS of the firm insisted that Anson should go abroad for the summer. He had scarcely had a vacation in seven years, they said. He was stale and needed a change. Anson resisted.

"If I go," he declared, "I won't come back any more."

"That's absurd, old man. You'll be back in three months with all this depression gone. Fit as ever."

"No." He shook his head stubbornly. "If I stop, I won't go back to work. If I stop, that means I've given up – I'm through."

"We'll take a chance on that. Stay six months if you like – we're not afraid you'll leave us. Why, you'd be miserable if you didn't work."

They arranged his passage for him. They liked Anson – everyone liked Anson – and the change that had been coming over him cast a sort of pall over the office. The enthusiasm that had invariably signalled up business, the consideration towards his equals and his inferiors, the lift of his vital presence – within the past four months his intense nervousness had melted down these qualities into the fussy pessimism of a man of forty. On every transaction in which he was involved he acted as a drag and a strain.

"If I go I'll never come back," he said.

Three days before he sailed, Paula Legendre Hagerty died in childbirth. I was with him a great deal then, for we were crossing together, but for the first time in our friendship he told me not a word of how he felt, nor did I see the slightest sign of emotion. His chief preoccupation was with the fact that he was thirty years old – he would turn the conversation to the point where he could remind you of it and then fall silent, as if he assumed that the statement would start a chain of thought sufficient to itself. Like his partners I was amazed at the change in him, and I was glad when the *Paris* moved off into the wet space between the worlds, leaving his principality behind.

"How about a drink?" he suggested.

We walked into the bar with that defiant feeling that characterizes the day of departure and ordered four martinis. After one cocktail a change came over him – he suddenly reached across and slapped my knee with the first joviality I had seen him exhibit for months.

"Did you see that girl in the red tam?" he demanded. "The one with the high colour who had the two police dogs down to bid her goodbye."

"She's pretty," I agreed.

"I looked her up in the purser's office and found out that she's alone. I'm going down to see the steward in a few minutes. We'll have dinner with her tonight."

After a while he left me and within an hour he was walking up and down the deck with her, talking to her in his strong, clear voice. Her red tam was a bright spot of colour against the steel-green sea, and from time to time she looked up with a flashing bob of her head, and smiled with amusement and interest, and anticipation. At dinner we had champagne, and were very joyous – afterwards Anson ran the pool with infectious gusto, and several people who had seen me with him asked me his name. He and the girl were talking and laughing together on a lounge in the bar when I went to bed.

I saw less of him on the trip than I had hoped. He wanted to arrange a foursome, but there was no one available, so I saw him only at meals. Sometimes, though, he would have a cocktail in the bar, and he told me about the girl in the red tam, and his adventures with her, making them all bizarre and amusing, as he had a way of doing, and I was glad that he was himself again, or at least the self that I knew, and with which I felt at home. I don't think he was ever happy unless someone was in love with him, responding to him like filings to a magnet, helping him to explain himself, promising him something. What it was I do not know. Perhaps they promised that there would always be women in the world who would spend their brightest, freshest, rarest hours to nurse and protect that superiority he cherished in his heart.

Winter Dreams

I

SOME OF THE CADDIES were poor as sin and lived in one-room houses with a neurasthenic cow in the front yard, but Dexter Green's father owned the second-best grocery store in Black Bear – the best one was "The Hub", patronized by the wealthy people from Sherry Island – and Dexter caddied only for pocket money.

In the fall when the days became crisp and grey and the long Minnesota winter shut down like the white lid of a box, Dexter's skis moved over the snow that hid the fairways of the golf course. At these times the country gave him a feeling of profound melancholy – it offended him that the links should lie in enforced fallowness, haunted by ragged sparrows for the long season. It was dreary, too, that on the tees where the gay colours fluttered in summer there were now only the desolate sandboxes knee-deep in crusted ice. When he crossed the hills the wind blew cold as misery, and if the sun was out he tramped with his eyes squinted up against the hard dimensionless glare.

In April the winter ceased abruptly. The snow ran down into Black Bear Lake scarcely tarrying for the early golfers to brave the season with red and black balls. Without elation, without an interval of moist glory, the cold was gone.

Dexter knew that there was something dismal about this northern spring, just as he knew there was something gorgeous about the fall. Fall made him clench his hands and tremble and repeat idiotic sentences to himself and make brisk abrupt gestures of command to imaginary audiences and armies. October filled him with hope which November raised to a sort of ecstatic triumph, and in this mood the fleeting brilliant impressions of the summer at Sherry Island were ready grist to his mill. He became a golf champion and defeated Mr T.A. Hedrick in a marvellous match played a hundred times over the fairways of his imagination, a match each detail of which he changed about untiringly – sometimes he won with almost laughable ease, sometimes he came up magnificently from behind. Again, stepping from a Pierce-Arrow automobile, like Mr Mortimer Jones, he strolled frigidly into the lounge of the Sherry Island Golf Club – or perhaps, surrounded by an admiring crowd, he gave an exhibition of fancy diving from the springboard of the club raft… Among those who watched him in open-mouthed wonder was Mr Mortimer Jones.

And one day it came to pass that Mr Jones – himself and not his ghost – came up to Dexter with tears in his eyes and said that Dexter was the — best caddy in the club and wouldn't he decide not to quit if Mr Jones made it worth his while, because every other — caddy in the club lost one ball a hole for him – regularly.

"No, sir," said Dexter decisively, "I don't want to caddy any more." Then, after a pause: "I'm too old."

"You're not more than fourteen. Why the devil did you decide just this morning that you wanted to quit? You promised that next week you'd go over to the state tournament with me."

"I decided I was too old."

Dexter handed in his "A Class" badge, collected what money was due him from the caddy master and walked home to Black Bear Village.

"The best — caddy I ever saw," shouted Mr Mortimer Jones over a drink that afternoon. "Never lost a ball! Willing! Intelligent! Quiet! Honest! Grateful!…"

The little girl who had done this was eleven – beautifully ugly as little girls are apt to be who are destined after a few years to be inexpressibly lovely and bring no end of misery to a great number of men. The spark, however, was perceptible. There was a general ungodliness in the way her lips twisted down at the corners when she smiled and in the – Heaven help us! – in the almost passionate quality of her eyes. Vitality is born early in such women. It was utterly in evidence now, shining through her thin frame in a sort of glow.

She had come eagerly out onto the course at nine o'clock with a white linen nurse and five small new golf clubs in a white canvas bag which the nurse was carrying. When Dexter first saw her she was standing by the caddy house, rather ill at ease and trying to conceal the fact by engaging her nurse in an obviously unnatural conversation graced by startling and irrelevant grimaces from herself.

"Well, it's certainly a nice day, Hilda," Dexter heard her say. She drew down the corners of her mouth, smiled and glanced furtively around, her eyes in transit falling for an instant on Dexter.

Then to the nurse:

"Well, I guess there aren't very many people out here this morning, are there?"

The smile again – radiant, blatantly artificial – convincing.

"I don't know what we're supposed to do now," said the nurse, looking nowhere in particular.

"Oh, that's all right. I'll fix it up."

Dexter stood perfectly still, his mouth slightly ajar. He knew that if he moved forward a step his stare would be in her line of vision – if he moved backwards he would lose his full view of her face. For a moment he had not realized how young she was. Now he remembered having seen her several times the year before – in bloomers.

Suddenly, involuntarily, he laughed, a short abrupt laugh – then, startled by himself, he turned and began to walk quickly away.

"Boy!"

Dexter stopped.

"Boy—"

Beyond question he was addressed. Not only that, but he was treated to that absurd smile, that preposterous smile – the memory of which at least a dozen men were to carry into middle age.

"Boy, do you know where the golf teacher is?"

"He's giving a lesson."

"Well, do you know where the caddy master is?"

"He isn't here yet this morning."

"Oh." For a moment this baffled her. She stood alternately on her right and left foot.

44

"We'd like to get a caddy," said the nurse. "Mrs Mortimer Jones sent us out to play golf and we don't know how without we get a caddy."

Here she was stopped by an ominous glance from Miss Jones, followed immediately by the smile.

"There aren't any caddies here except me," said Dexter to the nurse, "and I got to stay here in charge until the caddy master gets here."

"Oh."

Miss Jones and her retinue now withdrew and at a proper distance from Dexter became involved in a heated conversation, which was concluded by Miss Jones taking one of the clubs and hitting it on the ground with violence. For further emphasis she raised it again and was about to bring it down smartly upon the nurse's bosom, when the nurse seized the club and twisted it from her hands.

"You damn little mean old *thing*!" cried Miss Jones wildly.

Another argument ensued. Realizing that the elements of the comedy were implied in the scene, Dexter several times began to laugh, but each time restrained the laugh before it reached audibility. He could not resist the monstrous conviction that the little girl was justified in beating the nurse.

The situation was resolved by the fortuitous appearance of the caddy master, who was appealed to immediately by the nurse.

"Miss Jones is to have a little caddy and this one says he can't go."

"Mr McKenna said I was to wait here till you came," said Dexter quickly.

"Well, he's here now." Miss Jones smiled cheerfully at the caddy master. Then she dropped her bag and set off at a haughty mince towards the first tee.

"Well?" The caddymaster turned to Dexter. "What you standing there like a dummy for? Go pick up the young lady's clubs."

"I don't think I'll go out today," said Dexter.

"You don't—"

"I think I'll quit."

The enormity of his decision frightened him. He was a favourite caddy and the thirty dollars a month he earned through the summer were not to be made elsewhere around the lake. But he had received a strong emotional shock and his perturbation required a violent and immediate outlet.

It is not so simple as that, either. As so frequently would be the case in the future, Dexter was unconsciously dictated to by his winter dreams.

II

NOW, OF COURSE, THE QUALITY and the seasonability of these winter dreams varied, but the stuff of them remained. They persuaded Dexter several years later to pass up a business course at the state university – his father, prospering now, would have paid his way – for the precarious advantage of attending an older and more famous university in the East, where he was bothered by his scanty funds. But do not get the impression, because his winter dreams happened to be concerned at first with musings on the rich, that there was anything merely snobbish in the boy. He wanted not association with glittering things and glittering people – he wanted the glittering things themselves. Often he reached out for the best without knowing why he wanted it – and sometimes he ran up against the mysterious denials and prohibitions in which life indulges. It is with one of those denials and not with his career as a whole that this story deals.

He made money. It was rather amazing. After college he went to the city from which Black Bear Lake draws its wealthy patrons. When he was only twenty-three and had been there not quite two years, there were already people who liked to say: "Now *there's* a boy..." All about him rich men's sons were peddling bonds precariously, or investing patrimonies precariously, or plodding through the two dozen volumes of the *George Washington Commercial Course*, but Dexter borrowed a thousand dollars on his college degree and his confident mouth, and bought a partnership in a laundry.

It was a small laundry when he went into it, but Dexter made a specialty of learning how the English washed fine woollen golf stockings without shrinking them, and within a year he was catering to the trade that wore knickerbockers. Men were insisting that their Shetland hose and sweaters go to his laundry just as they had insisted on a caddy who could find golf balls. A little later he was doing their wives' lingerie as well – and running five branches in different parts of the city. Before he was twenty-seven he owned the largest string of laundries in his section of the country. It was then that he sold out and went to New York. But the part of his story that concerns us goes back to the days when he was making his first big success.

When he was twenty-three Mr Hart – one of the grey-haired men who liked to say "Now there's a boy" – gave him a guest card to the Sherry Island Golf Club for a weekend. So he signed his name one day on the register, and that afternoon played golf in a foursome with Mr Hart and Mr Sandwood and Mr T.A. Hedrick. He did not consider it necessary to remark that he had once carried Mr Hart's bag over these same links and that he knew every trap and gully with his eyes shut – but he found himself glancing at the four caddies who trailed them, trying to catch a gleam or gesture that would remind him of himself, that would lessen the gap which lay between his present and his past.

It was a curious day, slashed abruptly with fleeting, familiar impressions. One minute he had the sense of being a trespasser – in the next he was impressed by the tremendous superiority he felt towards Mr T.A. Hedrick, who was a bore and not even a good golfer any more.

Then, because of a ball Mr Hart lost near the fifteenth green, an enormous thing happened. While they were searching the stiff grasses of the rough there was a clear call of "Fore!" from behind a hill in their rear. And as they all turned abruptly from their search a bright new ball sliced abruptly over the hill and caught Mr T.A. Hedrick in the abdomen.

"By Gad!" cried Mr T.A. Hedrick. "They ought to put some of these crazy women off the course. It's getting to be outrageous."

A head and a voice came up together over the hill:

"Do you mind if we go through?"

"You hit me in the stomach!" declared Mr Hedrick wildly.

"Did I?" The girl approached the group of men. "I'm sorry. I yelled 'Fore!'"

Her glance fell casually on each of the men – then scanned the fairway for her ball.

"Did I bounce into the rough?"

It was impossible to determine whether this question was ingenuous or malicious. In a moment, however, she left no doubt, for as her partner came up over the hill she called cheerfully:

"Here I am! I'd have gone on the green except that I hit something."

As she took her stance for a short mashie shot, Dexter looked at her closely. She wore a blue gingham dress, rimmed at throat and shoulders with a white edging that accentuated her tan. The quality of exaggeration, of thinness, which had made her passionate eyes and down-turning mouth absurd at eleven, was gone now. She was arrestingly beautiful. The colour in her cheeks was centred like the colour in a picture – it was not a "high" colour, but a sort of fluctuating and feverish warmth, so shaded that it seemed at any moment it would recede and disappear. This colour and the mobility of her mouth gave a continual impression of flux, of intense life, of passionate vitality – balanced only partially by the sad luxury of her eyes.

She swung her mashie impatiently and without interest, pitching the ball into a sandpit on the other side of the green. With a quick insincere smile and a careless "Thank you!" she went on after it.

"That Judy Jones!" remarked Mr Hedrick on the next tee, as they waited – some moments – for her to play on ahead. "All she needs is to be turned up and spanked for six months and then to be married off to an old-fashioned cavalry captain."

"My God, she's good-looking!" said Mr Sandwood, who was just over thirty.

"Good-looking!" cried Mr Hedrick contemptuously. "She always looks as if she wanted to be kissed! Turning those big cow-eyes on every calf in town!"

It was doubtful if Mr Hedrick intended a reference to the maternal instinct.

"She'd play pretty good golf if she'd try," said Mr Sandwood.

"She has no form," said Mr Hedrick solemnly.

"She has a nice figure," said Mr Sandwood.

"Better thank the Lord she doesn't drive a swifter ball," said Mr Hart, winking at Dexter.

Later in the afternoon the sun went down with a riotous swirl of gold and varying blues and scarlets, and left the dry rustling night of western summer. Dexter watched from the veranda of the golf club, watched the even overlap of the waters in the little wind, silver molasses under the harvest moon. Then the moon held a finger to her lips and the lake became a clear pool, pale and quiet. Dexter put on his bathing suit and swam out to the farthest raft, where he stretched dripping on the wet canvas of the springboard.

There was a fish jumping and a star shining and the lights around the lake were gleaming. Over on a dark peninsula a piano was playing the songs of last summer and of summers before that – songs from 'Chin-Chin' and *The Count of Luxembourg* and *The Chocolate Soldier** – and because the sound of a piano over a stretch of water had always seemed beautiful to Dexter he lay perfectly quiet and listened.

The tune the piano was playing at that moment had been gay and new five years before when Dexter was a sophomore at college. They had played it at a prom once when he could not afford the luxury of proms, and he had stood outside the gymnasium and listened. The sound of the tune precipitated in him a sort of ecstasy and it was with that ecstasy he viewed what happened to him now. It was a mood of intense appreciation, a sense that, for once, he was magnificently attuned to life and that everything about him was radiating a brightness and a glamour he might never know again.

A low pale oblong detached itself suddenly from the darkness of the island, spitting forth the reverberate sound of a racing motorboat. Two white streamers of cleft water rolled themselves out behind it and almost immediately the boat was beside him, drowning out the hot tinkle of the piano in the drone of its spray. Dexter, raising himself on his arms, was aware of a figure standing at the wheel, of two dark eyes regarding him over the lengthening space of water – then the boat had gone by and was sweeping in an immense and purposeless circle of spray round and round in the middle of the lake. With equal eccentricity one of the circles flattened out and headed back towards the raft.

"Who's that?" she called, shutting off her motor. She was so near now that Dexter could see her bathing suit, which consisted apparently of pink rompers.

The nose of the boat bumped the raft, and as the latter tilted rakishly he was precipitated towards her. With different degrees of interest they recognized each other.

"Aren't you one of those men we played through this afternoon?" she demanded.

He was.

"Well, do you know how to drive a motorboat? Because if you do I wish you'd drive this one so I can ride on the surfboard behind. My name is Judy Jones" – she favoured him with an absurd smirk – rather, what tried to be a smirk, for, twist her mouth as she might, it was not grotesque, it was merely beautiful – "and I live in a house over there on the island, and in that house there is a man waiting for me. When he drove up at the door I drove out of the dock, because he says I'm his ideal."

There was a fish jumping and a star shining and the lights around the lake were gleaming. Dexter sat beside Judy Jones and she explained how her boat was driven. Then she was in the water, swimming to the floating surfboard with a sinuous crawl. Watching her was without effort to the eye, watching a branch waving or a seagull flying. Her arms, burnt to butternut, moved sinuously among the dull platinum ripples, elbow appearing first, casting the forearm back with a cadence of falling water, then reaching out and down, stabbing a path ahead.

They moved out into the lake; turning, Dexter saw that she was kneeling on the low rear of the now up-tilted surfboard.

"Go faster," she called, "fast as it'll go."

Obediently he jammed the lever forward and the white spray mounted at the bow. When he looked around again the girl was

standing up on the rushing board, her arms spread wide, her eyes
lifted towards the moon.

"It's awful cold," she shouted. "What's your name?"

He told her.

"Well, why don't you come to dinner tomorrow night?"

His heart turned over like the flywheel of the boat and, for the
second time, her casual whim gave a new direction to his life.

III

NEXT EVENING WHILE HE WAITED for her to come downstairs, Dexter peopled the soft deep summer room and the
sun porch that opened from it with the men who had already
loved Judy Jones. He knew the sort of men they were – the men
who when he first went to college had entered from the great prep
schools with graceful clothes and the deep tan of healthy summers.
He had seen that, in one sense, he was better than these men. He
was newer and stronger. Yet in acknowledging to himself that he
wished his children to be like them he was admitting that he was
but the rough, strong stuff from which they eternally sprang.

When the time had come for him to wear good clothes, he had
known who were the best tailors in America, and the best tailors
in America had made him the suit he wore this evening. He had
acquired that particular reserve peculiar to his university that set it
off from other universities. He recognized the value to him of such
a mannerism and he had adopted it; he knew that to be careless
in dress and manner required more confidence than to be careful.
But carelessness was for his children. His mother's name had been
Krimslich. She was a Bohemian of the peasant class and she had
talked broken English to the end of her days. Her son must keep
to the set patterns.

At a little after seven Judy Jones came downstairs. She wore a
blue silk afternoon dress, and he was disappointed at first that she
had not put on something more elaborate. This feeling was accentuated when, after a brief greeting, she went to the door of a butler's
pantry and pushing it open called: "You can serve dinner, Martha."

He had rather expected that a butler would announce dinner, that there would be a cocktail. Then he put these thoughts behind him as they sat down side by side on a lounge and looked at each other.

"Father and Mother won't be here," she said thoughtfully.

He remembered the last time he had seen her father, and he was glad the parents were not to be here tonight – they might wonder who he was. He had been born in Keeble, a Minnesota village fifty miles farther north, and he always gave Keeble as his home instead of Black Bear Village. Country towns were well enough to come from if they weren't inconveniently in sight and used as footstools by fashionable lakes.

They talked of his university, which she had visited frequently during the past two years, and of the nearby city which supplied Sherry Island with its patrons, and whither Dexter would return next day to his prospering laundries.

During dinner she slipped into a moody depression which gave Dexter a feeling of uneasiness. Whatever petulance she uttered in her throaty voice worried him. Whatever she smiled at – at him, at a chicken liver, at nothing – it disturbed him that her smile could have no root in mirth, or even in amusement. When the scarlet corners of her lips curved down, it was less a smile than an invitation to a kiss.

Then, after dinner, she led him out on the dark sun porch and deliberately changed the atmosphere.

"Do you mind if I weep a little?" she said.

"I'm afraid I'm boring you," he responded quickly.

"You're not. I like you. But I've just had a terrible afternoon. There was a man I cared about, and this afternoon he told me out of a clear sky that he was poor as a church mouse. He'd never even hinted it before. Does this sound horribly mundane?"

"Perhaps he was afraid to tell you."

"Suppose he was," she answered. "He didn't start right. You see, if I'd thought of him as poor – well, I've been mad about loads of poor men, and fully intended to marry them all. But in this case, I hadn't thought of him that way and my interest in him wasn't strong enough to survive the shock. As if a girl calmly informed her fiancé that she was a widow. He might not object to widows, but—

"Let's start right," she interrupted herself suddenly. "Who are you, anyhow?"

For a moment Dexter hesitated. Then:

"I'm nobody," he announced. "My career is largely a matter of futures."

"Are you poor?"

"No," he said frankly, "I'm probably making more money than any man my age in the North-west. I know that's an obnoxious remark, but you advised me to start right."

There was a pause. Then she smiled and the corners of her mouth drooped and an almost imperceptible sway brought her closer to him, looking up into his eyes. A lump rose in Dexter's throat, and he waited breathless for the experiment, facing the unpredictable compound that would form mysteriously from the elements of their lips. Then he saw – she communicated her excitement to him, lavishly, deeply, with kisses that were not a promise but a fulfilment. They aroused in him not hunger demanding renewal but surfeit that would demand more surfeit... kisses that were like charity, creating want by holding back nothing at all.

It did not take him many hours to decide that he had wanted Judy Jones ever since he was a proud, desirous little boy.

IV

IT BEGAN LIKE THAT – AND CONTINUED, with varying shades of intensity, on such a note, right up to the denouement. Dexter surrendered a part of himself to the most direct and unprincipled personality with which he had ever come in contact. Whatever Judy wanted, she went after with the full pressure of her charm. There was no divergence of method, no jockeying for position or premeditation of effects – there was a very little mental side to any of her affairs. She simply made men conscious to the highest degree of her physical loveliness. Dexter had no desire to change her. Her deficiencies were knit up with a passionate energy that transcended and justified them.

When, as Judy's head lay against his shoulder that first night, she whispered, "I don't know what's the matter with me. Last night I thought I was in love with a man and tonight I think I'm in love with you..." – it seemed to him a beautiful and romantic thing to say. It was the exquisite excitability that for the moment he controlled and owned. But a week later he was compelled to view this same quality in a different light. She took him in her roadster to a picnic supper, and after supper she disappeared, likewise in her roadster, with another man. Dexter became enormously upset and was scarcely able to be decently civil to the other people present. When she assured him that she had not kissed the other man, he knew she was lying – yet he was glad that she had taken the trouble to lie to him.

He was, as he found before the summer ended, one of a varying dozen who circulated about her. Each of them had at one time been favoured above all others – about half of them still basked in the solace of occasional sentimental revivals. Whenever one showed signs of dropping out through long neglect, she granted him a brief honeyed hour, which encouraged him to tag along for a year or so longer. Judy made these forays upon the helpless and defeated without malice, indeed half unconscious that there was anything mischievous in what she did.

When a new man came to town everyone dropped out – dates were automatically cancelled.

The helpless part of trying to do anything about it was that she did it all herself. She was not a girl who could be "won" in the kinetic sense – she was proof against cleverness, she was proof against charm; if any of these assailed her too strongly she would immediately resolve the affair to a physical basis, and under the magic of her physical splendour the strong as well as the brilliant played her game and not their own. She was entertained only by the gratification of her desires and by the direct exercise of her own charm. Perhaps from so much youthful love, so many youthful lovers, she had come, in self-defence, to nourish herself wholly from within.

Succeeding Dexter's first exhilaration came restlessness and dissatisfaction. The helpless ecstasy of losing himself in her was opiate rather than tonic. It was fortunate for his work during the winter that those moments of ecstasy came infrequently. Early in their acquaintance it had seemed for a while that there was a deep and spontaneous mutual attraction – that first August, for example – three days of long evenings on her dusky veranda, of strange wan kisses through the late afternoon, in shadowy alcoves or behind the protecting trellises of the garden arbours, of mornings when she was fresh as a dream and almost shy at meeting him in the clarity of the rising day. There was all the ecstasy of an engagement about it, sharpened by his realization that there was no engagement. It was during those three days that, for the first time, he had asked her to marry him. She said "maybe some day", she said "kiss me", she said "I'd like to marry you", she said "I love you" – she said – nothing.

The three days were interrupted by the arrival of a New York man who visited at her house for half September. To Dexter's agony, rumour engaged them. The man was the son of the president of a great trust company. But at the end of a month it was reported that Judy was yawning. At a dance one night she sat all evening in a motorboat with a local beau, while the New Yorker searched the club for her frantically. She told the local beau that she was bored with her visitor and two days later he left. She was seen with him at the station and it was reported that he looked very mournful indeed.

On this note the summer ended. Dexter was twenty-four and he found himself increasingly in a position to do as he wished. He joined two clubs in the city and lived at one of them. Though he was by no means an integral part of the stag lines at these clubs, he managed to be on hand at dances where Judy Jones was likely to appear. He could have gone out socially as much as he liked – he was an eligible young man now, and popular with downtown fathers. His confessed devotion to Judy Jones had rather solidified his position. But he had no social aspirations and rather despised the dancing men who were always on tap for the Thursday or Saturday parties and who filled in at dinners with the younger married set. Already he was playing with the idea of going east to

New York. He wanted to take Judy Jones with him. No disillusion as to the world in which she had grown up could cure his illusion as to her desirability.

Remember that – for only in the light of it can what he did for her be understood.

Eighteen months after he first met Judy Jones he became engaged to another girl. Her name was Irene Scheerer, and her father was one of the men who had always believed in Dexter. Irene was light-haired and sweet and honourable, and a little stout, and she had two suitors whom she pleasantly relinquished when Dexter formally asked her to marry him.

Summer, fall, winter, spring, another summer, another fall – so much he had given of his active life to the incorrigible lips of Judy Jones. She had treated him with interest, with encouragement, with malice, with indifference, with contempt. She had inflicted on him the innumerable little slights and indignities possible in such a case – as if in revenge for having ever cared for him at all. She had beckoned him and yawned at him and beckoned him again and he had responded often with bitterness and narrowed eyes. She had brought him ecstatic happiness and intolerable agony of spirit. She had caused him untold inconvenience and not a little trouble. She had insulted him and she had ridden over him and she had played his interest in her against his interest in his work – for fun. She had done everything to him except to criticize him – this she had not done – it seemed to him only because it might have sullied the utter indifference she manifested and sincerely felt towards him.

When autumn had come and gone again it occurred to him that he could not have Judy Jones. He had to beat this into his mind, but he convinced himself at last. He lay awake at night for a while and argued it over. He told himself the trouble and the pain she had caused him, he enumerated her glaring deficiencies as a wife. Then he said to himself that he loved her, and after a while he fell asleep. For a week, lest he imagined her husky voice over the telephone or her eyes opposite him at lunch, he worked hard and late and at night he went to his office and plotted out his years.

At the end of a week he went to a dance and cut in on her once. For almost the first time since they had met he did not ask her to sit out with him or tell her that she was lovely. It hurt him that she did not miss these things – that was all. He was not jealous when he saw that there was a new man tonight. He had been hardened against jealousy long before.

He stayed late at the dance. He sat for an hour with Irene Scheerer and talked about books and about music. He knew very little about either. But he was beginning to be master of his own time now, and he had a rather priggish notion that he – the young and already fabulously successful Dexter Green – should know more about such things.

That was in October when he was twenty-five. In January, Dexter and Irene became engaged. It was to be announced in June and they were to be married three months later.

The Minnesota winter prolonged itself interminably, and it was almost May when the winds came soft and the snow ran down into Black Bear Lake at last. For the first time in over a year Dexter was enjoying a certain tranquillity of spirit. Judy Jones had been in Florida and afterwards in Hot Springs and somewhere she had been engaged and somewhere she had broken it off. At first, when Dexter had definitely given her up, it had made him sad that people still linked them together and asked for news of her, but when he began to be placed at dinner next to Irene Scheerer people didn't ask him about her any more – they told him about her. He ceased to be an authority on her.

May at last. Dexter walked the streets at night when the darkness was damp as rain, wondering that so soon, with so little done, so much of ecstasy had gone from him. May one year back had been marked by Judy's poignant, unforgivable yet forgiven turbulence – it had been one of those rare times when he fancied she had grown to care for him. That old penny's worth of happiness he had spent for this bushel of content. He knew that Irene would be no more than a curtain spread behind him, a hand moving among gleaming teacups, a voice calling to children... fire and loveliness were gone, the magic of nights and the wonder of the varying hours and seasons… slender lips, downturning, dropping to his lips and bearing him up into a heaven of eyes… The thing was deep in him. He was too strong and alive for it to die lightly.

In the middle of May, when the weather balanced for a few days on the thin bridge that led to deep summer, he turned in one night at Irene's house. Their engagement was to be announced in a week now – no one would be surprised at it. And tonight they would sit together on the lounge at the University Club and look on for an hour at the dancers. It gave him a sense of solidity to go with her – she was so sturdily popular, so intensely "great".

He mounted the steps of the brownstone house and stepped inside.

"Irene," he called.

Mrs Scheerer came out of the living room to meet him.

"Dexter," she said, "Irene's gone upstairs with a splitting headache. She wanted to go with you but I made her go to bed."

"Nothing serious, I—"

"Oh, no. She's going to play golf with you in the morning. You can spare her for just one night, can't you, Dexter?"

Her smile was kind. She and Dexter liked each other. In the living room he talked for a moment before he said goodnight.

Returning to the University Club, where he had rooms, he stood in the doorway for a moment and watched the dancers. He leant against the doorpost, nodded at a man or two – yawned.

"Hello, darling."

The familiar voice at his elbow startled him. Judy Jones had left a man and crossed the room to him – Judy Jones, a slender enamelled doll in cloth of gold: gold in a band at her head, gold in two slipper points at her dress's hem. The fragile glow of her face seemed to blossom as she smiled at him. A breeze of warmth and light blew through the room. His hands in the pockets of his dinner jacket tightened spasmodically. He was filled with a sudden excitement.

"When did you get back?" he asked casually.

"Come here and I'll tell you about it."

She turned and he followed her. She had been away – he could have wept at the wonder of her return. She had passed through enchanted streets, doing things that were like provocative music. All mysterious happenings, all fresh and quickening hopes, had gone away with her, come back with her now.

She turned in the doorway.

"Have you a car here? If you haven't, I have."

"I have a coupé."

In then, with a rustle of golden cloth. He slammed the door. Into so many cars she had stepped – like this – like that – her back against the leather, so – her elbow resting on the door – waiting. She would have been soiled long since, had there been anything to soil her – except herself – but this was her own self outpouring.

With an effort he forced himself to start the car and back into the street. This was nothing, he must remember. She had done this before and he had put her behind him as he would have crossed a bad account from his books.

He drove slowly downtown and, affecting abstraction, traversed the deserted streets of the business section, peopled here and there where a movie was giving out its crowd or where consumptive or pugilistic youth lounged in front of pool halls. The clink of glasses and the slap of hands on the bars issued from saloons, cloisters of glazed glass and dirty yellow light.

She was watching him closely and the silence was embarrassing, yet in this crisis he could find no casual word with which to profane the hour. At a convenient turning he began to zigzag back towards the University Club.

"Have you missed me?" she asked suddenly.

"Everybody missed you."

He wondered if she knew of Irene Scheerer. She had been back only a day – her absence had been almost contemporaneous with his engagement.

"What a remark!" Judy laughed sadly – without sadness. She looked at him searchingly. He became absorbed in the dashboard.

"You're handsomer than you used to be," she said thoughtfully. "Dexter, you have the most rememberable eyes."

He could have laughed at this, but he did not laugh. It was the sort of thing that was said to sophomores. Yet it stabbed at him.

"I'm awfully tired of everything, darling." She called everyone darling, endowing the endearment with careless, individual cama-raderie. "I wish you'd marry me."

The directness of this confused him. He should have told her now that he was going to marry another girl, but he could not tell her. He could as easily have sworn that he had never loved her.

"I think we'd get along," she continued, on the same note, "unless probably you've forgotten me and fallen in love with another girl."

Her confidence was obviously enormous. She had said, in effect, that she found such a thing impossible to believe, that if it were true he had merely committed a childish indiscretion – and probably to show off. She would forgive him, because it was not a matter of any moment but rather something to be brushed aside lightly.

"Of course you could never love anybody but me," she contin-ued. "I like the way you love me. Oh, Dexter, have you forgotten last year?"

"No, I haven't forgotten."

"Neither have I!"

Was she sincerely moved – or was she carried along by the wave of her own acting?

"I wish we could be like that again," she said, and he forced himself to answer:

"I don't think we can."

"I suppose not... I hear you're giving Irene Scheerer a violent rush."

There was not the faintest emphasis on the name, yet Dexter was suddenly ashamed.

"Oh, take me home," cried Judy suddenly. "I don't want to go back to that idiotic dance – with those children."

Then, as he turned up the street that led to the residence dis-trict, Judy began to cry quietly to herself. He had never seen her cry before.

The dark street lightened, the dwellings of the rich loomed up around them, he stopped his coupé in front of the great white bulk of the Mortimer Jones house, somnolent, gorgeous, drenched with the splendour of the damp moonlight. Its solidity startled him. The strong walls, the steel of the girders, the breadth and beam and pomp of it were there only to bring out the contrast with the young beauty beside him. It was sturdy to accentuate her slightness – as if to show what a breeze could be generated by a butterfly's wing.

He sat perfectly quiet, his nerves in wild clamour, afraid that if he moved he would find her irresistibly in his arms. Two tears had rolled down her wet face and trembled on her upper lip.

"I'm more beautiful than anybody else," she said brokenly. "Why can't I be happy?" Her moist eyes tore at his stability – her mouth turned slowly downward with an exquisite sadness: "I'd like to marry you if you'll have me, Dexter. I suppose you think I'm not worth having, but I'll be so beautiful for you, Dexter."

A million phrases of anger, pride, passion, hatred, tenderness fought on his lips. Then a perfect wave of emotion washed over him, carrying off with it a sediment of wisdom, of convention, of doubt, of honour. This was his girl who was speaking, his own, his beautiful, his pride.

"Won't you come in?" He heard her draw in her breath sharply. Waiting.

"All right," his voice was trembling, "I'll come in."

V

IT WAS STRANGE THAT NEITHER when it was over nor a long time afterwards did he regret that night. Looking at it from the perspective of ten years, the fact that Judy's flare for him endured just one month seemed of little importance. Nor did it matter that by his yielding he subjected himself to a deeper agony in the end and gave serious hurt to Irene Scheerer and to Irene's parents, who had befriended him. There was nothing sufficiently pictorial about Irene's grief to stamp itself on his mind.

Dexter was at bottom hard-minded. The attitude of the city on his action was of no importance to him, not because he was going to leave the city, but because any outside attitude on the situation seemed superficial. He was completely indifferent to popular opinion. Nor, when he had seen that it was no use, that he did not possess in himself the power to move fundamentally or to hold Judy Jones, did he bear any malice towards her. He loved her and he would love her until the day he was too old for loving – but he could not have her. So he tasted the deep pain that is reserved only for the strong, just as he had tasted for a little while the deep happiness.

Even the ultimate falsity of the grounds upon which Judy terminated the engagement, that she did not want to "take him away" from Irene – Judy, who had wanted nothing else – did not revolt him. He was beyond any revulsion or any amusement.

He went east in February with the intention of selling out his laundries and settling in New York – but the war came to America in March and changed his plans. He returned to the West, handed over the management of the business to his partner, and went into the first officers' training camp in late April. He was one of those young thousands who greeted the war with a certain amount of relief, welcoming the liberation from webs of tangled emotion.

VI

THIS STORY IS NOT HIS BIOGRAPHY, remember, although things creep into it which have nothing to do with those dreams he had when he was young. We are almost done with them and with him now. There is only one more incident to be related here, and it happens seven years further on.

It took place in New York, where he had done well – so well that there were no barriers too high for him. He was thirty-two years old and, except for one flying trip immediately after the war, he had not been west in seven years. A man named Devlin from Detroit came into his office to see him in a business way, and then and there this incident occurred, and closed out, so to speak, this particular side of his life.

"So you're from the Middle West," said the man Devlin with careless curiosity. "That's funny – I thought men like you were probably born and raised on Wall Street. You know ——, wife of one of my best friends in Detroit came from your city. I was an usher at the wedding."

Dexter waited with no apprehension of what was coming.

"Judy Simms," said Devlin with no particular interest. "Judy Jones she was once."

"Yes, I knew her." A dull impatience spread over him. He had heard, of course, that she was married – perhaps deliberately he had heard no more.

"Awfully nice girl," brooded Devlin meaninglessly. "I'm sort of sorry for her."

"Why?" Something in Dexter was alert, receptive, at once.

"Oh, Lud Simms has gone to pieces in a way. I don't mean he ill-uses her, but he drinks and runs around—"

"Doesn't she run around?"

"No. Stays at home with her kids."

"Oh."

"She's a little too old for him," said Devlin.

"Too old!" cried Dexter. "Why, man, she's only twenty-seven."

He was possessed with a wild notion of rushing out into the streets and taking a train to Detroit. He rose to his feet spasmodically.

"I guess you're busy," Devlin apologized quickly. "I didn't realize—"

"No, I'm not busy," said Dexter, steadying his voice. "I'm not busy at all. Not busy at all. Did you say she was – twenty-seven? No, I said she was twenty-seven."

"Yes, you did," agreed Devlin drily.

"Go on, then. Go on."

"What do you mean?"

"About Judy Jones."

Devlin looked at him helplessly.

"Well, that's – I told you all there is to it. He treats her like the devil. Oh, they're not going to get divorced or anything. When he's particularly outrageous she forgives him. In fact, I'm inclined to think she loves him. She was a pretty girl when she first came to Detroit."

A pretty girl! The phrase struck Dexter as ludicrous.

"Isn't she – a pretty girl, any more?"

"Oh, she's all right."

"Look here," said Dexter, sitting down suddenly, "I don't understand. You say she was a 'pretty girl' and now you say she's 'all right'. I don't understand what you mean – Judy Jones wasn't a pretty girl, at all. She was a great beauty. Why, I knew her, I knew her. She was——"

Devlin laughed pleasantly.

"I'm not trying to start a row," he said. "I think Judy's a nice girl and I like her. I can't understand how a man like Lud Simms could fall madly in love with her, but he did." Then he added: "Most of the women like her."

Dexter looked closely at Devlin, thinking wildly that there must be a reason for this, some insensitivity in the man or some private malice.

"Lots of women fade just like *that*," Devlin snapped his fingers. "You must have seen it happen. Perhaps I've forgotten how pretty she was at her wedding. I've seen her so much since then, you see. She has nice eyes."

A sort of dullness settled down upon Dexter. For the first time in his life he felt like getting very drunk. He knew that he was laughing loudly at something Devlin had said, but he did not know what it was or why it was funny. When, in a few minutes, Devlin went, he lay down on his lounge and looked out the window at the New York skyline into which the sun was sinking in dull lovely shades of pink and gold.

He had thought that having nothing else to lose he was invulnerable at last – but he knew that he had just lost something more, as surely as if he had married Judy Jones and seen her fade away before his eyes.

The dream was gone. Something had been taken from him. In a sort of panic he pushed the palms of his hands into his eyes and tried to bring up a picture of the waters lapping on Sherry Island and the moonlit veranda, and gingham on the golf links and the dry sun and the gold colour of her neck's soft down. And her mouth damp to his kisses and her eyes plaintive with melancholy and her freshness like new fine linen in the morning. Why, these things were no longer in the world! They had existed and they existed no longer.

For the first time in years the tears were streaming down his face. But they were for himself now. He did not care about mouth and eyes and moving hands. He wanted to care and he could not care. For he had gone away and he could never go back any more. The gates were closed, the sun was gone down and there was no beauty but the grey beauty of steel that withstands all time. Even the grief he could have borne was left behind in the country of illusion, of youth, of the richness of life, where his winter dreams had flourished.

"Long ago," he said, "long ago, there was something in me, but now that thing is gone. Now that thing is gone, that thing is gone. I cannot cry. I cannot care. That thing will come back no more."

The Baby Party

WHEN JOHN ANDROS FELT OLD he found solace in the thought of life continuing through his child. The dark trumpets of oblivion were less loud at the patter of his child's feet or at the sound of his child's voice babbling mad non sequiturs to him over the telephone. The latter incident occurred every afternoon at three when his wife called the office from the country, and he came to look forward to it as one of the vivid minutes of his day.

He was not physically old, but his life had been a series of struggles up a series of rugged hills, and here at thirty-eight, having won his battles against ill health and poverty, he cherished less than the usual number of illusions. Even his feeling about his little girl was qualified. She had interrupted his rather intense love affair with his wife, and she was the reason for their living in a suburban town, where they paid for country air with endless servant troubles and the weary merry-go-round of the commuting train.

It was little Ede as a definite piece of youth that chiefly interested him. He liked to take her on his lap and examine minutely her fragrant, downy scalp and her eyes with their irises of morning blue. Having paid this homage John was content that the nurse should take her away. After ten minutes the very vitality of the child irritated him; he was inclined to lose his temper when things were broken, and one Sunday afternoon when she had disrupted a bridge game by permanently hiding the ace of spades, he had made a scene that had reduced his wife to tears.

This was absurd and John was ashamed of himself. It was inevitable that such things would happen, and it was impossible that little Ede should spend all her indoor hours in the nursery upstairs when she was becoming, as her mother said, more nearly a "real person" every day.

She was two and a half and this afternoon, for instance, she was going to a baby party. Grown-up Edith, her mother, had telephoned the information to the office, and little Ede had confirmed the business by shouting "I yam going to a *pantry*!" into John's unsuspecting left ear.

"Drop in at the Markeys' when you get home, won't you, dear?" resumed her mother. "It'll be funny. Ede's going to be all dressed up in her new pink dress—"

The conversation terminated abruptly with a squawk which indicated that the telephone had been pulled violently to the floor. John laughed and decided to get an early train out; the prospect of a baby party in someone else's house amused him.

"What a peach of a mess!" he thought humorously. "A dozen mothers and each one looking at nothing but her own child. All the babies breaking things and grabbing at the cake, and each mama going home thinking about the subtle superiority of her own child to every other child there."

He was in a good humour today – all the things in his life were going better than they had ever gone before. When he got off the train at his station he shook his head at an importunate taxi man and began to walk up the long hill towards his house through the crisp December twilight. It was only six o'clock but the moon was out, shining with proud brilliance on the thin sugary snow that lay over the lawns.

As he walked along drawing his lungs full of cold air his happiness increased, and the idea of a baby party appealed to him more and more. He began to wonder how Ede compared to other children of her own age and if the pink dress she was to wear was something radical and mature. Increasing his gait he came in sight of his own house, where the lights of a defunct Christmas tree still blossomed in the window, but he continued on past the walk. The party was at the Markeys' next door.

As he mounted the brick step and rang the bell he became aware of voices inside, and he was glad he was not too late. Then he raised his head and listened – the voices were not children's voices, but they were loud and pitched high with anger; there were at least three of them and one, which rose as he listened to a hysterical sob, he recognized immediately as his wife's.

"There's been some trouble," he thought quickly.

Trying the door he found it unlocked and pushed it open.

The baby party began at half-past four, but Edith Andros, calculating shrewdly that the new dress would stand out more sensationally against vestments already rumpled, planned the arrival of herself and little Ede for five. When they appeared it was already a flourishing affair. Four baby girls and nine baby boys, each one curled and washed and dressed with all the care of a proud and jealous heart, were dancing to the music of a phonograph. Never more than two or three were dancing at once, but as all were continually in motion, running to and from their mothers for encouragement, the general effect was the same.

As Edith and her daughter entered, the music was temporarily drowned out by a sustained chorus, consisting largely of the word *cute* and directed towards little Ede, who stood looking timidly about and fingering the edges of her pink dress. She was not kissed – this is the sanitary age – but she was passed along a row of mamas each one of whom said "cu-u-ute" to her and held her pink little hand before passing her on to the next. After some encouragement and a few mild pushes she was absorbed into the dance and became an active member of the party.

Edith stood near the door talking to Mrs Markey and keeping one eye on the tiny figure in the pink dress. She did not care for Mrs Markey; she considered her both snippy and common, but John and Joe Markey were congenial and went in together on the commuting train every morning, so the two women kept up an elaborate pretence of warm amity. They were always reproaching each other for "not coming to see me", and they were always planning the kind of parties that began with "You'll have to come to dinner with us soon, and we'll go in to the theatre", but never matured further.

"Little Ede looks perfectly darling," said Mrs Markey, smiling and moistening her lips in a way that Edith found particularly repulsive. "So *grown up* – I can't *believe* it!"

Edith wondered if "little Ede" referred to the fact that Billy Markey, though several months younger, weighed almost five pounds more. Accepting a cup of tea, she took a seat with two other ladies on a divan and launched into the real business of the afternoon, which of course lay in relating the recent accomplishments and insouciances of her child.

An hour passed. Dancing palled and the babies took to sterner sport. They ran into the dining room, rounded the big table and essayed the kitchen door, from which they were rescued by an expeditionary force of mothers. Having been rounded up they immediately broke loose, and rushing back to the dining room tried the familiar swinging door again. The word "overheated" began to be used, and small white brows were dried with small white handkerchiefs. A general attempt to make the babies sit down began, but the babies squirmed off laps with peremptory cries of "Down! Down!" and the rush into the fascinating dining room began anew.

This phase of the party came to an end with the arrival of refreshments, a large cake with two candles and saucers of vanilla ice cream. Billy Markey, a stout laughing baby with red hair and legs somewhat bowed, blew out the candles and placed an experimental thumb on the white frosting. The refreshments were distributed, and the children ate greedily but without confusion – they had behaved remarkably well all afternoon. They were modern babies who ate and slept at regular hours, so their dispositions were good and their faces healthy and pink – such a peaceful party would not have been possible thirty years ago.

After the refreshments a gradual exodus began. Edith glanced anxiously at her watch – it was almost six and John had not arrived. She wanted him to see Ede with the other children – to see how dignified and polite and intelligent she was, and how the only ice-cream spot on her dress was some that had dropped from her chin when she was joggled from behind.

"You're a darling," she whispered to her child, drawing her suddenly against her knee. "Do you know you're a darling? Do you *know* you're a darling?"

Ede laughed. "Bow-wow," she said suddenly.

"Bow-wow?" Edith looked around. "There isn't any bow-wow."

"Bow-wow," repeated Ede. "I want a bow-wow."

Edith followed the small pointing finger.

"That isn't a bow-wow, dearest, that's a teddy bear."

"Bear?"

"Yes, that's a teddy bear, and it belongs to Billy Markey. You don't want Billy Markey's teddy bear, do you?"

Ede did want it.

She broke away from her mother and approached Billy Markey, who held the toy closely in his arms. Ede stood regarding him with inscrutable eyes and Billy laughed.

Grown-up Edith looked at her watch again, this time impatiently.

The party had dwindled until, besides Ede and Billy, there were only two babies remaining – and one of the two remained only by virtue of having hidden himself under the dining-room table. It was selfish of John not to come. It showed so little pride in the child. Other fathers had come, half a dozen of them, to call for their wives, and they had stayed for a while and looked on.

There was a sudden wail. Ede had obtained Billy's teddy bear by pulling it forcibly from his arms, and on Billy's attempt to recover it she had pushed him casually to the floor.

"Why, Ede!" cried her mother, repressing an inclination to laugh.

Joe Markey, a handsome, broad-shouldered man of thirty-five, picked up his son and set him on his feet. "You're a fine fellow," he said jovially. "Let a girl knock you over! You're a fine fellow."

"Did he bump his head?" Mrs Markey returned anxiously from bowing the next to last remaining mother out the door.

"No-o-o-o," exclaimed Markey. "He bumped something else, didn't you, Billy? He bumped something else."

Billy had so far forgotten the bump that he was already making an attempt to recover his property. He seized a leg of the bear which projected from Ede's enveloping arms and tugged at it but without success.

"No," said Ede emphatically.

Suddenly, encouraged by the success of her former half-accidental manoeuvre, Ede dropped the teddy bear, placed her hands on Billy's shoulders and pushed him backwards off his feet.

This time he landed less harmlessly; his head hit the bare floor just off the rug with a dull hollow sound, whereupon he drew in his breath and delivered an agonized yell.

Immediately the room was in confusion. With an exclamation Markey hurried to his son, but his wife was first to reach the injured baby and catch him up into her arms.

"Oh, *Billy*," she cried, "what a terrible bump! She ought to be spanked."

Edith, who had rushed immediately to her daughter, heard this remark and her lips came sharply together.

"Why, Ede," she whispered perfunctorily, "you bad girl!"

Ede put back her little head suddenly and laughed. It was a loud laugh, a triumphant laugh with victory in it and challenge and contempt. Unfortunately it was also an infectious laugh. Before her mother realized the delicacy of the situation, she too had laughed, an audible, distinct laugh not unlike the baby's and partaking of the same overtones.

Then, as suddenly, she stopped.

Mrs Markey's face had grown red with anger, and Markey, who had been feeling the back of the baby's head with one finger, looked at her, frowning.

"It's swollen already," he said with a note of reproof in his voice. "I'll get some witch hazel."

But Mrs Markey had lost her temper. "I don't see anything funny about a child being hurt!" she said in a trembling voice.

Little Ede meanwhile had been looking at her mother curiously. She noted that her own laugh had produced her mother's, and she wondered if the same cause would always produce the same effect. So she chose this moment to throw back her head and laugh again.

To her mother the additional mirth added the final touch of hysteria to the situation. Pressing her handkerchief to her mouth she giggled irrepressibly. It was more than nervousness – she felt

71

that in a peculiar way she was laughing with her child – they were laughing together.

It was in a way a defiance – those two against the world.

While Markey rushed upstairs to the bathroom for ointment, his wife was walking up and down rocking the yelling boy in her arms.

"Please go home!" she broke out suddenly. "The child's badly hurt, and if you haven't the decency to be quiet, you'd better go home."

"Very well," said Edith, her own temper rising. "I've never seen anyone make such a mountain out of—"

"Get out!" cried Mrs Markey frantically. "There's the door, get out – I never want to see you in our house again. You or your brat either!"

Edith had taken her daughter's hand and was moving quickly towards the door, but at this remark she stopped and turned around, her face contracting with indignation.

"Don't you dare call her that!"

Mrs Markey did not answer but continued walking up and down, muttering to herself and to Billy in an inaudible voice.

Edith began to cry.

"I will get out!" she sobbed. "I've never heard anybody so rude and c-common in my life. I'm glad your baby did get pushed down – he's nothing but a f-fat little fool anyhow."

Joe Markey reached the foot of the stairs just in time to hear this remark.

"Why, Mrs Andros," he said sharply, "can't you see the child's hurt? You really ought to control yourself."

"Control m-myself!" exclaimed Edith brokenly. "You better ask her to c-control herself. I've never heard anybody so c-common in my life."

"She's insulting me!" Mrs Markey was now livid with rage. "Did you hear what she said, Joe? I wish you'd put her out. If she won't go, just take her by the shoulders and put her out!"

"Don't you dare touch me!" cried Edith. "I'm going just as quick as I can find my c-coat!"

Blind with tears she took a step towards the hall. It was just at this moment that the door opened and John Andros walked anxiously in.

"John!" cried Edith and fled to him wildly.

"What's the matter? Why, what's the matter?"

"They're – they're putting me out!" she wailed, collapsing against him. "He'd just started to take me by the shoulders and put me out. I want my coat!"

"That's not true," objected Markey hurriedly. "Nobody's going to put you out." He turned to John. "Nobody's going to put her out," he repeated. "She's—"

"What do you mean 'put her out'?" demanded John abruptly. "What's all this talk, anyhow?"

"Oh, let's go!" cried Edith. "I want to go. They're so *common*, John!"

"Look here!" Markey's face darkened. "You've said that about enough. You're acting sort of crazy."

"They called Ede a brat!"

For the second time that afternoon little Ede expressed emotion at an inopportune moment. Confused and frightened at the shouting voices, she began to cry, and her tears had the effect of conveying that she felt the insult in her heart.

"What's the idea of this?" broke out John. "Do you insult your guests in your own house?"

"It seems to me it's your wife that's done the insulting!" answered Markey crisply. "In fact, your baby there started all the trouble."

John gave a contemptuous snort. "Are you calling names at a little baby?" he enquired. "That's a fine manly business!"

"Don't talk to him, John," insisted Edith. "Find my coat!"

"You must be in a bad way," went on John angrily, "if you have to take out your temper on a helpless little baby."

"I never heard anything so damn twisted in my life," shouted Markey. "If that wife of yours would shut her mouth for a minute—"

"Wait a minute! You're not talking to a woman and child now—"

There was an incidental interruption. Edith had been fumbling on a chair for her coat, and Mrs Markey had been watching her with hot angry eyes. Suddenly she laid Billy down on the sofa, where he immediately stopped crying and pulled himself upright, and coming into the hall she quickly found Edith's coat and handed it to her without a word. Then she went back to the sofa, picked up Billy, and rocking him in her arms looked again at Edith with hot angry eyes. The interruption had taken less than half a minute.

"Your wife comes in here and begins shouting around about how common we are!" burst out Markey violently. "Well, if we're so damn common you'd better stay away! And what's more you'd better get out now!"

Again John gave a short, contemptuous laugh.

"You're not only common," he returned. "You're evidently an awful bully – when there's any helpless women and children around." He felt for the knob and swung the door open. "Come on, Edith."

Taking up her daughter in her arms, his wife stepped outside and John, still looking contemptuously at Markey, started to follow.

"Wait a minute!" Markey took a step forward; he was trembling slightly, and two large veins on his temple were suddenly full of blood. "You don't think you can get away with that, do you? With me?"

Without a word John walked out the door, leaving it open.

Edith, still weeping, had started for home. After following her with his eyes until she reached her own walk, John turned back towards the lighted doorway where Markey was slowly coming down the slippery steps. He took off his overcoat and hat, tossed them off the path onto the snow. Then, sliding a little on the iced walk, he took a step forward.

At the first blow, they both slipped and fell heavily to the sidewalk, half rising then, and again pulling each other to the ground. They found a better foothold in the thin snow to the side of the walk and rushed at each other, both swinging wildly and pressing out the snow into a pasty mud underfoot.

The street was deserted, and except for their short tired gasps and the padded sound as one or the other slipped down into the slushy mud, they fought in silence, clearly defined to each other by the full moonlight as well as by the amber glow that shone out of the open door. Several times they both slipped down together, and then for a while the conflict threshed about wildly on the lawn.

For ten, fifteen, twenty minutes they fought there senselessly in the moonlight. They had both taken off coats and vests at some silently agreed upon interval, and now their shirts dripped from their backs in wet pulpy shreds. Both were torn and bleeding and so exhausted that they could stand only when by their position they mutually supported each other – the impact, the mere effort of a blow, would send them both to their hands and knees.

But it was not weariness that ended the business, and the very meaninglessness of the fight was a reason for not stopping. They stopped because once when they were straining at each other on the ground, they heard a man's footsteps coming along the sidewalk. They had rolled somehow into the shadow, and when they heard these footsteps they stopped fighting, stopped moving, stopped breathing, lay huddled together like two boys playing Indian until the footsteps had passed. Then, staggering to their feet, they looked at each other like two drunken men.

"I'll be damned if I'm going on with this thing any more," cried Markey thickly.

"I'm not going on any more either," said John Andros. "I've had enough of this thing."

Again they looked at each other, sulkily this time, as if each suspected the other of urging him to a renewal of the fight. Markey spat out a mouthful of blood from a cut lip; then he cursed softly and, picking up his coat and vest, shook off the snow from them in a surprised way, as if their comparative dampness was his only worry in the world.

"Want to come in and wash up?" he asked suddenly.

"No thanks," said John. "I ought to be going home – my wife'll be worried."

He too picked up his coat and vest and then his overcoat and hat. Soaking wet and dripping with perspiration, it seemed absurd that less than half an hour ago he had been wearing all these clothes.

"Well – goodnight," he said hesitantly.

Suddenly they both walked towards each other and shook hands. It was no perfunctory handshake: John Andros's arm went around Markey's shoulder, and he patted him softly on the back for a little while.

"No harm done," he said brokenly.

"No – you?"

"No, no harm done."

"Well," said John Andros after a minute, "I guess I'll say goodnight."

"Goodnight."

Limping slightly and with his clothes over his arm, John Andros turned away. The moonlight was still bright as he left the dark patch of trampled ground and walked over the intervening lawn. Down at the station, half a mile away, he could hear the rumble of the seven-o'clock train.

"But you must have been crazy," cried Edith brokenly. "I thought you were going to fix it all up there and shake hands. That's why I went away."

"Did you want us to fix it up?"

"Of course not, I never want to see them again. But I thought of course that was what you were going to do." She was touching the bruises on his neck and back with iodine as he sat placidly in a hot bath. "I'm going to get the doctor," she said insistently. "You may be hurt internally."

He shook his head. "Not a chance," he answered. "I don't want this to get all over town."

"I don't understand yet how it all happened."

"Neither do I." He smiled grimly. "I guess these baby parties are pretty rough affairs."

"Well, one thing…" suggested Edith hopefully. "I'm certainly glad we have beefsteak in the house for tomorrow's dinner."

"Why?"

"For your eye, of course. Do you know I came within an ace of ordering veal? Wasn't that the luckiest thing?"

Half an hour later, dressed except that his neck would accommodate no collar, John moved his limbs experimentally before the glass. "I believe I'll get myself in better shape," he said thoughtfully. "I must be getting old."

"You mean so that next time you can beat him?"

"I did beat him," he announced. "At least, I beat him as much as he beat me. And there isn't going to be any next time. Don't you go calling people common any more. If you get in any trouble, you just take your coat and go home. Understand?"

"Yes, dear," she said meekly. "I was very foolish and now I understand."

Out in the hall, he paused abruptly by the baby's door.

"Is she asleep?"

"Sound asleep. But you can go in and peek at her – just to say goodnight."

They tiptoed in and bent together over the bed. Little Ede, her cheeks flushed with health, her pink hands clasped tight together, was sleeping soundly in the cool dark room. John reached over the railing of the bed and passed his hand lightly over the silken hair.

"She's asleep," he murmured in a puzzled way.

"Naturally, after such an afternoon."

"Miz Andros," the coloured maid's stage whisper floated in from the hall, "Mr and Miz Markey downstairs an' want to see you. Mr Markey he's all cut up in pieces, mam'n. His face look like a roast beef. An' Miz Markey she 'pear mighty mad."

"Why, what incomparable nerve!" exclaimed Edith. "Just tell them we're not home. I wouldn't go down for anything in the world."

"You most certainly will." John's voice was hard and set.

"What?"

"You'll go down right now, and what's more, whatever that other woman does, you'll apologize for what you said this afternoon. After that you don't ever have to see her again."

"Why – John, I can't."

"You've got to. And just remember that she probably hated to come over here just twice as much as you hate to go downstairs."

"Aren't you coming? Do I have to go alone?"

"I'll be down – in just a minute."

John Andros waited until she had closed the door behind her; then he reached over into the bed, and picking up his daughter, blankets and all, sat down in the rocking chair holding her tightly in his arms. She moved a little and he held his breath, but she was sleeping soundly and in a moment she was resting quietly in the hollow of his elbow. Slowly he bent his head until his cheek was against her bright hair. "Dear little girl," he whispered. "Dear little girl, dear little girl."

John Andros knew at length what it was he had fought for so savagely that evening. He had it now, he possessed it for ever, and for some time he sat there rocking very slowly to and fro in the darkness.

Absolution

I

T HERE WAS ONCE A PRIEST with cold, watery eyes, who, in the still of the night, wept cold tears. He wept because the afternoons were warm and long, and he was unable to attain a complete mystical union with our Lord. Sometimes, near four o'clock, there was a rustle of Swede girls along the path by his window, and in their shrill laughter he found a terrible dissonance that made him pray aloud for the twilight to come. At twilight the laughter and the voices were quieter, but several times he had walked past Romberg's Drug Store when it was dusk and the yellow lights shone inside and the nickel taps of the soda fountain were gleaming, and he had found the scent of cheap toilet soap desperately sweet upon the air. He passed that way when he returned from hearing confessions on Saturday nights, and he grew careful to walk on the other side of the street so that the smell of the soap would float upwards before it reached his nostrils as it drifted, rather like incense, towards the summer moon.

But there was no escape from the hot madness of four o'clock. From his window, as far as he could see, the Dakota wheat thronged the valley of the Red River. The wheat was terrible to look upon and the carpet pattern to which in agony he bent his eyes sent his thoughts brooding through grotesque labyrinths, open always to the unavoidable sun.

One afternoon when he had reached the point where the mind runs down like an old clock, his housekeeper brought into his study a beautiful, intense little boy of eleven named Rudolph Miller. The little boy sat down in a patch of sunshine and the priest, at his walnut desk, pretended to be very busy. This was to conceal his relief that someone had come into his haunted room.

Presently he turned around and found himself staring into two enormous, staccato eyes, lit with gleaming points of cobalt light. For a moment their expression startled him – then he saw that his visitor was in a state of abject fear.

"Your mouth is trembling," said Father Schwartz in a haggard voice.

The little boy covered his quivering mouth with his hand.

"Are you in trouble?" asked Father Schwartz sharply. "Take your hand away from your mouth and tell me what's the matter."

The boy – Father Schwartz recognized him now as the son of a parishioner, Mr Miller, the freight agent – moved his hand reluctantly off his mouth and became articulate in a despairing whisper.

"Father Schwartz – I've committed a terrible sin."

"A sin against purity?"

"No, Father... worse."

Father Schwartz's body jerked sharply.

"Have you killed somebody?"

"No – but I'm afraid..." the voice rose to a shrill whimper.

"Do you want to go to confession?"

The little boy shook his head miserably. Father Schwartz cleared his throat so that he could make his voice soft and say some quiet, kind thing. In this moment he should forget his own agony and try to act like God. He repeated to himself a devotional phrase, hoping that in return God would help him to act correctly.

"Tell me what you've done," said his new soft voice.

The little boy looked at him through his tears and was reassured by the impression of moral resiliency which the distraught priest had created. Abandoning as much of himself as he was able to this man, Rudolph Miller began to tell his story.

"On Saturday, three days ago, my father he said I had to go to confession, because I hadn't been for a month, and the family they go every week, and I hadn't been. So I just as leave go, I didn't care. So I put it off till after supper because I was playing with a bunch of kids and Father asked me if I went and I said 'no', and he took me by the neck and he said, 'You go now,' so I said, 'All right,' so I went over to church. And he yelled after me: 'Don't come back till you go'…"

II
"On Saturday, Three Days Ago"

THE PLUSH CURTAIN OF THE CONFESSIONAL rearranged its dismal creases, leaving exposed only the bottom of an old man's old shoe. Behind the curtain an immortal soul was alone with God and the Reverend Adolphus Schwartz, priest of the parish. Sound began, a laboured whispering, sibilant and discreet, broken at intervals by the voice of the priest in audible question.

Rudolph Miller knelt in the pew beside the confessional and waited, straining nervously to hear and yet not to hear what was being said within. The fact that the priest was audible alarmed him. His own turn came next, and the three or four others who waited might listen unscrupulously while he admitted his violations of the Sixth and Ninth Commandments.

Rudolph had never committed adultery, nor even coveted his neighbour's wife – but it was the confession of the associate sins that was particularly hard to contemplate. In comparison he relished the less shameful fallings-away – they formed a greyish background which relieved the ebony mark of sexual offences upon his soul.

He had been covering his ears with his hands, hoping that his refusal to hear would be noticed, and a like courtesy rendered to him in turn, when a sharp movement of the penitent in the confessional made him sink his face precipitately into the crook of his elbow. Fear assumed solid form and pressed out a lodging between his heart and his lungs. He must try now with all his might to be sorry for his sins – not because he was afraid, but because he had offended God. He must convince God that he was sorry and to do so he must first convince himself. After a tense emotional struggle he achieved a tremulous self-pity, and decided that he was now ready.

If, by allowing no other thought to enter his head, he could preserve this state of emotion unimpaired until he went into that large coffin set on end, he would have survived another crisis in his religious life.

For some time, however, a demoniac notion had partially possessed him. He could go home now, before his turn came, and tell his mother that he had arrived too late and found the priest gone. This, unfortunately, involved the risk of being caught in a lie. As an alternative he could say that he *had* gone to confession, but this meant that he must avoid Communion next day, for Communion taken upon an uncleansed soul would turn to poison in his mouth, and he would crumple limp and damned from the altar rail.

Again Father Schwartz's voice became audible.

"And for your..."

The words blurred to a husky mumble and Rudolph got excitedly to his feet. He felt that it was impossible for him to go to confession this afternoon. He hesitated tensely. Then from the confessional came a tap, a creak and a sustained rustle. The slide had fallen and the plush curtain trembled. Temptation had come to him too late...

"Bless me, Father, for I have sinned... I confess to Almighty God and to you, Father, that I have sinned... Since my last confession it has been one month and three days... I accuse myself of... taking the Name of the Lord in vain..."

This was an easy sin. His curses had been but bravado – telling of them was little less than a brag.

"...of being mean to an old lady."

The wan shadow moved a little on the latticed slat.

"How, my child?"

"Old lady Swenson," Rudolph's murmur soared jubilantly. "She got our baseball that we knocked in her window, and she wouldn't give it back, so we yelled 'Twenty-three Skidoo' at her all afternoon. Then about five o'clock she had a fit and they had to have the doctor."

"Go on, my child."

"Of... of not believing I was the son of my parents."

"What?" The interrogator was distinctly startled.

"Of not believing that I was the son of my parents."

"Why not?"

"Oh, just pride," answered the penitent airily.

"You mean you thought you were too good to be the son of your parents?"

"Yes, Father." On a less jubilant note.

"Go on."

"Of being disobedient and calling my mother names. Of slandering people behind my back. Of smoking…"

Rudolph had now exhausted the minor offences and was approaching the sins it was agony to tell. He held his fingers against his face like bars as if to press out between them the shame in his heart.

"Of dirty words and immodest thoughts and desires," he whispered very low.

"How often?"

"I don't know."

"Once a week? Twice a week?"

"Twice a week."

"Did you yield to these desires?"

"No, Father."

"Were you alone when you had them?"

"No, Father. I was with two boys and a girl."

"Don't you know, my child, that you should avoid the occasions of sin as well as the sin itself? Evil companionship leads to evil desires and evil desires to evil actions. Where were you when this happened?"

"In a barn in back of—"

"I don't want to hear any names," interrupted the priest sharply.

"Well, it was up in the loft of this barn and this girl and… a fella, they were saying things… saying immodest things, and I stayed."

"You should have gone – you should have told the girl to go."

He should have gone! He could not tell Father Schwartz how his pulse had bumped in his wrist, how a strange, romantic excitement had possessed him when those curious things had been said. Perhaps in the houses of delinquency among the dull and hard-eyed incorrigible girls can be found those for whom has burned the whitest fire.

"Have you anything else to tell me?"

"I don't think so, Father."

Rudolph felt a great relief. Perspiration had broken out under his tight-pressed fingers.

"Have you told any lies?"

The question startled him. Like all those who habitually and instinctively lie, he had an enormous respect and awe for the truth. Something almost exterior to himself dictated a quick, hurt answer.

"Oh, no, Father, I never tell lies."

For a moment, like the commoner in the king's chair, he tasted the pride of the situation. Then as the priest began to murmur conventional admonitions he realized that in heroically denying he had told lies, he had committed a terrible sin – he had told a lie in confession.

In automatic response to Father Schwartz's "Make an act of contrition", he began to repeat aloud meaninglessly:

"Oh, my God, I am heartily sorry for having offended Thee..."

He must fix this now – it was a bad mistake – but as his teeth shut on the last words of his prayer there was a sharp sound, and the slat was closed.

A minute later when he emerged into the twilight, the relief in coming from the muggy church into an open world of wheat and sky postponed the full realization of what he had done. Instead of worrying he took a deep breath of the crisp air and began to say over and over to himself the words "Blatchford Sarnemington, Blatchford Sarnemington!"

Blatchford Sarnemington was himself, and these words were in effect a lyric. When he became Blatchford Sarnemington a suave nobility flowed from him. Blatchford Sarnemington lived in great sweeping triumphs. When Rudolph half-closed his eyes it meant that Blatchford had established dominance over him and, as he went by, there were envious mutters in the air: "Blatchford Sarnemington! There goes Blatchford Sarnemington."

He was Blatchford now for a while as he strutted homewards along the staggering road, but when the road braced itself in macadam in order to become the main street of Ludwig, Rudolph's exhilaration faded out and his mind cooled and he felt the horror of his lie. God, of course, already knew of it – but Rudolph reserved a corner of his mind where he was safe from God, where he prepared the subterfuges with which he often tricked God. Hiding now in this corner he considered how he could best avoid the consequences of his misstatement.

At all costs he must avoid communion next day. The risk of angering God to such an extent was too great. He would have to drink water "by accident" in the morning and thus, in accordance with a Church law, render himself unfit to receive communion that day. In spite of its flimsiness, this subterfuge was the most feasible that occurred to him. He accepted its risks and was concentrating on how best to put it into effect, as he turned the corner by Romberg's Drug Store and came in sight of his father's house.

III

R UDOLPH'S FATHER, the local freight agent, had floated with the second wave of German and Irish stock to the Minnesota-Dakota country. Theoretically, great opportunities lay ahead of a young man of energy in that day and place, but Carl Miller had been incapable of establishing either with his superiors or his subordinates the reputation for approximate immutability which is essential to success in a hierarchic industry. Somewhat gross, he was, nevertheless, insufficiently hard-headed and unable to take fundamental relationships for granted, and this inability made him suspicious, unrestful and continually dismayed.

His two bonds with the colourful life were his faith in the Roman Catholic Church and his mystical worship of the Empire Builder, James J. Hill.* Hill was the apotheosis of that quality in which Miller himself was deficient – the sense of things, the feel of things, the hint of rain in the wind on the cheek. Miller's mind worked late on the old decisions of other men, and he had never in his life felt the balance of any single thing in his hands. His weary, sprightly, undersized body was growing old in Hill's gigantic shadow. For twenty years he had lived alone with Hill's name and God.

On Sunday morning Carl Miller awoke in the dustless quiet of six o'clock. Kneeling by the side of the bed he bent his yellow-grey hair and the full dapple bangs of his moustache into the pillow, and prayed for several minutes. Then he drew off his nightshirt – like the rest of his generation he had never been able to endure pyjamas – and clothed his thin, white, hairless body in woollen underwear.

He shaved. Silence in the other bedroom where his wife lay nervously asleep. Silence from the screened-off corner of the hall where his son's cot stood, and his son slept among his Alger* books, his collection of cigar bands, his mothy pennants – "Cornell", "Hamline" and "Greetings from Pueblo, New Mexico" – and the other possessions of his private life. From outside Miller could hear the shrill birds and the whirring movement of the poultry and, as an undertone, the low, swelling click-a-tick of the six-fifteen through train for Montana and the green coast beyond. Then as the cold water dripped from the washrag in his hand he raised his head suddenly – he had heard a furtive sound from the kitchen below.

He dried his razor hastily, slipped his dangling suspenders to his shoulders, and listened. Someone was walking in the kitchen, and he knew by the light footfall that it was not his wife. With his mouth faintly ajar he ran quickly down the stairs and opened the kitchen door.

Standing by the sink, with one hand on the still-dripping faucet and the other clutching a full glass of water, stood his son. The boy's eyes, still heavy with sleep, met his father's with a frightened, reproachful beauty. He was barefooted and his pyjamas were rolled up at the knees and sleeves.

For a moment they both remained motionless – Carl Miller's brow went down and his son's went up, as though they were striking a balance between the extremes of emotion which filled them. Then the bangs of the parent's moustache descended portentously until they obscured his mouth, and he gave a short glance around to see if anything had been disturbed.

The kitchen was garnished with sunlight which beat on the pans and made the smooth boards of the floor and table yellow and clean as wheat. It was the centre of the house where the fire burned and the tins fitted into tins like toys, and the steam whistled all day on a thin pastel note. Nothing was moved, nothing touched – except the faucet where beads of water still formed and dripped with a white flash into the sink below.

"What are you doing?"

"I got awful thirsty, so I thought I'd just come down and get—"

"I thought you were going to communion."

A look of vehement astonishment spread over his son's face.

"I forgot all about it."

"Have you drunk any water?"

"No—"

As the word left his mouth Rudolph knew it was the wrong answer, but the faded indignant eyes facing him had signalled up the truth before the boy's will could act. He realized, too, that he should never have come downstairs; some vague necessity for verisimilitude had made him want to leave a wet glass as evidence by the sink; the honesty of his imagination had betrayed him.

"Pour it out," commanded his father, "that water!"

Rudolph despairingly inverted the tumbler.

"What's the matter with you, anyways?" demanded Miller angrily.

"Nothing."

"Did you go to confession yesterday?"

"Yes."

"Then why were you going to drink water?"

"I don't know – I forgot."

"Maybe you care more about being a little bit thirsty than you do about your religion."

"I forgot." Rudolph could feel the tears straining in his eyes.

"That's no answer."

"Well, I did."

"You better look out!" His father held to a high, persistent, inquisitory note: "If you're so forgetful that you can't remember your religion, something better be done about it."

Rudolph filled a sharp pause with:

"I can remember it all right."

"First you begin to neglect your religion," cried his father, fanning his own fierceness, "the next thing you'll begin to lie and steal, and the *next* thing is the *reform* school!"

Not even this familiar threat could deepen the abyss that Rudolph saw before him. He must either tell all now, offering his body for what he knew would be a ferocious beating, or else tempt the thunderbolts by receiving the Body and Blood of Christ with sacrilege upon his soul. And of the two the former seemed more terrible – it was not so much the beating he dreaded as the savage ferocity, outlet of the ineffectual man, which would lie behind it.

"Put down that glass and go upstairs and dress!" his father ordered. "And when we get to church, before you go to communion, you better kneel down and ask God to forgive you for your carelessness."

Some accidental emphasis in the phrasing of this command acted like a catalytic agent on the confusion and terror of Rudolph's mind. A wild, proud anger rose in him, and he dashed the tumbler passionately into the sink.

His father uttered a strained, husky sound, and sprang for him. Rudolph dodged to the side, tipped over a chair, and tried to get beyond the kitchen table. He cried out sharply when a hand grasped his pyjama shoulder, then he felt the dull impact of a fist against the side of his head and glancing blows on the upper part of his body. As he slipped here and there in his father's grasp, dragged or lifted when he clung instinctively to an arm, aware of sharp smarts and strains, he made no sound except that he laughed hysterically several times. Then in less than a minute the blows abruptly ceased. After a lull during which Rudolph was tightly held and during which they both trembled violently and uttered strange, truncated words, Carl Miller half dragged, half threatened his son upstairs.

"Put on your clothes!"

Rudolph was now both hysterical and cold. His head hurt him, and there was a long, shallow scratch on his neck from his father's fingernail, and he sobbed and trembled as he dressed. He was aware of his mother standing at the doorway in a wrapper, her wrinkled face compressing and squeezing and opening out into a new series of wrinkles which floated and eddied from neck to brow. Despising her nervous ineffectuality and avoiding her rudely when she tried to touch his neck with witch hazel, he made a hasty, choking toilet. Then he followed his father out of the house and along the road towards the Catholic church.

IV

THEY WALKED WITHOUT SPEAKING, except when Carl Miller acknowledged automatically the existence of passers-by. Rudolph's uneven breathing alone ruffled the hot Sunday silence.

His father stopped decisively at the door of the church.

"I've decided you'd better go to confession again. Go in and tell Father Schwartz what you did and ask God's pardon."

"You lost your temper too!" said Rudolph quickly.

Carl Miller took a step towards his son, who moved cautiously backwards.

"All right, I'll go."

"Are you going to do what I say?" cried his father in a hoarse whisper.

"All right."

Rudolph walked into the church and for the second time in two days entered the confessional and knelt down. The slat went up almost at once.

"I accuse myself of missing my morning prayers."

"Is that all?"

"That's all."

A maudlin exultation filled him. Not easily ever again would he be able to put an abstraction before the necessities of his ease and pride. An invisible line had been crossed and he had become aware of his isolation – aware that it applied not only to those moments when he was Blatchford Sarnemington, but that it applied to all his inner life. Hitherto such phenomena as "crazy" ambitions and petty shames and fears had been but private reservations, unacknowledged before the throne of his official soul. Now he realized unconsciously that his private reservations were himself – and all the rest a garnished front and a conventional flag. The pressure of his environment had driven him into the lonely secret road of adolescence.

He knelt in the pew beside his father. Mass began. Rudolph knelt up – when he was alone he slumped his posterior back against the seat – and tasted the consciousness of a sharp, subtle revenge. Beside him his father prayed that God would forgive Rudolph, and asked also that his own outbreak of temper would be pardoned. He glanced sidewise at this son and was relieved to see that the strained, wild look had gone from his face and that he had ceased sobbing. The Grace of God, inherent in the Sacrament, would do the rest, and perhaps after Mass everything would be better. He was proud of Rudolph in his heart and beginning to be truly as well as formally sorry for what he had done.

Usually, the passing of the collection box was a significant point for Rudolph in the services. If, as was often the case, he had no money to drop in he would be furiously ashamed and bow his head and pretend not to see the box, lest Jeanne Brady in the pew behind should take notice and suspect an acute family poverty. But today he glanced coldly into it as it skimmed under his eyes, noting with casual interest the large number of pennies it contained.

When the bell rang for communion, however, he quivered. There was no reason why God should not stop his heart. During the past twelve hours he had committed a series of mortal sins increasing in gravity, and he was now to crown them all with a blasphemous sacrilege.

"*Domine, non sum dignus, ut intres sub tectum meum: sed tantum dic verbo, et sanabitur anima mea...*"*

There was a rustle in the pews and the communicants worked their ways into the aisle with downcast eyes and joined hands. Those of larger piety pressed together their fingertips to form steeples. Among these latter was Carl Miller. Rudolph followed him towards the altar rail and knelt down, automatically taking up the napkin under his chin. The bell rang sharply, and the priest turned from the altar with the white Host held above the chalice:

"*Corpus Domini nostri Jesu Christi custodiat animam meam in vitam æternam.*"*

A cold sweat broke out on Rudolph's forehead as the communion began. Along the line Father Schwartz moved, and with gathering nausea Rudolph felt his heart valves weakening at the will of God. It seemed to him that the church was darker and that a great quiet had fallen, broken only by the inarticulate mumble which announced the approach of the Creator of Heaven and Earth. He dropped his head down between his shoulders and waited for the blow.

Then he felt a sharp nudge in his side. His father was poking him to sit up, not to slump against the rail; the priest was only two places away.

"*Corpus Domini nostri Jesu Christi custodiat animam meam in vitam æternam.*"

Rudolph opened his mouth. He felt the sticky wax taste of the wafer on his tongue. He remained motionless for what seemed an interminable period of time, his head still raised, the wafer undissolved in his mouth. Then again he started at the pressure of his father's elbow, and saw that the people were falling away from the altar like leaves and turning with blind downcast eyes to their pews, alone with God.

Rudolph was alone with himself, drenched with perspiration and deep in mortal sin. As he walked back to his pew the sharp taps of his cloven hoofs were loud upon the floor, and he knew that it was a dark poison he carried in his heart.

V

"*Sagitta volante in die*"*

THE BEAUTIFUL LITTLE BOY with eyes like blue stones, and lashes that sprayed open from them like flower petals, had finished telling his sin to Father Schwartz – and the square of sunshine in which he sat had moved forward half an hour into the room. Rudolph had become less frightened now; once eased of the story a reaction had set in. He knew that as long as he was in the room with this priest God would not stop his heart, so he sighed and sat quietly, waiting for the priest to speak.

Father Schwartz's cold watery eyes were fixed upon the carpet pattern on which the sun had brought out the swastikas and the flat bloomless vines and the pale echoes of flowers. The hall clock ticked insistently towards sunset, and from the ugly room and from the afternoon outside the window arose a stiff monotony, shattered now and then by the reverberate clapping of a faraway hammer on the dry air. The priest's nerves were strung thin and the beads of his rosary were crawling and squirming like snakes upon the green felt of his tabletop. He could not remember now what it was he should say.

Of all the things in this lost Swede town he was most aware of this little boy's eyes – the beautiful eyes, with lashes that left them reluctantly and curved back as though to meet them once more.

For a moment longer the silence persisted while Rudolph waited, and the priest struggled to remember something that was slipping farther and farther away from him, and the clock ticked in the broken house. Then Father Schwartz stared hard at the little boy and remarked in a peculiar voice:

"When a lot of people get together in the best places things go glimmering."

Rudolph started and looked quickly at Father Schwartz's face.

"I said…" began the priest, and paused, listening. "Do you hear the hammer and the clock ticking and the bees? Well, that's no good. The thing is to have a lot of people in the centre of the world, wherever that happens to be. Then" – his watery eyes widened knowingly – "things go glimmering."

"Yes, Father," agreed Rudolph, feeling a little frightened.

"What are you going to be when you grow up?"

"Well, I was going to be a baseball player for a while," answered Rudolph nervously, "but I don't think that's a very good ambition, so I think I'll be an actor or a navy officer."

Again the priest stared at him.

"I see *exactly* what you mean," he said, with a fierce air.

Rudolph had not meant anything in particular, and at the implication that he had, he became more uneasy.

"This man is crazy," he thought, "and I'm scared of him. He wants me to help him out some way, and I don't want to."

"You look as if things went glimmering," cried Father Schwartz wildly. "Did you ever go to a party?"

"Yes, Father."

"And did you notice that everybody was properly dressed? That's what I mean. Just as you went into the party there was a moment when everybody was properly dressed. Maybe two little girls were standing by the door and some boys were leaning over the banisters, and there were bowls around full of flowers."

"I've been to a lot of parties," said Rudolph, rather relieved that the conversation had taken this turn.

"Of course," continued Father Schwartz triumphantly, "I knew you'd agree with me. But my theory is that when a whole lot of people get together in the best places things go glimmering all the time."

Rudolph found himself thinking of Blatchford Sarnemington.

"Please listen to me!" commanded the priest impatiently. "Stop worrying about last Saturday. Apostasy implies an absolute damnation only on the supposition of a previous perfect faith. Does that fix it?"

Rudolph had not the faintest idea what Father Schwartz was talking about, but he nodded, and the priest nodded back at him and returned to his mysterious preoccupation.

"Why," he cried, "they have lights now as big as stars – do you realize that? I heard of one light they had in Paris or somewhere that was as big as a star. A lot of people had it – a lot of gay people. They have all sorts of things now that you never dreamt of.

"Look here..." He came nearer to Rudolph, but the boy drew away, so Father Schwartz went back and sat down in his chair, his eyes dried out and hot.

"Did you ever see an amusement park?"

"No, Father."

"Well, go and see an amusement park." The priest waved his hand vaguely. "It's a thing like a fair, only much more glittering. Go to one at night and stand a little way off from it in a dark place – under dark trees. You'll see a big wheel made of lights turning in the air and a long slide shooting boats down into the water. A band playing somewhere and a smell of peanuts – and everything will twinkle. But it won't remind you of anything, you see. It will all just hang out there in the night like a coloured balloon – like a big yellow lantern on a pole."

Father Schwartz frowned as he suddenly thought of something.

"But don't get up close," he warned Rudolph, "because if you do you'll only feel the heat and the sweat and the life."

All this talking seemed particularly strange and awful to Rudolph, because this man was a priest. He sat there, half-terrified, his beautiful eyes open wide and staring at Father Schwartz. But underneath his terror he felt that his own inner convictions were confirmed. There was something ineffably gorgeous somewhere that had nothing to do with God. He no longer thought that God was angry at him about the original lie, because He must have understood that Rudolph had done it to make things finer in the confessional, brightening up the dinginess of his admissions by saying a thing radiant and proud. At the moment when he had affirmed immaculate honour a silver pennon had flapped out into the breeze somewhere and there had been the crunch of leather and the shine of silver spurs and a troop of horsemen waiting for dawn on a low green hill. The sun had made stars of light on their breastplates like the picture at home of the German cuirassiers at Sedan.

But now the priest was muttering inarticulate and heartbroken words, and the boy became wildly afraid. Horror entered suddenly in at the open window, and the atmosphere of the room changed. Father Schwartz collapsed precipitously down on his knees and let his body settle back against a chair.

"Oh, my God!" he cried out, in a strange voice, and wilted to the floor.

Then a human oppression rose from the priest's worn clothes and mingled with the faint smell of old food in the corners. Rudolph gave a sharp cry and ran in a panic from the house – while the collapsed man lay there quite still, filling his room, filling it with voices and faces until it was crowded with echolalia, and rang loud with a steady, shrill note of laughter.

Outside the window the blue sirocco trembled over the wheat, and girls with yellow hair walked sensuously along roads that bounded the fields, calling innocent, exciting things to the young men who were working in the lines between the grain. Legs were shaped under starchless gingham, and rims of the necks of dresses were warm and damp. For five hours now hot fertile life had burnt in the afternoon. It would be night in three hours, and all along the land there would be these blonde northern girls and the tall young men from the farms lying out beside the wheat, under the moon.

Rags Martin-Jones and
the Pr–nce of W–les

I

T HE MAJESTIC CAME GLIDING into New York harbour on an
April morning. She sniffed at the tugboats and turtle-gaited
ferries, winked at a gaudy young yacht, and ordered a cattle boat
out of her way with a snarling whistle of steam. Then she parked at
her private dock with all the fuss of a stout lady sitting down, and
announced complacently that she had just come from Cherbourg
and Southampton with a cargo of the very best people in the world.

The very best people in the world stood on the deck and waved
idiotically to their poor relations who were waiting on the dock for
gloves from Paris. Before long a great toboggan had connected the
Majestic with the North American continent and the ship began
to disgorge these very best people in the world – who turned out to
be Gloria Swanson, two buyers from Lord & Taylor, the financial
minister from Graustark* with a proposal for funding the debt,
and an African king who had been trying to land somewhere all
winter and was feeling violently seasick.

The photographers worked passionately as the stream of passengers flowed onto the dock. There was a burst of cheering at
the appearance of a pair of stretchers laden with two Middle-
Westerners who had drunk themselves delirious on the last night
out.

The deck gradually emptied, but when the last bottle of
Benedictine had reached shore the photographers still remained
at their posts. And the officer in charge of debarkation still stood
at the foot of the gangway, glancing first at his watch and then at
the deck as if some important part of the cargo was still on board.

At last from the watchers on the pier there arose a long-drawn "Ah-h-h!" as a final entourage began to stream down from deck B.

First came two French maids, carrying small, purple dogs, and followed by a squad of porters, blind and invisible under innumerable bunches and bouquets of fresh flowers. Another maid followed, leading a sad-eyed orphan child of a French flavour, and close upon its heels walked the second officer pulling along three neurasthenic wolfhounds, much to their reluctance and his own.

A pause. Then the captain, Sir Howard George Witchcraft, appeared at the rail, with something that might have been a pile of gorgeous silver fox fur standing by his side...

Rags Martin-Jones, after five years in the capitals of Europe, was returning to her native land!

Rags Martin-Jones was not a dog. She was half a girl and half a flower, and as she shook hands with Captain Sir Howard George Witchcraft she smiled as if someone had told her the newest, freshest joke in the world. All the people who had not already left the pier felt that smile trembling on the April air and turned around to see.

She came slowly down the gangway. Her hat, an expensive, inscrutable experiment, was crushed under her arm so that her scant boy's hair, convict's hair, tried unsuccessfully to toss and flop a little in the harbour wind. Her face was like seven o'clock on a wedding morning, save where she had slipped a preposterous monocle into an eye of clear childish blue. At every few steps her long lashes would tilt out the monocle and she would laugh, a bored, happy laugh, and replace the supercilious spectacle in the other eye.

Tap! Her one hundred and five pounds reached the pier and it seemed to sway and bend from the shock of her beauty. A few porters fainted. A large, sentimental shark which had followed the ship across made a despairing leap to see her once more, and then dove, broken-hearted, back into the deep sea. Rags Martin-Jones had come home.

There was no member of her family there to meet her for the simple reason that she was the only member of her family left alive. In 1912 her parents had gone down on the *Titanic* together rather than be separated in this world, and so the Martin-Jones fortune of seventy-five millions had been inherited by a very little girl on her tenth birthday. It was what the consumer always refers to as a "shame".

Rags Martin-Jones (everybody had forgotten her real name long ago) was now photographed from all sides. The monocle persistently fell out and she kept laughing and yawning and replacing it, so no very clear picture of her was taken – except by the motion-picture camera. All the photographs, however, included a flustered handsome young man, with an almost ferocious love light burning in his eyes, who had met her on the dock. His name was John M. Chestnut, he had already written the story of his success for the *American Magazine* and he had been hopelessly in love with Rags ever since the time when she, like the tides, had come under the influence of the summer moon.

When Rags became really aware of his presence they were walking down the pier, and she looked at him blankly as though she had never seen him before in this world.

"Rags," he began, "Rags—"

"John M. Chestnut?" she enquired, inspecting him with great interest.

"Of course!" he exclaimed angrily. "Are you trying to pretend you don't know me? That you didn't write me to meet you here?"

She laughed. A chauffeur appeared at her elbow and she twisted out of her coat, revealing a dress made in great splashy checks of sea blue and grey. She shook herself like a wet bird.

"I've got a lot of junk to declare," she remarked absently.

"So have I," said Chestnut anxiously, "and the first thing I want to declare is that I've loved you, Rags, every minute since you've been away."

She stopped him with a groan.

"Please! There were some young Americans on the boat. The subject has become a bore."

"My God!" cried Chestnut. "Do you mean to say that you class *my* love with what was said to you on a *boat*?"

His voice had risen and several people in the vicinity turned to hear.

"Sh!" she warned him. "I'm not giving a circus. If you want me to even see you while I'm here you'll have to be less violent."

But John M. Chestnut seemed unable to control his voice.

"Do you mean to say" – it trembled to a carrying pitch – "that you've forgotten what you said on this very pier five years ago last Thursday?"

Half the passengers from the ship were now watching the scene on the dock and another little eddy drifted out of the customs house to see.

"John" – her displeasure was increasing – "if you raise your voice again I'll arrange it so you'll have plenty of chance to cool off. I'm going to the Ritz. Come and see me there this afternoon."

"But, Rags!..." he protested hoarsely. "Listen to me. Five years ago—"

Then the watchers on the dock were treated to a curious sight. A beautiful lady in a chequered dress of sea blue and grey took a brisk step forward so that her hands came into contact with an excited young man by her side. The young man retreating instinctively reached back with his foot but, finding nothing, relapsed gently off the thirty-foot dock and plopped, after a not ungraceful revolution, into the Hudson River.

A shout of alarm went up and there was a rush to the edge, just as his head appeared above water. He was swimming easily and, perceiving this, the young lady who had apparently been the cause of the accident leant over the pier and made a megaphone of her hands.

"I'll be in at half-past four," she cried.

And with a cheerful wave of her hand, which the engulfed gentleman was unable to return, she adjusted her monocle, threw one haughty glance at the gathered crowd and walked leisurely from the scene.

II

THE FIVE DOGS, THE THREE MAIDS and the French orphan were installed in the largest suite at the Ritz, and Rags tumbled lazily into a steaming bath, fragrant with herbs, where she dozed for the greater part of an hour. At the end of that time she received business calls from a masseuse, a manicure and finally a Parisian hairdresser, who restored her haircut to criminal's length. When John M. Chestnut arrived at four he found half a dozen lawyers and bankers, the administrators of the Martin-Jones trust fund, waiting in the hall. They had been there since half-past one and were now in a state of considerable agitation.

After one of the maids had subjected him to a severe scrutiny, possibly to be sure that he was thoroughly dry, John was conducted immediately into the presence of M'selle. M'selle was in her bedroom reclining on the chaise longue among two dozen silk pillows that had accompanied her from the other side. John came into the room somewhat stiffly and greeted her with a formal bow.

"You look better," she said, raising herself from her pillows and staring at him appraisingly. "It gave you a colour."

He thanked her coldly for the compliment.

"You ought to go in every morning." And then she added irrelevantly, "I'm going back to Paris tomorrow."

John Chestnut gasped.

"I wrote you that I didn't intend to stay more than a week anyhow," she added.

"But, Rags—"

"Why should I? There isn't an amusing man in New York."

"But listen, Rags, won't you give me a chance? Won't you stay for, say, ten days and get to know me a little?"

"Know you!" Her tone implied that he was already a far too open book. "I want a man who's capable of a gallant gesture."

"Do you mean you want me to express myself entirely in pantomime?"

Rags uttered a disgusted sigh.

"I mean you haven't any imagination," she explained patiently. "No Americans have any imagination. Paris is the only large city where a civilized woman can breathe."

"Don't you care for me at all any more?"

"I wouldn't have crossed the Atlantic to see you if I didn't. But as soon as I looked over the Americans on the boat I knew I couldn't marry one. I'd just hate you, John, and the only fun I'd have out of it would be the fun of breaking your heart."

She began to twist herself down among the cushions until she almost disappeared from view.

"I've lost my monocle," she explained.

After an unsuccessful search in the silken depths she discovered the elusive glass hanging down the back of her neck.

"I'd love to be in love," she went on, replacing the monocle in her childish eye. "Last spring in Sorrento I almost eloped with an Indian raja, but he was half a shade too dark, and I took an intense dislike to one of his other wives."

"Don't talk that rubbish!" cried John, sinking his face into his hands.

"Well, I didn't marry him," she protested. "But in one way he had a lot to offer. He was the third richest subject of the British Empire. That's another thing – are you rich?"

"Not as rich as you."

"There you are. What have you to offer me?"

"Love."

"Love!" She disappeared again among the cushions. "Listen, John. Life to me is a series of glistening bazaars with a merchant in front of each one rubbing his hands together and saying 'Patronize this place here. Best bazaar in the world.' So I go in with my purse full of beauty and money and youth, all prepared to buy. 'What have you got for sale?' I ask him, and he rubs his hands together and says: 'Well, Mademoiselle, today we have some perfectly be-oo-tiful love.' Sometimes he hasn't even got that in stock, but he sends out for it when he finds I have so much money to spend. Oh, he always gives me love before I go – and for nothing. That's the one revenge I have."

John Chestnut rose despairingly to his feet and took a step towards the window.

"Don't throw yourself out," Rags exclaimed quickly.

"All right." He tossed his cigarette down into Madison Avenue.

"It isn't just you," she said in a softer voice. "Dull and uninspired as you are, I care for you more than I can say. But life's so endless here. Nothing ever comes off."

"Loads of things come off," he insisted. "Why, today there was an intellectual murder in Hoboken and a suicide by proxy in Maine. A bill to sterilize agnostics is before Congress—"

"I have no interest in humour," she objected, "but I have an almost archaic predilection for romance. Why, John, last month I sat at a dinner table while two men flipped a coin for the kingdom of Schwartzberg-Rhineminster. In Paris I knew a man named Blutchdak who really started the war, and has a new one planned for year after next."

"Well, just for a rest you come out with me tonight," he said doggedly.

"Where to?" demanded Rags with scorn. "Do you think I still thrill at a nightclub and a bottle of sugary mousseux? I prefer my own gaudy dreams."

"I'll take you to the most highly strung place in the city."

"What'll happen? You've got to tell me what'll happen."

John Chestnut suddenly drew a long breath and looked cautiously around as if he were afraid of being overheard.

"Well, to tell you the truth," he said in a low worried tone, "if everything was known, something pretty awful would be liable to happen to *me*."

She sat upright and the pillows tumbled about her like leaves.

"Do you mean to imply that there's anything shady in your life?" she cried, with laughter in her voice. "Do you expect me to believe that? No, John, you'll have your fun by plugging ahead on the beaten path – just plugging ahead."

Her mouth, a small insolent rose, dropped the words on him like thorns. John took his hat and coat from the chair and picked up his cane.

"For the last time – will you come along with me tonight and see what you will see?"

"See what? See who? Is there anything in this country worth seeing?"

"Well," he said, in a matter-of-fact tone, "for one thing you'll see the Prince of Wales."

"What?" She left the chaise longue at a bound. "Is he back in New York?"

"He will be tonight. Would you care to see him?"

"Would I? I've never seen him. I've missed him everywhere. I'd give a year of my life to see him for an hour." Her voice trembled with excitement.

"He's been in Canada. He's down here incognito for the big prizefight this afternoon. And I happen to know where he's going to be tonight."

Rags gave a sharp ecstatic cry:

"Dominique! Louise! Germaine!"

The three maids came running. The room filled suddenly with vibrations of wild, startled light.

"Dominique, the car!" cried Rags in French. "St Raphael, my gold dress and the slippers with the real gold heels. The big pearls too – all the pearls, and the egg diamond and the stockings with the sapphire clocks. Germaine – send for a beauty parlour on the run. My bath again – ice cold and half full of almond cream. Dominique – Tiffany's, like lightning, before they close! Find me a brooch, a pendant, a tiara, anything – it doesn't matter – with the arms of the House of Windsor."

She was fumbling at the buttons of her dress – and as John turned quickly to go it was already sliding from her shoulders.

"Orchids!" she called after him. "Orchids, for the love of Heaven! Four dozen, so I can choose four."

And then maids flew here and there about the room like frightened birds. "Perfume, St Raphael, open the perfume trunk, and my rose-coloured sables, and my diamond garters, and the sweet oil for my hands! Here, take these things! This too – and this – ouch! – and this!"

With becoming modesty John Chestnut closed the outside door. The six trustees in various postures of fatigue, of ennui, of resignation, of despair, were still cluttering up the outer hall.

"Gentlemen," announced John Chestnut, "I fear that Miss Martin-Jones is much too weary from her trip to talk to you this afternoon."

III

"THIS PLACE, for no particular reason, is called the Hole in the Sky."

Rags looked around her. They were on a roof garden wide open to the April night. Overhead the true stars winked cold and there was a lunar sliver of ice in the dark west. But where they stood it was warm as June, and the couples dining or dancing on the opaque glass floor were unconcerned with the forbidding sky.

"What makes it so warm?" she whispered as they moved towards a table.

"It's some new invention that keeps the warm air from rising. I don't know the principle of the thing, but I know that they can keep it open like this even in the middle of winter—"

"Where's the Prince of Wales?" she demanded tensely.

John looked around.

"He hasn't arrived yet. He won't be here for about half an hour."

She sighed profoundly.

"It's the first time I've been excited in four years."

Four years – one year less than he had loved her. He wondered if when she was sixteen, a wild lovely child, sitting up all night in restaurants with officers who were to leave for Brest next day, losing the glamour of life too soon in the old, sad, poignant days of the war, she had ever been so lovely as under these amber lights and this dark sky. From her excited eyes to her tiny slipper heels, which were striped with layers of real silver and gold, she was like one of those amazing ships that are carved complete in a bottle. She was finished with that delicacy, with that care, as though the long lifetime of some worker in fragility had been used to make her so. John Chestnut wanted to take her up in his hands, turn her this way and that, examine the tip of a slipper or the tip of an ear or squint closely at the fairy stuff from which her lashes were made.

"Who's that?" She pointed suddenly to a handsome Latin at a table over the way.

"That's Roderigo Minerlino, the movie and face-cream star. Perhaps he'll dance after a while."

Rags became suddenly aware of the sound of violins and drums, but the music seemed to come from far away, seemed to float over the crisp night and onto the floor with the added remoteness of a dream.

"The orchestra's on another roof," explained John. "It's a new idea – look, the entertainment's beginning."

A Negro girl, thin as a reed, emerged suddenly from a masked entrance into a circle of harsh barbaric light, startled the music to a wild minor and commenced to sing a rhythmic, tragic song. The pipe of her body broke abruptly and she began a slow incessant step, without progress and without hope, like the failure of a savage insufficient dream. She had lost Papa Jack, she cried over and over with a hysterical monotony at once despairing and unreconciled. One by one the loud horns tried to force her from the steady beat of madness, but she listened only to the mutter of the drums which were isolating her in some lost place in time, among many thousand forgotten years. After the failure of the piccolo, she made herself again into a thin brown line, wailed once with a sharp and terrible intensity, then vanished into sudden darkness.

"If you lived in New York you wouldn't need to be told who she is," said John when the amber light flashed on. "The next fella is Sheik B. Smith, a comedian of the fatuous, garrulous sort…"

He broke off. Just as the lights went down for the second number Rags had given a long sigh and leant forward tensely in her chair. Her eyes were rigid like the eyes of a pointer dog, and John saw that they were fixed on a party that had come through a side entrance and were arranging themselves around a table in the half-darkness.

The table was shielded with palms, and Rags at first made out only three dim forms. Then she distinguished a fourth who seemed to be placed well behind the other three – a pale oval of a face topped with a glimmer of dark-yellow hair.

"Hello!" ejaculated John. "There's His Majesty now."

Her breath seemed to die murmurously in her throat. She was dimly aware that the comedian was now standing in a glow of white light on the dancing floor, that he had been talking for some moments, and that there was a constant ripple of laughter in the air. But her eyes remained motionless, enchanted. She saw one of the party bend and whisper to another, and, after the low glitter of a match, the bright button of a cigarette end gleamed in the background. How long it was before she moved she did not know. Then something seemed to happen to her eyes, something white, something terribly urgent, and she wrenched about sharply to find herself full in the centre of a baby spotlight from above. She became aware that words were being said to her from somewhere and that a quick trail of laughter was circling the roof, but the light blinded her and instinctively she made a half-movement from her chair.

"Sit still!" John was whispering across the table. "He picks somebody out for this every night."

Then she realized – it was the comedian, Sheik B. Smith. He was talking to her, arguing with her – about something that seemed incredibly funny to everyone else, but came to her ears only as a blur of muddled sound. Instinctively she had composed her face at the first shock of the light and now she smiled. It was a gesture of rare self-possession. Into this smile she insinuated a vast impersonality, as if she were unconscious of the light, unconscious of his attempt to play upon her loveliness – but amused at an infinitely removed *him*, whose darts might have been thrown just as successfully at the moon. She was no longer a "lady" – a lady would have been harsh or pitiful or absurd; Rags stripped her attitude to a sheer consciousness of her own impervious beauty, sat there glittering until the comedian began to feel alone as he had never felt alone before. At a signal from him the spotlight was switched suddenly out. The moment was over.

The moment was over, the comedian left the floor and the faraway music began. John leant towards her.

"I'm sorry. There really wasn't anything to do. You were wonderful."

She dismissed the incident with a casual laugh – then she started, there were now only two men sitting at the table across the floor.

"He's gone!" she exclaimed in quick distress.

"Don't worry – he'll be back. He's got to be awfully careful, you see, so he's probably waiting outside with one of his aides until it gets dark again."

"Why has he got to be careful?"

"Because he's not supposed to be in New York. He's even under one of his second-string names."

The lights dimmed again and almost immediately a tall man appeared out of the darkness and approached their table.

"May I introduce myself?" he said rapidly to John in a supercilious British voice. "Lord Charles Este, of Baron Marchbanks' party." He glanced at John closely as if to be sure that he appreciated the significance of the name.

John nodded.

"That is between ourselves, you understand."

"Of course."

Rags groped on the table for her untouched champagne and tipped the glassful down her throat.

"Baron Marchbanks requests that your companion will join his party during this number."

Both men looked at Rags. There was a moment's pause.

"Very well," she said, and glanced back again interrogatively at John. Again he nodded. She rose and, with her heart beating wildly, threaded the tables, making the half-circuit of the room; then melted, a slim figure in shimmering gold, into the table set in half darkness.

IV

THE NUMBER DREW TO A CLOSE and John Chestnut sat alone at his table, stirring auxiliary bubbles in his glass of champagne. Just before the lights went on there was a soft rasp of gold cloth, and Rags, flushed and breathing quickly, sank into her chair. Her eyes were shining with tears.

John looked at her moodily.

"Well, what did he say?"

"He was very quiet."

"Didn't he say a word?"

Her hand trembled as she took up her glass of champagne.

"He just looked at me while it was dark. And he said a few conventional things. He was like his pictures, only he looks very bored and tired. He didn't even ask my name."

"Is he leaving New York tonight?"

"In half an hour. He and his aides have a car outside, and they expect to be over the border before dawn."

"Did you find him – fascinating?"

She hesitated and then slowly nodded her head.

"That's what everybody says," admitted John glumly. "Do they expect you back there?"

"I don't know." She looked uncertainly across the floor, but the celebrated personage had again withdrawn from his table to some retreat outside. As she turned back an utterly strange young man who had been standing for a moment in the main entrance came towards them hurriedly. He was a deathly-pale person in a dishevelled and inappropriate business suit, and he laid a trembling hand on John Chestnut's shoulder.

"Monte!" exclaimed John, starting up so suddenly that he upset his champagne. "What is it? What's the matter?"

"They've picked up the trail!" said the young man in a shaken whisper. He looked around. "I've got to speak to you alone."

John Chestnut jumped to his feet, and Rags noticed that his face too had become white as the napkin in his hand. He excused himself and they retreated to an unoccupied table a few feet away. Rags watched them curiously for a moment, then she resumed her scrutiny of the table across the floor. Would she be asked to come back? The Prince had simply risen and bowed and gone outside. Perhaps she should have waited until he returned, but though she was still tense with excitement she had, to some extent, become Rags Martin-Jones again. Her curiosity was satisfied – any new urge must come from him. She wondered if she had really felt an intrinsic charm – she wondered especially if he had in any marked way responded to her beauty.

The pale person called Monte disappeared and John returned to the table. Rags was startled to find that a tremendous change had come over him. He lurched into his chair like a drunken man.

"John! What's the matter?"

Instead of answering he reached for the champagne bottle, but his fingers were trembling so that the splattered wine made a wet yellow ring around his glass.

"Are you sick?"

"Rags," he said unsteadily, "I'm all through."

"What do you mean?"

"I'm all through, I tell you." He managed a sickly smile. "There's been a warrant out for me for over an hour."

"What have you done?" she demanded in a frightened voice. "What's the warrant for?"

The lights went out for the next number and he collapsed suddenly over the table.

"What is it?" she insisted, with rising apprehension. She leant forward – his answer was barely audible.

"Murder?" She could feel her body grow cold as ice.

He nodded. She took hold of both arms and tried to shake him upright, as one shakes a coat into place. His eyes were rolling in his head.

"Is it true? Have they got proof?"

Again he nodded drunkenly.

"Then you've got to get out of the country now! Do you understand, John? You've got to get out *now*, before they come looking for you here!"

He loosed a wild glance of terror towards the entrance.

"Oh, God!" cried Rags. "Why don't you do something?" Her eyes strayed here and there in desperation, became suddenly fixed. She drew in her breath sharply, hesitated and then whispered fiercely into his ear.

"If I arrange it, will you go to Canada tonight?"

"How?"

"I'll arrange it – if you'll pull yourself together a little. This is Rags talking to you, don't you understand, John? I want you to sit here and not move until I come back!"

A minute later she had crossed the room under cover of the darkness.

"Baron Marchbanks," she whispered softly, standing just behind his chair.

He motioned her to sit down.

"Have you room in your car for two more passengers tonight?"

One of the aides turned around abruptly.

"His Lordship's car is full," he said shortly.

"It's terribly urgent." Her voice was trembling.

"Well," said the Prince hesitantly, "I don't know."

Lord Charles Este looked at the Prince and shook his head.

"I don't think it's advisable. This is a ticklish business anyhow with contrary orders from home. You know we agreed there'd be no complications."

The Prince frowned.

"This isn't a complication," he objected.

Este turned frankly to Rags.

"Why is it urgent?"

Rags hesitated.

"Why" – she flushed suddenly – "it's a runaway marriage."

The Prince laughed.

"Good!" he exclaimed. "That settles it. Este is just being official. Bring him over right away. We're leaving shortly, what?"

Este looked at his watch.

"Right now!"

Rags rushed away. She wanted to move the whole party from the roof while the lights were still down.

"Hurry!" she cried in John's ear. "We're going over the border – with the Prince of Wales. You'll be safe by morning."

He looked up at her with dazed eyes. She hurriedly paid the check and, seizing his arm, piloted him as inconspicuously as possible to the other table, where she introduced him with a word. The Prince acknowledged his presence by shaking hands – the aides nodded, only faintly concealing their displeasure.

"We'd better start," said Este, looking impatiently at his watch.

They were on their feet when suddenly an exclamation broke from all of them – two policemen and a red-haired man in plain clothes had come in at the main door.

"Out we go," breathed Este, impelling the party towards the side entrance. "There's going to be some kind of riot here." He swore – two more bluecoats barred the exit there. They paused uncertainly. The plain-clothes man was beginning a careful inspection of the people at the tables.

Este looked sharply at Rags and then at John, who shrank back behind the palms.

"Is that one of your revenue fellas out there?" demanded Este.

"No," whispered Rags. "There's going to be trouble. Can't we get out this entrance?"

The Prince, with rising impatience, sat down again in his chair.

"Let me know when you chaps are ready to go." He smiled at Rags. "Now just suppose we all get in trouble just for that jolly face of yours."

Then suddenly the lights went up. The plain-clothes man whirled around quickly and sprang to the middle of the cabaret floor.

"Nobody try to leave this room!" he shouted. "Sit down, that party behind the palms! Is John M. Chestnut in this room?"

Rags gave a short involuntary cry.

"Here!" cried the detective to the policeman behind him. "Take a look at that funny bunch over there. Hands up, you men!"

"My God!" whispered Este. "We've got to get out of here!" He turned to the Prince. "This won't do, Ted. You can't be seen here. I'll stall them off while you get down to the car."

He took a step towards the side entrance.

"Hands up, there!" shouted the plain-clothes man. "And when I say hands up I mean it! Which one of you's Chestnut?"

"You're mad!" cried Este. "We're British subjects. We're not involved in this affair in any way!"

A woman screamed somewhere and there was a general movement towards the elevator, a movement which stopped short before the muzzles of two automatic pistols. A girl next to Rags collapsed in a dead faint to the floor, and at the same moment the music on the other roof began to play.

"Stop that music!" bellowed the plain-clothes man. "And get some earrings* on that whole bunch – quick!"

Two policemen advanced towards the party, and simultaneously Este and the other aides drew their revolvers and, shielding the Prince as they best could, began to edge towards the side. A shot rang out and then another, followed by a crash of silver and china as half a dozen diners overturned their tables and dropped quickly behind.

The panic became general. There were three shots in quick succession and then a fusillade. Rags saw Este firing coolly at the eight amber lights above, and a thick fume of grey smoke began to fill the air. As a strange undertone to the shouting and screaming came the incessant clamour of the distant jazz band.

Then in a moment it was all over. A shrill whistle rang out over the roof, and through the smoke Rags saw John Chestnut advancing towards the plain-clothes man, his hands held out in a gesture of surrender. There was a last nervous cry, a chill clatter as someone inadvertently stepped into a pile of dishes, and then a heavy silence fell on the roof – even the band seemed to have died away.

"It's all over!" John Chestnut's voice rang out wildly on the night air. "The party's over. Everybody who wants to can go home!"

Still there was silence – Rags knew it was the silence of awe – the strain of guilt had driven John Chestnut insane.

"It was a great performance," he was shouting. "I want to thank you one and all. If you can find any tables still standing, champagne will be served as long as you care to stay."

It seemed to Rags that the roof and the high stars suddenly began to swim round and round. She saw John take the detective's hand and shake it heartily, and she watched the detective grin and pocket his gun. The music had recommenced, and the girl who had fainted was suddenly dancing with Lord Charles Este in the corner. John was running here and there patting people on the back, and laughing and shaking hands. Then he was coming towards her, fresh and innocent as a child.

"Wasn't it wonderful?" he cried.

Rags felt a faintness stealing over her. She groped backwards with her hand towards a chair.

"What was it?" she cried dazedly. "Am I dreaming?"

"Of course not! You're wide awake. I made it up, Rags, don't you see? I made up the whole thing for you. I had it invented! The only thing real about it was my name!"

She collapsed suddenly against his coat, clung to his lapels and would have wilted to the floor if he had not caught her quickly in his arms.

"Some champagne – quick!" he called, and then he shouted at the Prince of Wales, who stood nearby. "Order my car quick, you! Miss Martin-Jones has fainted from excitement."

V

THE SKYSCRAPER ROSE BULKILY through thirty tiers of windows before it attenuated itself to a graceful sugarloaf of shining white. Then it darted up again another hundred feet, thinned to a mere oblong tower in its last fragile aspiration towards the sky. At the highest of its high windows Rags Martin-Jones stood full in the stiff breeze, gazing down at the city.

"Mr Chestnut wants to know if you'll come right into his private office."

Obediently her slim feet moved along the carpet into a high cool chamber overlooking the harbour and the wide sea.

John Chestnut sat at his desk, waiting, and Rags walked to him and put her arms around his shoulder.

"Are you sure *you*'re real?" she asked anxiously. "Are you absolutely *sure*?"

"You only wrote me a week before you came," he protested modestly, "or I could have arranged a revolution."

"Was the whole thing just *mine*?" she demanded. "Was it a perfectly useless, gorgeous thing, just for me?"

"Useless?" He considered. "Well, it started out to be. At the last minute I invited a big restaurant man to be there, and while you were at the other table I sold him the whole idea of the nightclub."

He looked at his watch.

"I've got one more thing to do – and then we've got just time to be married before lunch." He picked up his telephone. "Jackson?... Send a triplicated cable to Paris, Berlin and Budapest and have those two bogus dukes who tossed up for Schwartzberg-Rhineminster chased over the Polish border. If the Duchy won't act, lower the rate of exchange to point triple zero naught two. Also, that idiot Blutchdak is in the Balkans again, trying to start a new war. Put him on the first boat for New York or else throw him in a Greek jail."

He rang off, turned to the startled cosmopolite with a laugh.

"The next stop is the City Hall. Then if you like we'll run over to Paris."

"John," she asked him intently, "who was the Prince of Wales?"

He waited till they were in the elevator, dropping twenty floors at a swoop. Then he leant forward and tapped the lift boy on the shoulder.

"Not so fast, Cedric. This lady isn't used to falls from high places."

The elevator boy turned around, smiled. His face was pale, oval, framed in yellow hair. Rags blushed like fire.

"Cedric's from Wessex," explained John. "The resemblance is, to say the least, amazing. Princes are not particularly discreet, and I suspect Cedric of being a Guelf* in some left-handed way."

Rags took the monocle from around her neck and threw the ribbon over Cedric's head.

"Thank you," she said simply, "for the second-greatest thrill of my life."

John Chestnut began rubbing his hands together in a commercial gesture.

"Patronize this place, lady," he besought her. "Best bazaar in the city!"

"What have you got for sale?"

"Well, M'selle, today we have some perfectly bee-*oo*-tiful love."

"Wrap it up, Mr Merchant," cried Rags Martin-Jones. "It looks like a bargain to me."

The Adjuster

I

A T FIVE O'CLOCK THE SOMBRE egg-shaped room at the Ritz ripens to a subtle melody – the light *clat-clat* of one lump, two lumps, into the cup and the *ding* of the shining teapots and cream pots as they kiss elegantly in transit upon a silver tray. There are those who cherish that amber hour above all other hours, for now the pale pleasant toil of the lilies who inhabit the Ritz is over – the singing decorative part of the day remains.

Moving your eyes around the slightly raised horseshoe balcony you might, one spring afternoon, have seen young Mrs Alphonse Karr and young Mrs Charles Hemple at a table for two. The one in the dress was Mrs Hemple – when I say "the dress" I refer to that black immaculate affair with the big buttons and the red ghost of a cape at the shoulders, a gown suggesting with faint and fashionable irreverence the garb of a French cardinal, as it was meant to do when it was invented in the Rue de la Paix. Mrs Karr and Mrs Hemple were twenty-three years old and their enemies said that they had done very well for themselves. Either might have had her limousine waiting at the hotel door, but both of them much preferred to walk home (up Park Avenue) through the April twilight.

Luella Hemple was tall, with the sort of flaxen hair that English country girls should have, but seldom do. Her skin was radiant and there was no need of putting anything on it at all, but in deference to an antiquated fashion – this was the year 1920 – she had powdered out its high roses and drawn on it a new mouth and new eyebrows – which were no more successful than such meddling deserves. This, of course, is said from the vantage point of 1925. In those days the effect she gave was exactly right.

"I've been married three years," she was saying as she squashed out a cigarette in an exhausted lemon. "The baby will be two years old tomorrow. I must remember to get…"

She took a gold pencil from her case and wrote "Candles" and "Things you pull, with paper caps" on an ivory date pad. Then, raising her eyes, she looked at Mrs Karr and hesitated.

"Shall I tell you something outrageous?"

"Try," said Mrs Karr cheerfully.

"Even my baby bores me. That sounds unnatural, Ede, but it's true. He doesn't *begin* to fill my life. I love him with all my heart, but when I have him to take care of for an afternoon I get so nervous that I want to scream. After two hours I begin praying for the moment the nurse'll walk in the door."

When she had made this confession Luella breathed quickly and looked closely at her friend. She didn't really feel unnatural at all. This was the truth. There couldn't be anything vicious in the truth.

"It may be because you don't love Charles," ventured Mrs Karr, unmoved.

"But I do! I hope I haven't given you that impression with all this talk." She decided that Ede Karr was stupid. "It's the very fact that I do love Charles that complicates matters. I cried myself to sleep last night because I know we're drifting slowly but surely towards a divorce. It's the baby that keeps us together."

Ede Karr, who had been married five years, looked at her critically to see if this was a pose, but Luella's lovely eyes were grave and sad.

"And what is the trouble?" Ede enquired.

"It's plural," said Luella, frowning. "First there's food. I'm a vile housekeeper and I have no intention of turning into a good one. I hate to order groceries, and I hate to go into the kitchen and poke around to see if the icebox is clean, and I hate to pretend to the servants that I'm interested in their work, when really I never want to hear about food until it comes on the table. You see, I never learnt to cook, and consequently a kitchen is about as interesting to me as a… as a boiler room. It's simply a machine that I don't understand. It's easy to say 'Go to cooking school', the way people do in books – but, Ede, in real life does anybody ever change into a model *Hausfrau** – unless they have to?"

"Go on," said Ede noncommittally. "Tell me more."

"Well, as a result the house is always in a riot. The servants leave every week. If they're young and incompetent I can't train them, so we have to let them go. If they're experienced, they hate a house where a woman doesn't take an intense interest in the price of asparagus. So they leave – and half the time we eat at restaurants and hotels."

"I don't suppose Charles likes that."

"Hates it. In fact he hates about everything that I like. He's lukewarm about the theatre, hates the opera, hates dancing, hates cocktail parties – sometimes I think he hates everything pleasant in the world. I sat home for a year or so. While Chuck was on the way, and while I was nursing him, I didn't mind. But this year I told Charles frankly that I was still young enough to want some fun. And since then we've been going out whether he wants to or not." She paused, brooding. "I'm so sorry for him I don't know what to do, Ede – but if we sat home I'd just be sorry for myself. And to tell you another true thing, I'd rather that he'd be unhappy than me."

Luella was not so much stating a case as thinking aloud. She considered that she was being very fair. Before her marriage men had always told her that she was "a good sport", and she had tried to carry this fairness into her married life. So she always saw Charley's point of view as clearly as she saw her own.

If she had been a pioneer wife she would probably have fought the fight side by side with her husband. But here in New York there wasn't any fight. They weren't struggling together to obtain a far-off peace and leisure – she had more of either than she could use. Luella, like several thousand other young wives in New York, honestly wanted something to do. If she had had a little more money and a little less love, she could have gone in for horses or for vagarious amour. Or if they had had a little less money, her surplus energy would have been absorbed by hope and even by effort. But the Charles Hemples were in between. They were of that enormous American class who wander over Europe every summer, sneering rather pathetically and wistfully at the customs and traditions and pastimes of other countries, because they have no customs or traditions or pastimes of their own. It is a class sprung yesterday from fathers and mothers who might just as well have lived two hundred years ago.

The tea hour had turned abruptly into the before-dinner hour. Most of the tables had emptied until the room was dotted rather than crowded with shrill isolated voices and remote, surprising laughter – in one corner the waiters were already covering the tables with white for dinner.

"Charles and I are on each other's nerves." In the new silence Luella's voice rang out with startling clearness, and she lowered it precipitately. "Little things. He keeps rubbing his face with his hand – all the time, at table, at the theatre – even when he's in bed. It drives me wild, and when things like that begin to irritate you, it's nearly over." She broke off and, reaching backwards, drew up a light fur around her neck. "I hope I haven't bored you, Ede. It's on my mind because tonight tells the story. I made an engagement for tonight – an interesting engagement, a supper after the theatre to meet some Russians, singers or dancers or something, and Charles says he won't go. If he doesn't – then I'm going alone. And that's the end."

She put her elbows on the table suddenly and, bending her eyes down into her smooth gloves, began to cry, stubbornly and quietly. There was no one near to see, but Ede Karr wished that she had taken her gloves off. She would have reached out consolingly and touched her bare hand. But the gloves were a symbol of the difficulty of sympathizing with a woman to whom life had given so much. Ede wanted to say that it would "come out all right", that it wasn't "so bad as it seemed", but she said nothing. Her only reaction was impatience and distaste.

A waiter stepped near and laid a folded paper on the table, and Mrs Karr reached for it.

"No, you mustn't," murmured Luella brokenly. "No, I invited *you*! I've got the money right here."

II

THE HEMPLES' APARTMENT – they owned it – was in one of those impersonal white palaces that are known by number instead of name. They had furnished it on their honeymoon, gone to England for the big pieces, to Florence for the bric-a-brac and to Venice for the lace and sheer linen of the curtains and for the glass of many colours which littered the table when they entertained. Luella enjoyed choosing things on her honeymoon. It gave a purposeful air to the trip and saved it from ever turning into the rather dismal wandering among big hotels and desolate ruins which European honeymoons are apt to be.

They returned and life began. On the grand scale. Luella found herself a lady of substance. It amazed her sometimes that the specially created apartment and the specially created limousine were hers, just as indisputably as the mortgaged suburban bungalow out of the *Ladies' Home Journal* and the last year's car that fate might have given her instead. She was even more amazed when it all began to bore her. But it did…

The evening was at seven when she turned out of the April dusk, let herself into the hall and saw her husband waiting in the living room before an open fire. She came in without a sound, closed the door noiselessly behind her and stood watching him for a moment through the pleasant effective vista of the small salon which intervened. Charles Hemple was in the middle thirties, with a young serious face and distinguished iron-grey hair which would be white in ten years more. That and his deep-set, dark-grey eyes were his most noticeable features – women always thought his hair was romantic; most of the time Luella thought so too.

At this moment she found herself hating him a little, for she saw that he had raised his hand to his face and was rubbing it nervously over his chin and mouth. It gave him an air of unflattering abstraction and sometimes even obscured his words so that she was continually saying "What?" She had spoken about it several times, and he had apologized in a surprised way. But obviously he didn't realize how noticeable and how irritating it was, for he continued to do it. Things had now reached such a precarious state that Luella dreaded speaking of such matters any more – a certain sort of word might precipitate the imminent scene.

Luella tossed her gloves and purse abruptly on the table. Hearing the faint sound, her husband looked out towards the hall.

"Is that you, dear?"

"Yes, dear."

She went into the living room, and walked into his arms and kissed him tensely. Charles Hemple responded with unusual formality and then turned her slowly around so that she faced across the room.

"I've brought someone home to dinner."

She saw then that they were not alone, and her first feeling was of strong relief; the rigid expression on her face softened into a shy charming smile as she held out her hand.

"This is Doctor Moon – this is my wife."

A man a little older than her husband, with a round, pale, slightly lined face, came forward to meet her.

"Good evening, Mrs Hemple," he said. "I hope I'm not interfering with any arrangement of yours."

"Oh, no," Luella cried quickly. "I'm delighted that you're coming to dinner. We're quite alone."

Simultaneously she thought of her engagement tonight and wondered if this could be a clumsy trap of Charles's to keep her at home. If it were, he had chosen his bait badly. This man – a tired placidity radiated from him, from his face, from his heavy, leisurely voice, even from the three-year-old shine of his clothes.

Nevertheless she excused herself and went into the kitchen to see what was planned for dinner. As usual they were trying a new pair of servants, the luncheon had been ill cooked and ill served – she would let them go tomorrow. She hoped Charles would talk to them – she hated to get rid of servants. Sometimes they wept and sometimes they were insolent, but Charles had a way with them. And they were always afraid of a man.

The cooking on the stove, however, had a soothing savour. Luella gave instructions about "which china" and unlocked a bottle of precious Chianti from the buffet. Then she went in to kiss young Chuck good night.

"Has he been good?" she demanded as he crawled enthusiastically into her arms.

"Very good," said the governess. "We went for a long walk over by Central Park."

"Well aren't you a smart boy!" She kissed him ecstatically.

"And he put his foot into the fountain, so we had to come home in a taxi right away and change his little shoe and stocking."

"That's right. Here, wait a minute, *Chuck*!" Luella unclasped the great yellow beads from around her neck and handed them to him. "You mustn't break Mamma's beads." She turned to the nurse. "Put them on my dresser, will you, after he's asleep?"

She felt a certain compassion for her son as she went away – the small enclosed life he led, that all children led, except in big families. He was a dear little rose, except on the days when she took care of him. His face was the same shape as hers; she was thrilled sometimes and formed new resolves about life when his heart beat against her own.

In her own pink and lovely bedroom she confined her attentions to her face, which she washed and restored. Doctor Moon didn't deserve a change of dress, and Luella found herself oddly tired, though she had done very little all day. She returned to the living room and they went in to dinner.

"Such a nice house, Mrs Hemple," said Doctor Moon impersonally, "and let me congratulate you on your fine little boy."

"Thanks. Coming from a doctor, that's a nice compliment." She hesitated. "Do you specialize in children?"

"I'm not a specialist at all," he said. "I'm about the last of my kind – a general practitioner."

"The last in New York anyhow," remarked Charles. He had begun rubbing his face nervously and Luella fixed her eyes on Doctor Moon so that she wouldn't see. But at Charles's next words she looked back at him sharply.

"In fact," he said unexpectedly, "I've invited Doctor Moon here because I wanted you to have a talk with him tonight."

Luella sat up straight in her chair.

"A talk with *me*?"

"Doctor Moon's an old friend of mine and I think he can tell you a few things, Luella, that you ought to know."

"Why..." She tried to laugh but she was surprised and annoyed. "I don't see exactly what you mean. There's nothing the matter with me. I don't believe I've ever felt better in my life."

Doctor Moon looked at Charles, asking permission to speak. Charles nodded and his hand went up automatically to his face.

"Your husband has told me a great deal about your unsatisfactory life together," said Doctor Moon, still impersonally. "He wonders if I can be of any help in smoothing things out."

Luella's face was burning.

"I have no particular faith in psychoanalysis," she said coldly, "and I scarcely consider myself a subject for it."

"Neither have I," answered Doctor Moon, apparently unconscious of the snub. "I have no particular faith in anything but myself. I told you I am not a specialist, nor, I may add, a faddist of any sort. I promise nothing."

For a moment Luella considered leaving the room. But the effrontery of the suggestion aroused her curiosity too.

"I can't imagine what Charles has told you," she said, controlling herself with difficulty, "much less why. But I assure you that our affairs are a matter entirely between my husband and me. If you have no objections, Doctor Moon, I'd much prefer to discuss something less personal."

Doctor Moon nodded heavily and politely. He made no further attempt to open the subject, and dinner proceeded in what was little more than a defeated silence. Luella determined that whatever happened she would adhere to her plans for tonight. An hour ago her independence had demanded it, but now some gesture of defiance had become necessary to her self-respect. She would stay in the living room for a short moment after dinner; then when the coffee came she would excuse herself and dress to go out.

But when they did leave the dining room, it was Charles who, in a quick, unarguable way, vanished.

"I have a letter to write," he said. "I'll be back in a moment." Before Luella could make a diplomatic objection he went quickly down the corridor to his room and she heard him shut his door.

Angry and confused, Luella poured the coffee and sank into a corner of the couch, looking intently at the fire.

"Don't be afraid, Mrs Hemple," said Doctor Moon suddenly. "This was forced upon me. I do not act as a free agent—"

"I'm not afraid of you," she interrupted. But she knew that she was lying. She was a little afraid of him, if only for his dull insensitiveness to her distaste.

"Tell me about your trouble," he said very naturally, as though she were not a free agent either. He wasn't even looking at her, and except that they were alone in the room, he scarcely seemed to be addressing her at all.

The words that were in Luella's mind, her will, on her lips, were: "I'll do no such thing." What she actually said amazed her. It came out of her spontaneously, with apparently no cooperation of her own.

"Didn't you see him rubbing his face at dinner?" she said despairingly. "Are you blind? He's become so irritating to me that I think I'll go mad."

"I see." Doctor Moon's round face nodded.

"Don't you see I've had enough of home?" Her breasts seemed to struggle for air under her dress. "Don't you see how bored I am with keeping house, with the baby – everything seems as if it's going on for ever and ever? I want excitement, and I don't care what form it takes or what I pay for it, so long as it makes my heart beat."

"I see."

It infuriated Luella that he claimed to understand. Her feeling of defiance had reached such a pitch that she preferred that no one should understand. She was content to be justified by the impassioned sincerity of her desires.

"I've tried to be good, and I'm not going to try any more. If I'm one of those women who wreck their lives for nothing, then I'll do it now. You can call me selfish, or silly, and be quite right; but in five minutes I'm going out of this house and begin to be alive."

This time Doctor Moon didn't answer, but he raised his head as if he were listening to something that was taking place a little distance away.

"You're not going out," he said after a moment. "I'm quite sure you're not going out."

Luella laughed.

"I *am* going out."

He disregarded this.

"You see, Mrs Hemple, your husband isn't well. He's been trying to live your kind of life and the strain of it has been too much for him. When he rubs his mouth—"

Light steps came down the corridor and the maid, with a frightened expression on her face, tiptoed into the room.

"Mrs Hemple…"

Startled at the interruption Luella turned quickly.

"Yes?"

"Can I speak to—" Her fear broke precipitately through her slight training. "Mr Hemple, he's sick! He came into the kitchen a while ago and began throwing all the food out of the icebox, and now he's in his room, crying and singing…"

Suddenly Luella heard his voice.

III

CHARLES HEMPLE had had a nervous collapse. There were twenty years of almost uninterrupted toil upon his shoulders, and the recent pressure at home had been too much for him to bear. His attitude towards his wife was the weak point in what had otherwise been a strong-minded and well-organized career – he was aware of her intense selfishness, but it is one of the many flaws in the scheme of human relationships that selfishness in women has an irresistible appeal to many men. Luella's selfishness existed side by side with a childish beauty and, in consequence, Charles Hemple had begun to take the blame upon himself for situations which she had obviously brought about. It was an unhealthy attitude and his mind had sickened, at length, with his attempts to put himself in the wrong.

After the first shock and the momentary flush of pity that followed it, Luella looked at the situation with impatience. She was "a good sport" – she couldn't take advantage of Charles when he was sick. The question of her liberties had to be postponed until he was on his feet. Just when she had determined to be a wife no longer, Luella was compelled to be a nurse as well. She sat beside his bed while he talked about her in his delirium – about the days of their engagement, and how some friend had told him then that he was making a mistake, and about his happiness in the early months of their marriage, and his growing disquiet as the gap appeared. Evidently he had been more aware of it than she had thought – more than he ever said.

"Luella!" He would lurch up in bed. "Luella! Where *are* you?"

"I'm right here, Charles, beside you." She tried to make her voice cheerful and warm.

"If you want to go, Luella, you'd better go. I don't seem to be enough for you any more."

She denied this soothingly.

"I've thought it over, Luella, and I can't ruin my health on account of you…" Then quickly, and passionately: "Don't go, Luella, for God's sake, don't go away and leave me! Promise me you won't! I'll do anything you say if you won't go."

His humility annoyed her most; he was a reserved man, and she had never guessed at the extent of his devotion before.

"I'm only going for a minute. It's Doctor Moon, your friend, Charles. He came today to see how you were, don't you remember? And he wants to talk to me before he goes."

"You'll come back?" he persisted.

"In just a little while. There – lie quiet."

She raised his head and plumped his pillow into freshness. A new trained nurse would arrive tomorrow.

In the living room Doctor Moon was waiting – his suit more worn and shabby in the afternoon light. She disliked him inordinately, with an illogical conviction that he was in some way to blame for her misfortune, but he was so deeply interested that she couldn't refuse to see him. She hadn't asked him to consult with the specialists, though – a doctor who was so down at the heel...

"Mrs Hemple." He came forward, holding out his hand, and Luella touched it, lightly and uneasily.

"You seem well," he said.

"I am well, thank you."

"I congratulate you on the way you've taken hold of things."

"But I haven't taken hold of things at all," she said coldly. "I do what I have to—"

"That's just it."

Her impatience mounted rapidly.

"I do what I have to, and nothing more," she continued. "And with no particular goodwill."

Suddenly she opened up to him again, as she had the night of the catastrophe – realizing that she was putting herself on a footing of intimacy with him, yet unable to restrain her words.

"The house isn't going," she broke out bitterly. "I had to discharge the servants, and now I've got a woman in by the day. And the baby has a cold, and I've found out that his nurse doesn't know her business, and everything's just as messy and terrible as it can be!"

"Would you mind telling me how you found out the nurse didn't know her business?"

"You find out various unpleasant things when you're forced to stay around the house."

He nodded, his weary face turning here and there about the room.

"I feel somewhat encouraged," he said slowly. "As I told you, I promise nothing. I only do the best I can."

Luella looked up at him, startled.

"What do you mean?" she protested. "You've done nothing for me – nothing at all!"

"Nothing much – yet," he said heavily. "It takes time, Mrs Hemple."

The words were said in a dry monotone that was somehow without offence, but Luella felt that he had gone too far. She got to her feet.

"I've met your type before," she said coldly. "For some reason you seem to think that you have a standing here as 'the old friend of the family'. But I don't make friends quickly, and I haven't given you the privilege of being so" – she wanted to say "insolent", but the word eluded her – "so personal with me."

When the front door had closed behind him, Luella went into the kitchen to see if the woman understood about the three different dinners – one for Charles, one for the baby and one for herself. It was hard to do with only a single servant when things were so complicated. She must try another employment agency – this one had begun to sound bored.

To her surprise, she found the cook with hat and coat on, reading a newspaper at the kitchen table.

"Why" – Luella tried to think of the name – "why, what's the matter, Mrs—"

"Mrs Danski is my name."

"What's the matter?"

"I'm afraid I won't be able to accommodate you," said Mrs Danski. "You see, I'm only a plain cook, and I'm not used to preparing invalid's food."

"But I've counted on you."

"I'm very sorry." She shook her head stubbornly. "I've got my own health to think of. I'm sure they didn't tell me what kind of a job it was when I came. And when you asked me to clean out your husband's room, I knew it was way beyond my powers."

"I won't ask you to clean anything," said Luella desperately. "If you'll just stay until tomorrow. I can't possibly get anybody else tonight."

Mrs Danski smiled politely.

"I got my own children to think of, just like you."

It was on Luella's tongue to offer her more money, but suddenly her temper gave way.

"I've never heard of anything so selfish in my life!" she broke out. "To leave me at a time like this! You're an old fool!"

"If you'd pay me for my time, I'd go," said Mrs Danski calmly.

"I won't pay you a cent unless you'll stay!"

She was immediately sorry she had said this, but she was too proud to withdraw the threat.

"You will so pay me!"

"You go out that door!"

"I'll go when I get my money," asserted Mrs Danski indignantly. "I got my children to think of."

Luella drew in her breath sharply and took a step forward. Intimidated by her intensity, Mrs Danski turned and flounced, muttering, out of the door.

Luella went to the phone and, calling up the agency, explained that the woman had left.

"Can you send me someone right away? My husband is sick and the baby's sick——"

"I'm sorry, Mrs Hemple. There's no one in the office now. It's after four o'clock."

Luella argued for a while. Finally she obtained a promise that they would telephone to an emergency woman they knew. That was the best they could do until tomorrow.

She called several other agencies, but the servant industry had apparently ceased to function for the day. After giving Charles his medicine she tiptoed softly into the nursery.

"How's baby?" she asked abstractedly.

"Ninety-nine one," whispered the nurse, holding the thermometer to the light. "I just took it."

"Is that much?" asked Luella, frowning.

"It's just three fifths of a degree. That isn't so much for the afternoon. They often run up a little with a cold."

Luella went over to the cot and laid her hand on her son's flushed cheek, thinking, in the midst of her anxiety, how much he resembled the incredible cherub of the "Lux" advertisement in the bus.

She turned to the nurse.

"Do you know how to cook?"

"Why – I'm not a good cook."

"Well, can you do the baby's food tonight? That old fool has left and I can't get anyone and I don't know what to do."

"Oh yes, I can do the baby's food."

"That's all right, then. I'll try to fix something for Mr Hemple. Please have your door open so you can hear the bell when the doctor comes. And let me know."

So many doctors! There had scarcely been an hour all day when there wasn't a doctor in the house. The specialist and their family physician every morning, then the baby doctor – and this afternoon there had been Doctor Moon, placid, persistent, unwelcome, in the parlour. Luella went into the kitchen. She could cook bacon and eggs for herself – she had often done that after the theatre. But the vegetables for Charles were a different matter – they must be left to boil or stew or something, and the stove had so many doors and ovens that she couldn't decide which to use. She chose a blue pan that looked new, sliced carrots into it and covered them with a little water. As she put it on the stove and tried to remember what to do next, the phone rang. It was the agency.

"Yes, this is Mrs Hemple speaking."

"Why, the woman we sent to you has returned here with the claim that you refused to pay her for her time."

"I explained to you that she refused to stay," said Luella hotly. "She didn't keep her agreement and I didn't feel I was under any obligation—"

"We have to see that our people are paid," the agency informed her. "Otherwise we wouldn't be helping them at all, would we? I'm sorry, Mrs Hemple, but we won't be able to furnish you with anyone else until this little matter is arranged."

"Oh, I'll pay, I'll pay!" she cried.

"Of course we like to keep on good terms with our clients—"

"Yes – yes!"

"So if you'll send her money around tomorrow? It's seventy-five cents an hour."

"But how about tonight?" she exclaimed. "I've got to have someone tonight."

"Why – it's pretty late now. I was just going home myself."

"But I'm Mrs Charles Hemple! Don't you understand? I'm perfectly good for what I say I'll do. I'm the wife of Charles Hemple, of 14 Broadway—"

Simultaneously she realized that Charles Hemple of 14 Broadway was a helpless invalid – he was neither a reference nor a refuge any more. In despair at the sudden callousness of the world, she hung up the receiver.

After another ten minutes of frantic muddling in the kitchen she went to the baby's nurse, whom she disliked, and confessed that she was unable to cook her husband's dinner. The nurse announced that she had a splitting headache, and that with a sick child her hands were full already, but she consented, without enthusiasm, to show Luella what to do.

Swallowing her humiliation, Luella obeyed orders while the nurse experimented, grumbling, with the unfamiliar stove. Dinner was started after a fashion. Then it was time for the nurse to bathe Chuck, and Luella sat down alone at the kitchen table, and listened to the bubbling perfume that escaped from the pans.

"And women do this every day," she thought. "Thousands of women. Cook and take care of sick people – and go out to work too."

But she didn't think of those women as being like her, except in the superficial aspect of having two feet and two hands. She said it as she might have said "South Sea Islanders wear nose rings." She was merely slumming today in her own home and she wasn't enjoying it. For her, it was merely a ridiculous exception.

Suddenly she became aware of slow approaching steps in the dining room and then in the butler's pantry. Half-afraid that it was Doctor Moon coming to pay another call, she looked up – and saw the nurse coming through the pantry door. It flashed through Luella's mind that the nurse was going to be sick too. And she was right – the nurse had hardly reached the kitchen door when she lurched and clutched at the handle as a winged bird clings to a branch. Then she receded wordlessly to the floor. Simultaneously, the doorbell rang and Luella, getting to her feet, gasped with relief that the baby doctor had come.

"Fainted, that's all," he said, taking the girl's head into his lap. The eyes fluttered. "Yep, she fainted, that's all."

"Everybody's sick!" cried Luella with a sort of despairing humour. "Everybody's sick but me, doctor."

"This one's not sick," he said after a moment. "Her heart is normal already. She just fainted."

When she had helped the doctor raise the quickening body to a chair, Luella hurried into the nursery and bent over the baby's bed. She let down one of the iron sides quietly. The fever seemed to be gone now – the flush had faded away. She bent over to touch the small cheek.

Suddenly Luella began to scream.

IV

EVEN AFTER HER BABY'S FUNERAL, Luella still couldn't believe that she had lost him. She came back to the apartment and walked around the nursery in a circle, saying his name. Then, frightened by grief, she sat down and stared at his white rocker with the red chicken painted on the side.

"What will become of me now?" she whispered to herself. "Something awful is going to happen to me when I realize that I'll never see Chuck any more!"

She wasn't sure yet. If she waited here till twilight, the nurse might still bring him in from his walk. She remembered a tragic confusion in the midst of which someone had told her that Chuck was dead, but if that was so, then why was his room waiting, with his small brush and comb still on the bureau, and why was she here at all?

"Mrs Hemple."

She looked up. The weary, shabby figure of Doctor Moon stood in the door.

"You go away," Luella said dully.

"Your husband needs you."

"I don't care."

Doctor Moon came a little way into the room.

"I don't think you understand, Mrs Hemple. He's been calling for you. You haven't anyone now except him."

"I hate you," she said suddenly.

"If you like. I promised nothing, you know. I do the best I can. You'll be better when you realize that your baby is gone, that you're not going to see him any more."

Luella sprang to her feet.

"My baby isn't dead!" she cried. "You lie! You always lie!" Her flashing eyes looked into his and caught something there, at once brutal and kind, that awed her and made her impotent and acquiescent. She lowered her own eyes in tired despair.

"All right," she said wearily. "My baby is gone. What shall I do now?"

"Your husband is much better. All he needs is rest and kindness. But you must go to him and tell him what's happened."

"I suppose you think you made him better," said Luella bitterly.

"Perhaps. He's nearly well."

Nearly well – then the last link that held her to her home was broken. This part of her life was over – she could cut it off here, with its grief and oppression, and be off now, free as the wind.

"I'll go to him in a minute," Luella said in a faraway voice. "Please leave me alone."

Doctor Moon's unwelcome shadow melted into the darkness of the hall.

"I can go away," Luella whispered to herself. "Life has given me back freedom, in place of what it took away from me."

But she mustn't linger even a minute, or Life would bind her again and make her suffer once more. She called the apartment porter and asked that her trunk be brought up from the storeroom. Then she began taking things from the bureau and wardrobe, trying to approximate as nearly as possible the possessions that she had brought to her married life. She even found two old dresses that had formed part of her trousseau – out of style now, and a little tight in the hips – which she threw in with the rest. A new life. Charles was well again, and her baby, whom she had worshipped, and who had bored her a little, was dead.

When she had packed her trunk, she went into the kitchen automatically, to see about the preparations for dinner. She spoke to the cook about the special things for Charles and said that she herself was dining out. The sight of one of the small pans that had been used to cook Chuck's food caught her attention for a moment – but she stared at it unmoved. She looked into the icebox and saw it was clean and fresh inside. Then she went into Charles's room. He was sitting up in bed and the nurse was reading to him. His hair was almost white now, silvery white, and underneath it his eyes were huge and dark in his thin young face.

"The baby is sick?" he asked in his own natural voice.

She nodded.

He hesitated, closing his eyes for a moment. Then he asked: "The baby is dead?"

"Yes."

For a long time he didn't speak. The nurse came over and put her hand on his forehead. Two large, strange tears welled from his eyes.

"I knew the baby was dead."

After another long wait, the nurse spoke.

"The doctor said he could be taken out for a drive today while there was still sunshine. He needs a little change."

"Yes."

"I thought" – the nurse hesitated. "I thought perhaps it would do you both good, Mrs Hemple, if you took him instead of me."

Luella shook her head hastily.

"Oh no," she said. "I don't feel able to, today."

The nurse looked at her oddly. With a sudden feeling of pity for Charles, Luella bent down gently and kissed his cheek. Then, without a word, she went to her own room, put on her hat and coat, and with her suitcase started for the front door.

Immediately she saw that there was a shadow in the hall. If she could get past that shadow, she was free. If she could go to the right or left of it, or order it out of her way! But stubbornly, it refused to move, and with a little cry she sank down into a hall chair.

"I thought you'd gone," she wailed. "I told you to go away."

"I'm going soon," said Doctor Moon, "but I don't want you to make an old mistake."

"I'm not making a mistake – I'm leaving my mistakes behind."

"You're trying to leave yourself behind but you can't. The more you try to run away from yourself, the more you'll have yourself with you."

"But I've got to go away," she insisted wildly. "Out of this house of death and failure!"

"You haven't failed yet. You've only begun."

She stood up.

"Let me pass."

"No."

Abruptly she gave way, as she always did when he talked to her. She covered her face with her hands and burst into tears.

"Go back into that room and tell the nurse you'll take your husband for a drive," he suggested.

"I can't."

"Oh, yes."

Once more Luella looked at him and knew that she would obey. With the conviction that her spirit was broken at last, she took up her suitcase and walked back through the hall.

V

THE NATURE OF THE CURIOUS INFLUENCE that Doctor Moon exerted upon her Luella could not guess. But as the days passed, she found herself doing many things that had been repugnant to her before. She stayed at home with Charles, and when he grew better she went out with him sometimes to dinner, or the theatre, but only when he expressed a wish. She visited the kitchen every day, and kept an unwilling eye on the house, at first with a horror that it would go wrong again, then from habit. And she felt that it was all somehow mixed up with Doctor Moon – it was something he kept telling her about life, or almost telling her, and yet concealing from her as though he were afraid to have her know.

With the resumption of their normal life, she found that Charles was less nervous. His habit of rubbing his face had left him, and if the world seemed less gay and happy to her than it had before she experienced a certain peace, sometimes, that she had never known.

Then, one afternoon, Doctor Moon told her suddenly that he was going away.

"Do you mean for good?" she demanded with a touch of panic.

"For good."

For a strange moment she wasn't sure whether she was glad or sorry.

"You don't need me any more," he said quietly. "You don't realize it, but you've grown up."

He came over and, sitting on the couch beside her, took her hand. Luella sat silent and tense – listening.

"We make an agreement with children that they can sit in the audience without helping to make the play," he said, "but if they still sit in the audience after they're grown, somebody's got to work double time for them, so that they can enjoy the light and glitter of the world."

"But I want the light and glitter," she protested. "That's all there is in life. There can't be anything wrong in wanting to have things warm."

"Things will still be warm."

"How?"

"Things will warm themselves from you."

Luella looked at him, startled.

"It's your turn to be the centre, to give others what was given to you for so long. You've got to give security to young people and peace to your husband, and a sort of charity to the old. You've got to let the people who work for you depend on you. You've got to cover up a few more troubles than you show, and be a little more patient than the average person, and do a little more instead of a little less than your share. The light and glitter of the world is in your hands."

He broke off suddenly.

"Get up," he said, "and go to that mirror and tell me what you see."

Obediently Luella got up and went close to a purchase of her honeymoon, a Venetian pier glass on the wall.

"I see new lines in my face here," she said, raising her finger and placing it between her eyes, "and a few shadows at the sides that might be... that are little wrinkles."

"Do you care?"

She turned quickly. "No," she said.

"Do you realize that Chuck is gone? That you'll never see him any more?"

"Yes." She passed her hands slowly over her eyes. "But that all seems so vague and far away."

"Vague and far away," he repeated – and then: "And are you afraid of me now?"

"Not any longer," she said, and she added frankly, "now that you're going away."

He moved towards the door. He seemed particularly weary tonight, as though he could hardly move about at all.

"The household here is in your keeping," he said in a tired whisper. "If there is any light and warmth in it, it will be your light and warmth; if it is happy, it will be because you've made it so. Happy things may come to you in life, but you must never go seeking them any more. It is your turn to make the fire."

"Won't you sit down a moment longer?" Luella ventured.

"There isn't time." His voice was so low now that she could scarcely hear the words. "But remember that whatever suffering comes to you, I can always help you – if it is something that can be helped. I promise nothing."

He opened the door. She must find out now what she most wanted to know, before it was too late.

"What have you done to me?" she cried. "Why have I no sorrow left for Chuck – for anything at all? Tell me; I almost see, yet I can't see. Before you go – tell me who you are!"

"Who am I?..." His worn suit paused in the doorway. His round, pale face seemed to dissolve into two faces, a dozen faces, a score, each one different yet the same – sad, happy, tragic, indifferent, resigned – until threescore Doctor Moons were ranged like an infinite series of reflections, like months stretching into the vista of the past.

"Who am I?" he repeated. "I am five years."

The door closed.

At six o'clock Charles Hemple came home, and as usual Luella met him in the hall. Except that now his hair was dead white, his long illness of two years had left no mark upon him. Luella herself was more noticeably changed – she was a little stouter, and there were those lines around her eyes that had come when Chuck died one evening back in 1921. But she was still lovely, and there was a mature kindness about her face at twenty-eight, as if suffering had touched her only reluctantly and then hurried away.

"Ede and her husband are coming to dinner," she said. "I've got theatre tickets, but if you're tired, I don't care whether we go or not."

"I'd like to go."

She looked at him.

"You wouldn't."

"I really would."

"We'll see how you feel after dinner."

He put his arm around her waist. Together they walked into the nursery where the two children were waiting up to say goodnight.

Hot and Cold Blood

I

ONE DAY WHEN THE YOUNG MATHERS had been married for about a year, Jaqueline walked into the rooms of the hardware brokerage which her husband carried on with more than average success. At the open door of the inner office she stopped and said: "Oh, excuse me..." She had interrupted an apparently trivial yet somehow intriguing scene. A young man named Bronson whom she knew slightly was standing with her husband; the latter had risen from his desk. Bronson seized her husband's hand and shook it earnestly – something more than earnestly. When they heard Jaqueline's step in the doorway both men turned and Jaqueline saw that Bronson's eyes were red.

A moment later he came out, passing her with a somewhat embarrassed "How do you do?" She walked into her husband's office.

"What was Ed Bronson doing here?" she demanded curiously, and at once.

Jim Mather smiled at her, half-shutting his grey eyes, and drew her quietly to a sitting position on his desk.

"He just dropped in for a minute," he answered easily. "How's everything at home?"

"All right." She looked at him with curiosity. "What did he want?" she insisted.

"Oh, he just wanted to see me about something."

"What?"

"Oh, just something. Business."

"Why were his eyes red?"

"Were they?" He looked at her innocently – and then suddenly they both began to laugh. Jaqueline rose and walked around the desk and plumped down into his swivel chair.

"You might as well tell me," she announced cheerfully, "because I'm going to stay right here till you do."

"Well..." he hesitated, frowning. "He wanted me to do him a little favour."

Then Jaqueline understood – or rather her mind leapt half-accidentally to the truth.

"Oh." Her voice tightened a little. "You've been lending him some money."

"Only a little."

"How much?"

"Only three hundred."

"*Only* three hundred." The voice was of the texture of Bessemer cooled.* "How much do we spend a month, Jim?"

"Why... why, about five or six hundred, I guess." He shifted uneasily. "Listen, Jack. Bronson'll pay that back. He's in a little trouble. He's made a mistake about a girl out in Woodmere—"

"And he knows you're famous for being an easy mark, so he comes to you," interrupted Jaqueline.

"No." He denied this formally.

"Don't you suppose I could use that three hundred dollars?" she demanded. "How about that trip to New York we couldn't afford last November?"

The lingering smile faded from Mather's face. He went over and shut the door to the outer office.

"Listen, Jack," he began, "you don't understand this. Bronson's one of the men I eat lunch with almost every day. We used to play together when we were kids – we went to school together. Don't you see that I'm just the person he'd be right to come to in trouble? And that's just why I couldn't refuse."

Jaqueline gave her shoulders a twist as if to shake off this reasoning.

"Well," she answered decidedly, "all I know is that he's no good. He's always lit and if he doesn't choose to work he has no business living off the work you do."

They were sitting now on either side of the desk, each having adopted the attitude of one talking to a child. They began their sentences with "Listen!" and their faces wore expressions of rather tried patience.

"If you can't understand, I can't tell you," Mather concluded, at the end of fifteen minutes, on what was, for him, an irritated key. "Such obligations do happen to exist sometimes among men and they have to be met. It's more complicated than just refusing to lend money – especially in a business like mine where so much depends on the goodwill of men downtown."

Mather was putting on his coat as he said this. He was going home with her on the streetcar to lunch. They were between automobiles – they had sold their old one and were going to get a new one in the spring.

Now the streetcar, on this particular day, was distinctly unfortunate. The argument in the office might have been forgotten under other circumstances, but what followed irritated the scratch until it became a serious temperamental infection.

They found a seat near the front of the car. It was late February and an eager, unpunctilious sun was turning the scrawny street snow into dirty cheerful rivulets that echoed in the gutters. Because of this the car was less full than usual – there was no one standing. The motorman had even opened his window and a yellow breeze was blowing the late breath of winter from the car.

It occurred pleasurably to Jaqueline that her husband sitting beside her was handsome and kind above other men. It was silly to try to change him. Perhaps Bronson might return the money after all, and anyhow three hundred dollars wasn't a fortune. Of course he had no business doing it – but then—

Her musings were interrupted as an eddy of passengers pushed up the aisle. Jaqueline wished they'd put their hands over their mouths when they coughed, and she hoped that Jim would get a new machine pretty soon. You couldn't tell what disease you'd run into in these trolleys.

She turned to Jim to discuss the subject – but Jim had stood up and was offering his seat to a woman who had been standing beside him in the aisle. The woman, without so much as a grunt, sat down. Jaqueline frowned.

The woman was about fifty and enormous. When she first sat down she was content merely to fill the unoccupied part of the seat, but after a moment she began to expand and to spread her great rolls of fat over a larger and larger area until the process took on the aspect of violent trespassing. When the car rocked in Jaqueline's direction the woman slid with it, but when it rocked back she managed by some exercise of ingenuity to dig in and hold the ground won.

Jaqueline caught her husband's eye – he was swaying on a strap – and in an angry glance conveyed to him her entire disapproval of his action. He apologized mutely and became urgently engrossed in a row of car cards. The fat woman moved once more against Jaqueline – she was now practically overlapping her. Then she turned puffy, disagreeable eyes full on Mrs James Mather, and coughed rousingly in her face.

With a smothered exclamation Jaqueline got to her feet, squeezed with brisk violence past the fleshy knees and made her way, pink with rage, towards the rear of the car. There she seized a strap, and there she was presently joined by her husband in a state of considerable alarm.

They exchanged no word but stood silently side by side for ten minutes while a row of men sitting in front of them crackled their newspapers and kept their eyes fixed virtuously upon the day's cartoons.

When they left the car at last Jaqueline exploded.

"You big *fool!*" she cried wildly. "Did you see that horrible woman you gave your seat to? Why don't you consider *me* occasionally instead of every fat selfish washwoman you meet?"

"How should I know—"

But Jaqueline was as angry at him as she had ever been – it was unusual for anyone to get angry at him.

"You didn't see any of those men getting up for *me*, did you? No wonder you were too tired to go out last Monday night. You'd probably given your seat to some... to some horrible, Polish *wash*woman that's strong as an ox and *likes* to stand up!"

They were walking along the slushy street, stepping wildly into great pools of water. Confused and distressed, Mather could utter neither apology nor defence.

Jaqueline broke off and then turned to him with a curious light in her eyes. The words in which she couched her summary of the situation were probably the most disagreeable that had ever been addressed to him in his life.

"The trouble with you, Jim, the reason you're such an easy mark, is that you've got the ideas of a college freshman – you're a professional nice fellow."

II

THE INCIDENT AND THE UNPLEASANTNESS were forgotten. Mather's vast good nature had smoothed over the roughness within an hour. References to it fell with a dying cadence throughout several days – then ceased and tumbled into the limbo of oblivion. I say "limbo", for oblivion is, unfortunately, never quite oblivious. The subject was drowned out by the fact that Jaqueline with her customary spirit and coolness began the long, arduous, uphill business of bearing a child. Her natural traits and prejudices became intensified and she was less inclined to let things pass.

It was April now, and as yet they had not bought a car. Mather had discovered that he was saving practically nothing and that in another half-year he would have a family on his hands. It worried him. A wrinkle – small, tentative, undisturbing – appeared for the first time as a shadow around his honest, friendly eyes. He worked far into the spring twilight now and frequently brought home with him the overflow from his office day. The new car would have to be postponed for a while.

April afternoon, and all the city shopping on Washington Street. Jaqueline walked slowly past the shops, brooding without fear or depression on the shape into which her life was now being arbitrarily forced. Dry summer dust was in the wind; the sun bounded cheerily from the plate-glass windows and made radiant gasoline rainbows where automobile drippings had formed pools on the street.

Jaqueline stopped. Not six feet from her a bright new sport roadster was parked at the kerb. Beside it stood two men in conversation, and at the moment when she identified one of them as young Bronson she heard him say to the other in a casual tone:

"What do you think of it? Just got it this morning."

Jaqueline turned abruptly and walked with quick tapping steps to her husband's office. With her usual curt nod to the stenographer she strode by her to the inner room. Mather looked up from his desk in surprise at her brusque entry.

"Jim," she began breathlessly, "did Bronson ever pay you that three hundred?"

"Why – no," he answered hesitantly, "not yet. He was in here last week and he explained that he was a little bit hard up."

Her eyes gleamed with angry triumph.

"Oh, he did?" she snapped. "Well, he's just bought a new sport roadster that must have cost anyhow twenty-five hundred dollars." He shook his head, unbelieving.

"I saw it," she insisted. "I heard him say he'd just bought it."

"He *told* me he was hard up," repeated Mather helplessly.

Jaqueline audibly gave up by heaving a profound noise, a sort of groanish sigh.

"He was using you! He knew you were easy and he was using you. Can't you see? He wanted *you* to buy him the car and you *did*!" She laughed bitterly. "He's probably roaring his sides out to think how easily he worked you."

"Oh, no," protested Mather with a shocked expression, "you must have mistaken somebody for him—"

"We walk – and he rides on our money," she interrupted excitedly. "Oh, it's rich – it's rich. If it wasn't so maddening, it'd be just absurd. Look here!..." Her voice grew sharper, more restrained – there was a touch of contempt in it now. "You spend half your time doing things for people who don't give a damn about you or what becomes of you. You give up your seat on the streetcar to *hogs*, and come home too dead tired to even *move*. You're on all sorts of committees that take at least an hour a day out of your business and you don't get a cent out of them. You're – eternally – being *used*! I won't stand it! I thought I married a man – not a professional Samaritan who's going to fetch and carry for the world!"

As she finished her invective Jaqueline reeled suddenly and sank into a chair – nervously exhausted.

"Just at this time," she went on brokenly, "I need you. I need your strength and your health and your arms around me. And if you… if you just give it to *every*one, it's spread *so* thin when it reaches me…"

He knelt by her side, moving her tired young head until it lay against his shoulder.

"I'm sorry, Jaqueline," he said humbly. "I'll be more careful. I didn't realize what I was doing."

"You're the dearest person in the world," murmured Jaqueline huskily, "but I want all of you and the best of you for me."

He smoothed her hair over and over. For a few minutes they rested there silently, having attained a sort of nirvana of peace and understanding. Then Jaqueline reluctantly raised her head as they were interrupted by the voice of Miss Clancy in the doorway.

"Oh, I beg your pardon."

"What is it?"

"A boy's here with some boxes. It's COD."

Mather rose and followed Miss Clancy into the outer office.

"It's fifty dollars."

He searched his wallet – he had omitted to go to the bank that morning.

"Just a minute," he said abstractedly. His mind was on Jaqueline, Jaqueline who seemed forlorn in her trouble, waiting for him in the other room. He walked into the corridor, and opening the door of "Clayton and Drake, Brokers" across the way, swung wide a low gate and went up to a man seated at a desk.

"Morning, Fred," said Mather.

Drake, a little man of thirty with pince-nez and bald head, rose and shook hands.

"Morning, Jim. What can I do for you?"

"Why, a boy's in my office with some stuff COD and I haven't a cent. Can you let me have fifty till this afternoon?"

Drake looked closely at Mather. Then, slowly and startlingly, he shook his head – not up and down but from side to side.

"Sorry, Jim," he answered stiffly, "I've made a rule never to make a personal loan to anybody on any conditions. I've seen it break up too many friendships."

"What?"

Mather had come out of his abstraction now, and the monosyllable held an undisguised quality of shock. Then his natural tact acted automatically, springing to his aid and dictating his words, though his brain was suddenly numb. His immediate instinct was to put Drake at ease in his refusal.

"Oh, I see." He nodded his head as if in full agreement, as if he himself had often considered adopting just such a rule. "Oh, I see how you feel. Well – I just – I wouldn't have you break a rule like that for anything. It's probably a good thing."

They talked for a minute longer. Drake justified his position easily; he had evidently rehearsed the part a great deal. He treated Mather to an exquisitely frank smile.

Mather went politely back to his office leaving Drake under the impression that the latter was the most tactful man in the city. Mather knew how to leave people with that impression. But when he entered his own office and saw his wife staring dismally out the window into the sunshine he clenched his hands, and his mouth moved in an unfamiliar shape.

"All right, Jack," he said slowly, "I guess you're right about most things, and I'm wrong as hell."

III

DURING THE NEXT THREE MONTHS Mather thought back through many years. He had had an unusually happy life. Those frictions between man and man, between man and society, which harden most of us into a rough and cynical quarrelling trim, had been conspicuous by their infrequency in his life. It had never occurred to him before that he had paid a price for this immunity, but now he perceived how here and there, and constantly, he had taken the rough side of the road to avoid enmity or argument, or even question.

There was, for instance, much money that he had lent privately, about thirteen hundred dollars in all, which he realized, in his new enlightenment, he would never see again. It had taken Jaqueline's harder, feminine intelligence to know this. It was only now when he owed it to Jaqueline to have money in the bank that he missed these loans at all.

He realized too the truth of her assertions that he was continually doing favours – a little something here, a little something there – the sum total, in time and energy expended, was appalling. It had pleased him to do the favours. He reacted warmly to being thought well of, but he wondered now if he had not been merely indulging a selfish vanity of his own. In suspecting this, he was, as usual, not quite fair to himself. The truth was that Mather was essentially and enormously romantic.

He decided that these expenditures of himself made him tired at night, less efficient in his work and less of a prop to Jaqueline, who, as the months passed, grew more heavy and bored, and sat through the long summer afternoons on the screened veranda waiting for his step at the end of the walk.

Lest that step falter, Mather gave up many things – among them the presidency of his college alumni association. He let slip other labours less prized. When he was put on a committee, men had a habit of electing him chairman and retiring into a dim background, where they were inconveniently hard to find. He was done with such things now. Also he avoided those who were prone to ask favours – fleeing a certain eager look that would be turned on him from some group at his club.

The change in him came slowly. He was not exceptionally unworldly – under other circumstances Drake's refusal of money would not have surprised him. Had it come to him as a story he would scarcely have given it a thought. But it had broken in with harsh abruptness upon a situation existing in his own mind, and the shock had given it a powerful and literal significance.

It was mid-August now and the last of a baking week. The curtains of his wide-open office windows had scarcely rippled all the day, but lay like sails becalmed in warm juxtaposition with the smothering screens. Mather was worried – Jaqueline had overtired herself and was paying for it by violent sick headaches, and business seemed to have come to an apathetic standstill. That morning he had been so irritable with Miss Clancy that she had looked at him in surprise. He had immediately apologized, wishing afterwards that he hadn't. He was working at high speed through this heat – why shouldn't she?

She came to his door now, and he looked up faintly frowning.

"Mr Edward Lacy."

"All right," he answered listlessly. Old man Lacy – he knew him slightly. A melancholy figure – a brilliant start back in the Eighties, and now one of the city's failures. He couldn't imagine what Lacy wanted unless he were soliciting.

"Good afternoon, Mr Mather."

A little, solemn, grey-haired man stood on the threshold. Mather rose and greeted him politely.

"Are you busy, Mr Mather?"

"Well, not so *very*." He stressed the qualifying word slightly.

Mr Lacy sat down, obviously ill at ease. He kept his hat in his hands and clung to it tightly as he began to speak.

"Mr Mather, if you've got five minutes to spare, I'm going to tell you something that… that I find at present it's necessary for me to tell you."

Mather nodded. His instinct warned him that there was a favour to be asked, but he was tired, and with a sort of lassitude he let his chin sink into his hand, welcoming any distraction from his more immediate cares.

"You see," went on Mr Lacy – Mather noticed that the hands which fingered at the hat were trembling – "back in Eighty-four your father and I were very good friends. You've heard him speak of me no doubt."

Mather nodded.

"I was asked to be one of the pallbearers. Once we were – very close. It's because of that that I come to you now. Never before in my life have I ever had to come to anyone as I've come to you now, Mr Mather – come to a stranger. But as you grow older your friends die or move away or some misunderstanding separates you. And your children die unless you're fortunate enough to go first – and pretty soon you get to be alone, so that you don't have any friends at all. You're isolated." He smiled faintly. His hands were trembling violently now.

"Once upon a time almost forty years ago your father came to me and asked me for a thousand dollars. I was a few years older than he was, and though I knew him only slightly, I had a high opinion of him. That was a lot of money in those days, and he had no security – he had nothing but a plan in his head – but I liked the way he had of looking out of his eyes – you'll pardon me if I say you look not unlike him – so I gave it to him without security."

Mr Lacy paused.

"Without security," he repeated. "I could afford it then. I didn't lose by it. He paid it back with interest at six per cent before the year was up."

Mather was looking down at his blotter, tapping out a series of triangles with his pencil. He knew what was coming now, and his muscles physically tightened as he mustered his forces for the refusal he would have to make.

"I'm now an old man, Mr Mather," the cracked voice went on. "I've made a failure – I *am* a failure – only we needn't go into that now. I have a daughter, an unmarried daughter who lives with me. She does stenographic work and has been very kind to me. We live together, you know, on Selby Avenue – we have an apartment, quite a nice apartment."

The old man sighed quaveringly. He was trying – and at the same time was afraid – to get to his request. It was insurance, it seemed. He had a ten-thousand-dollar policy, he had borrowed on it up to the limit, and he stood to lose the whole amount unless he could raise four hundred and fifty dollars. He and his daughter had about seventy-five dollars between them. They had no friends – he had explained that – and they had found it impossible to raise the money...

Mather could stand the miserable story no longer. He could not spare the money, but he could at least relieve the old man of the blistered agony of asking for it.

"I'm sorry, Mr Lacy," he interrupted as gently as possible, "but I can't lend you that money."

"No?" The old man looked at him with faded, blinking eyes that were beyond all shock, almost, it seemed, beyond any human emotion except ceaseless care. The only change in his expression was that his mouth dropped slowly ajar.

Mather fixed his eyes determinately upon his blotter.

"We're going to have a baby in a few months, and I've been saving for that. It wouldn't be fair to my wife to take anything from her – or the child – right now."

His voice sank to a sort of mumble. He found himself saying platitudinously that business was bad – saying it with revolting facility.

Mr Lacy made no argument. He rose without visible signs of disappointment. Only his hands were still trembling and they worried Mather. The old man was apologetic – he was sorry to have bothered him at a time like this. Perhaps something would turn up. He had thought that if Mr Mather did happen to have a good deal extra – why, he might be the person to go to because he was the son of an old friend.

As he left the office he had trouble opening the outer door. Miss Clancy helped him. He went shabbily and unhappily down the corridor with his faded eyes blinking and his mouth still faintly ajar.

Jim Mather stood by his desk and put his hand over his face and shivered suddenly as if he were cold. But the five-o'clock air outside was hot as a tropic noon.

IV

THE TWILIGHT WAS HOTTER STILL an hour later as he stood at the corner waiting for his car. The trolley ride to his house was twenty-five minutes, and he bought a pink-jacketed newspaper to appetize his listless mind. Life had seemed less happy, less glamorous of late. Perhaps he had learnt more of the world's ways – perhaps its glamour was evaporating little by little with the hurried years.

Nothing like this afternoon, for instance, had ever happened to him before. He could not dismiss the old man from his mind. He pictured him plodding home in the weary heat – on foot, probably, to save car fare – opening the door of a hot little flat, and confessing to his daughter that the son of his friend had not been able to help him out. All evening they would plan helplessly until they said good night to each other – father and daughter, isolated by chance in this world – and went to lie awake with a pathetic loneliness in their two beds.

Mather's streetcar came along, and he found a seat near the front, next to an old lady who looked at him grudgingly as she moved over. At the next block a crowd of girls from the department-store district flowed up the aisle, and Mather unfolded his paper. Of late he had not indulged his habit of giving up his seat. Jaqueline was right – the average young girl was able to stand as well as he was. Giving up his seat was silly, a mere gesture. Nowadays not one woman in a dozen even bothered to thank him.

It was stifling hot in the car, and he wiped the heavy damp from his forehead. The aisle was thickly packed now, and a woman standing beside his seat was thrown momentarily against his shoulder as the car turned a corner. Mather took a long breath of the hot foul air, which persistently refused to circulate, and tried to centre his mind on a cartoon at the top of the sporting page.

"Move for'ard ina car, please!" The conductor's voice pierced the opaque column of humanity with raucous irritation. "Plen'y of room for'ard!"

The crowd made a feeble attempt to shove forward, but the unfortunate fact that there was no space into which to move precluded any marked success. The car turned another corner, and again the woman next to Mather swayed against his shoulder. Ordinarily he would have given up his seat if only to avoid this reminder that she was there. It made him feel unpleasantly cold-blooded. And the car was horrible – horrible. They ought to put more of them on the line these sweltering days.

For the fifth time he looked at the pictures in the comic strip. There was a beggar in the second picture, and the wavering image of Mr Lacy persistently inserted itself in the beggar's place. God! Suppose the old man really did starve to death – suppose he threw himself into the river.

"Once," thought Mather, "he helped my father. Perhaps if he hadn't my own life would have been different than it has been. But Lacy could afford it then – and I can't."

To force out the picture of Mr Lacy, Mather tried to think of Jaqueline. He said to himself over and over that he would have been sacrificing Jaqueline to a played-out man who had had his chance and failed. Jaqueline needed her chance now as never before.

Mather looked at his watch. He had been on the car ten minutes. Fifteen minutes still to ride, and the heat increasing with breathless intensity. The woman swayed against him once more, and looking out the window he saw that they were turning the last downtown corner.

It occurred to him that perhaps he ought, after all, to give the woman his seat – her last sway towards him had been a particularly tired sway. If he were sure she was an older woman – but the texture of her dress as it brushed his hand gave somehow the impression that she was a young girl. He did not dare look up to see. He was afraid of the appeal that might look out of her eyes if they were old eyes or the sharp contempt if they were young.

For the next five minutes his mind worked in a vague suffocated way on what now seemed to him the enormous problem of whether or not to give her the seat. He felt dimly that doing so would partially atone for his refusal to Mr Lacy that afternoon. It would be rather terrible to have done those two cold-blooded things in succession – and on such a day.

He tried the cartoon again, but in vain. He must concentrate on Jaqueline. He was dead tired now, and if he stood up he would be more tired. Jaqueline would be waiting for him, needing him. She would be depressed and she would want him to hold her quietly in his arms for an hour after dinner. When he was tired this was rather a strain. And afterwards when they went to bed she would ask him from time to time to get her her medicine or a glass of ice water. He hated to show any weariness in doing these things. She might notice and, needing something, refrain from asking for it.

The girl in the aisle swayed against him once more – this time it was more like a sag. She was tired too. Well, it was weary to work. The ends of many proverbs that had to do with toil and the long day floated fragmentarily through his mind. Everybody in the world was tired – this woman, for instance, whose body was sagging so wearily, so strangely against his. But his home came first and his girl that he loved was waiting for him there. He must keep his strength for her, and he said to himself over and over that he would not give up his seat.

Then he heard a long sigh, followed by a sudden exclamation, and he realized that the girl was no longer leaning against him. The exclamation multiplied into a clatter of voices – then came a pause – then a renewed clatter that travelled down the car in calls and little staccato cries to the conductor. The bell clanged violently, and the hot car jolted to a sudden stop.

"Girl fainted up here!"

"Too hot for her!"

"Just keeled right over!"

"Get back there! Gangway, you!"

The crowd eddied apart. The passengers in front squeezed back and those on the rear platform temporarily disembarked. Curiosity and pity bubbled out of suddenly conversing groups. People tried to help, got in the way. Then the bell rang and voices rose stridently again.

"Get her out all right?"

"Say, did you see that?"

"This damn company ought to—"

"Did you see the man that carried her out? He was pale as a ghost too."

"Yes, but did you hear—"

"What?"

"That fella. That pale fella that carried her out. He was sittin' beside her – he says she's his wife!"

The house was quiet. A breeze pressed back the dark vine leaves of the veranda, letting in thin yellow rods of moonlight on the wicker chairs. Jaqueline rested placidly on the long settee with her head in his arms. After a while she stirred lazily; her hand reaching up patted his cheek.

"I think I'll go to bed now. I'm so tired. Will you help me up?"

He lifted her and then laid her back among the pillows.

"I'll be with you in a minute," he said gently. "Can you wait for just a minute?"

He passed into the lighted living room, and she heard him thumbing the pages of a telephone directory; then she listened as he called a number.

"Hello, is Mr Lacy there? Why – yes, it *is* pretty important – if he hasn't gone to sleep."

A pause. Jaqueline could hear restless sparrows splattering through the leaves of the magnolia over the way. Then her husband at the telephone:

"Is this Mr Lacy? Oh, this is Mather. Why – why, in regard to that matter we talked about this afternoon, I think I'll be able to fix that up after all." He raised his voice a little as though someone at the other end found it difficult to hear. "James Mather's son, I said – About that little matter this afternoon…"

"The Sensible Thing"

I

A T THE GREAT AMERICAN LUNCH HOUR young George O'Kelly straightened his desk deliberately and with an assumed air of interest. No one in the office must know that he was in a hurry, for success is a matter of atmosphere, and it is not well to advertise the fact that your mind is separated from your work by a distance of seven hundred miles.

But once out of the building he set his teeth and began to run, glancing now and then at the gay noon of early spring which filled Times Square and loitered less than twenty feet over the heads of the crowd. The crowd all looked slightly upward and took deep March breaths, and the sun dazzled their eyes so that scarcely anyone saw anyone else but only their own reflection on the sky.

George O'Kelly, whose mind was over seven hundred miles away, thought that all outdoors was horrible. He rushed into the subway and for ninety-five blocks bent a frenzied glance on a car card which showed vividly how he had only one chance in five of keeping his teeth for ten years. At 137th Street he broke off his study of commercial art, left the subway and began to run again, a tireless, anxious run that brought him this time to his home – one room in a high, horrible apartment house in the middle of nowhere.

There it was on the bureau, the letter – in sacred ink, on blessed paper – all over the city, people, if they listened, could hear the beating of George O'Kelly's heart. He read the commas, the blots and the thumb smudge on the margin – then he threw himself hopelessly upon his bed.

He was in a mess, one of those terrific messes which are ordinary incidents in the life of the poor, which follow poverty like birds of prey. The poor go under or go up or go wrong or even go on, somehow, in a way the poor have – but George O'Kelly was so new to poverty that had anyone denied the uniqueness of his case he would have been astounded.

Less than two years ago he had been graduated with honours from the Massachusetts Institute of Technology and had taken a position with a firm of construction engineers in southern Tennessee. All his life he had thought in terms of tunnels and skyscrapers and great squat dams and tall, three-towered bridges that were like dancers holding hands in a row, with heads as tall as cities and skirts of cable strand. It had seemed romantic to George O'Kelly to change the sweep of rivers and the shape of mountains so that life could flourish in the old badlands of the world where it had never taken root before. He loved steel, and there was always steel near him in his dreams, liquid steel, steel in bars and blocks and beams and formless plastic masses, waiting for him, as paint and canvas to his hand. Steel inexhaustible, to be made lovely and austere in his imaginative fire...

At present he was an insurance clerk at forty dollars a week with his dream slipping fast behind him. The dark little girl who had made this mess, this terrible and intolerable mess, was waiting to be sent for in a town in Tennessee.

In fifteen minutes the woman from whom he sublet his room knocked and asked him with maddening kindness if, since he was home, he would have some lunch. He shook his head, but the interruption aroused him, and getting up from the bed he wrote a telegram.

"Letter depressed me have you lost your nerve you are foolish and just upset to think of breaking off why not marry me immediately sure we can make it all right..."

He hesitated for a wild minute and then added in a hand that could scarcely be recognized as his own: "In any case I will arrive tomorrow at six o'clock."

When he finished he ran out of the apartment and down to the telegraph office near the subway stop. He possessed in this world not quite one hundred dollars, but the letter showed that she was "nervous" and this left him no choice. He knew what "nervous" meant – that she was emotionally depressed, that the prospect of marrying into a life of poverty and struggle was putting too much strain upon her love.

George O'Kelly reached the insurance company at his usual run, the run that had become almost second nature to him, that seemed best to express the tension under which he lived. He went straight to the manager's office.

"I want to see you, Mr Chambers," he announced breathlessly.

"Well?" Two eyes, eyes like winter windows, glared at him with ruthless impersonality.

"I want to get four days' vacation."

"Why, you had a vacation just two weeks ago!" said Mr Chambers in surprise.

"That's true," admitted the distraught young man, "but now I've got to have another."

"Where'd you go last time? To your home?"

"No, I went to – a place in Tennessee."

"Well, where do you want to go this time?"

"Well, this time I want to go to – a place in Tennessee."

"You're consistent, anyhow," said the manager drily. "But I didn't realize you were employed here as a travelling salesman."

"I'm not," cried George desperately, "but I've got to go."

"All right," agreed Mr Chambers, "but you don't have to come back. So don't!"

"I won't." And to his own astonishment as well as Mr Chambers's, George's face grew pink with pleasure. He felt happy, exultant – for the first time in six months he was absolutely free. Tears of gratitude stood in his eyes, and he seized Mr Chambers warmly by the hand.

"I want to thank you," he said with a rush of emotion. "I don't want to come back. I think I'd have gone crazy if you'd said that I could come back. Only I couldn't quit myself, you see, and I want to thank you for... for quitting for me."

He waved his hand magnanimously, shouted aloud, "You owe me three days' salary but you can keep it!" and rushed from the office. Mr Chambers rang for his stenographer to ask if O'Kelly had seemed queer lately. He had fired many men in the course of his career, and they had taken it in many different ways, but none of them had thanked him – ever before.

II

JONQUIL CARY WAS HER NAME, and to George O'Kelly nothing had ever looked so fresh and pale as her face when she saw him and fled to him eagerly along the station platform. Her arms were raised to him, her mouth was half parted for his kiss, when she held him off suddenly and lightly and, with a touch of embarrassment, looked around. Two boys, somewhat younger than George, were standing in the background.

"This is Mr Craddock and Mr Holt," she announced cheerfully. "You met them when you were here before."

Disturbed by the transition of a kiss into an introduction and suspecting some hidden significance, George was more confused when he found that the automobile which was to carry them to Jonquil's house belonged to one of the two young men. It seemed to put him at a disadvantage. On the way Jonquil chattered between the front and back seats, and when he tried to slip his arm around her under cover of the twilight she compelled him with a quick movement to take her hand instead.

"Is this street on the way to your house?" he whispered. "I don't recognize it."

"It's the new boulevard. Jerry just got this car today, and he wants to show it to me before he takes us home."

When, after twenty minutes, they were deposited at Jonquil's house, George felt that the first happiness of the meeting, the joy he had recognized so surely in her eyes back in the station, had been dissipated by the intrusion of the ride. Something that he had looked forward to had been rather casually lost, and he was brooding on this as he said goodnight stiffly to the two young men. Then his ill humour faded as Jonquil drew him into a familiar embrace under the dim light of the front hall and told him in a dozen ways, of which the best was without words, how she had missed him. Her emotion reassured him, promised his anxious heart that everything would be all right.

They sat together on the sofa, overcome by each other's presence, beyond all except fragmentary endearments. At the supper hour Jonquil's father and mother appeared and were glad to see George. They liked him, and had been interested in his engineering career when he had first come to Tennessee over a year before. They had been sorry when he had given it up and gone to New York to look for something more immediately profitable, but while they deplored the curtailment of his career they sympathized with him and were ready to recognize the engagement. During dinner they asked about his progress in New York.

"Everything's going fine," he told them with enthusiasm. "I've been promoted – better salary."

He was miserable as he said this – but they were all *so* glad.

"They must like you," said Mrs Cary, "that's certain – or they wouldn't let you off twice in three weeks to come down here."

"I told them they had to," explained George hastily. "I told them if they didn't I wouldn't work for them any more."

"But you ought to save your money," Mrs Cary reproached him gently. "Not spend it all on this expensive trip."

Dinner was over – he and Jonquil were alone and she came back into his arms.

"So glad you're here," she sighed. "Wish you never were going away again, darling."

"Do you miss me?"

"Oh, so much, so much."

"Do you – do other men come to see you often? Like those two kids?"

The question surprised her. The dark velvet eyes stared at him.

"Why, of course they do. All the time. Why – I've told you in letters that they did, dearest."

This was true – when he had first come to the city there had been already a dozen boys around her, responding to her picturesque fragility with adolescent worship, and a few of them perceiving that her beautiful eyes were also sane and kind.

"Do you expect me never to go anywhere" – Jonquil demanded, leaning back against the sofa pillows until she seemed to look at him from many miles away – "and just fold my hands and sit still – for ever?"

"What do you mean?" he blurted out in a panic. "Do you mean you think I'll never have enough money to marry you?"

"Oh, don't jump at conclusions so, George."

"I'm not jumping at conclusions. That's what you said."

George decided suddenly that he was on dangerous ground. He had not intended to let anything spoil this night. He tried to take her again in his arms, but she resisted unexpectedly, saying:

"It's hot. I'm going to get the electric fan."

When the fan was adjusted they sat down again, but he was in a supersensitive mood and involuntarily he plunged into the specific world he had intended to avoid.

"When will you marry me?"

"Are you ready for me to marry you?"

All at once his nerves gave way, and he sprang to his feet.

"Let's shut off that damned fan," he cried. "It drives me wild. It's like a clock ticking away all the time I'll be with you. I came here to be happy and forget everything about New York and time…"

He sank down on the sofa as suddenly as he had risen. Jonquil turned off the fan, and drawing his head down into her lap began stroking his hair.

"Let's sit like this," she said softly. "Just sit quiet like this, and I'll put you to sleep. You're all tired and nervous and your sweetheart'll take care of you."

"But I don't want to sit like this," he complained, jerking up suddenly. "I don't want to sit like this at all. I want you to kiss me. That's the only thing that makes me rest. And anyway I'm not nervous – it's you that's nervous. I'm not nervous at all."

To prove that he wasn't nervous he left the couch and plumped himself into a rocking chair across the room.

"Just when I'm ready to marry you you write me the most nervous letters, as if you're going to back out, and I have to come rushing down here—"

"You don't have to come if you don't want to."

"But I *do* want to!" insisted George.

It seemed to him that he was being very cool and logical and that she was putting him deliberately in the wrong. With every word they were drawing farther and farther apart – and he was unable to stop himself or to keep worry and pain out of his voice.

But in a minute Jonquil began to cry sorrowfully and he came back to the sofa and put his arm around her. He was the comforter now, drawing her head close to his shoulder, murmuring old familiar things until she grew calmer and only trembled a little, spasmodically, in his arms. For over an hour they sat there, while the evening pianos thumped their last cadences into the street outside. George did not move, or think, or hope, lulled into numbness by the premonition of disaster. The clock would tick on, past eleven, past twelve, and then Mrs Cary would call down gently over the banister – beyond that he saw only tomorrow and despair.

III

I N THE HEAT OF THE NEXT DAY the breaking point came. They had each guessed the truth about the other, but of the two she was the more ready to admit the situation.

"There's no use going on," she said miserably. "You know you hate the insurance business, and you'll never do well in it."

"That's not it," he insisted stubbornly. "I hate going on alone. If you'll marry me and come with me and take a chance with me, I can make good at anything, but not while I'm worrying about you down here."

She was silent a long time before she answered, not thinking – for she had seen the end – but only waiting, because she knew that every word would seem more cruel than the last. Finally she spoke:

"George, I love you with all my heart, and I don't see how I can ever love anyone else but you. If you'd been ready for me two months ago I'd have married you – now I can't because it doesn't seem to be the sensible thing."

He made wild accusations – there was someone else – she was keeping something from him!

"No, there's no one else."

This was true. But reacting from the strain of this affair she had found relief in the company of young boys like Jerry Holt, who had the merit of meaning absolutely nothing in her life.

George didn't take the situation well, at all. He seized her in his arms and tried literally to kiss her into marrying him at once. When this failed he broke into a long monologue of self-pity and ceased only when he saw that he was making himself despicable in her sight. He threatened to leave when he had no intention of leaving, and refused to go when she told him that, after all, it was best that he should.

For a while she was sorry, then for another while she was merely kind.

"You'd better go now!" she cried at last, so loud that Mrs Cary came downstairs in alarm.

"Is something the matter?"

"I'm going away, Mrs Cary," said George brokenly. Jonquil had left the room.

"Don't feel so badly, George." Mrs Cary blinked at him in helpless sympathy – sorry and, in the same breath, glad that the little tragedy was almost done. "If I were you I'd go home to your mother for a week or so. Perhaps after all this is the sensible thing—"

"Please don't talk!" he cried. "Please don't say anything to me now!"

Jonquil came into the room again, her sorrow and her nervousness alike tucked under powder and rouge and hat.

"I've ordered a taxicab," she said impersonally. "We can drive around until your train leaves."

She walked out on the front porch. George put on his coat and hat and stood for a minute exhausted in the hall – he had eaten scarcely a bite since he had left New York. Mrs Cary came over, drew his head down and kissed him on the cheek, and he felt very ridiculous and weak in his knowledge that the scene had been ridiculous and weak at the end. If he had only gone the night before – left her for the last time with a decent pride.

The taxi had come, and for an hour these two that had been lovers rode along the less frequented streets. He held her hand and grew calmer in the sunshine, seeing too late that there had been nothing all along to do or say.

"I'll come back," he told her.

"I know you will," she answered, trying to put a cheery faith into her voice. "And we'll write each other – sometimes."

"No," he said, "we won't write. I couldn't stand that. Some day I'll come back."

"I'll never forget you, George."

They reached the station, and she went with him while he bought his ticket...

"Why, George O'Kelly and Jonquil Cary!"

It was a man and a girl whom George had known when he had worked in town, and Jonquil seemed to greet their presence with relief. For an interminable five minutes they all stood there talking; then the train roared into the station, and with ill-concealed agony in his face George held out his arms towards Jonquil. She took an uncertain step towards him, faltered, and then pressed his hand quickly as if she were taking leave of a chance friend.

"Goodbye, George," she was saying, "I hope you have a pleasant trip."

"Goodbye, George. Come back and see us all again."

Dumb, almost blind with pain, he seized his suitcase, and in some dazed way got himself aboard the train.

Past clanging street crossings, gathering speed through wide suburban spaces towards the sunset. Perhaps she too would see the sunset and pause for a moment, turning, remembering, before he faded with her sleep into the past. This night's dusk would cover up for ever the sun and the trees and the flowers and laughter of his young world.

IV

ON A DAMP AFTERNOON in September of the following year a young man with his face burnt to a deep copper glow got off a train at a city in Tennessee. He looked around anxiously, and seemed relieved when he found that there was no one in the station to meet him. He taxied to the best hotel in the city, where he registered with some satisfaction as George O'Kelly, Cusco, Peru.

Up in his room he sat for a few minutes at the window looking down into the familiar street below. Then with his hand trembling faintly he took off the telephone receiver and called a number.

"Is Miss Jonquil in?"

"This is she."

"Oh…" His voice, after overcoming a faint tendency to waver, went on with friendly formality.

"This is George O'Kelly. Did you get my letter?"

"Yes. I thought you'd be in today."

Her voice, cool and unmoved, disturbed him, but not as he had expected. This was the voice of a stranger, unexcited, pleasantly glad to see him – that was all. He wanted to put down the telephone and catch his breath.

"I haven't seen you for… a long time." He succeeded in making this sound offhand. "Over a year."

He knew how long it had been – to the day.

"It'll be awfully nice to talk to you again."

"I'll be there in about an hour."

He hung up. For four long seasons every minute of his leisure had been crowded with anticipation of this hour, and now this hour was here. He had thought of finding her married, engaged, in love – he had not thought she would be unstirred at his return.

There would never again in his life, he felt, be another ten months like these he had just gone through. He had made an admittedly remarkable showing for a young engineer – stumbled into two unusual opportunities, one in Peru, whence he had just returned, and another, consequent upon it, in New York, whither he was bound. In this short time he had risen from poverty into a position of unlimited opportunity.

He looked at himself in the dressing-table mirror. He was almost black with tan, but it was a romantic black, and in the last week, since he had had time to think about it, it had given him considerable pleasure. The hardiness of his frame, too, he appraised with a sort of fascination. He had lost part of an eyebrow somewhere, and he still wore an elastic bandage on his knee, but he was too young not to realize that on the steamer many women had looked at him with unusual tributary interest.

His clothes, of course, were frightful. They had been made for him by a Greek tailor in Lima – in two days. He was young enough, too, to have explained this sartorial deficiency to Jonquil in his otherwise laconic note. The only further detail it contained was a request that he should *not* be met at the station.

George O'Kelly, of Cusco, Peru, waited an hour and a half in the hotel, until, to be exact, the sun had reached a midway position in the sky. Then, freshly shaven and talcum-powdered towards a somewhat more Caucasian hue, for vanity at the last minute had overcome romance, he engaged a taxicab and set out for the house he knew so well.

He was breathing hard – he noticed this but he told himself that it was excitement, not emotion. He was here; she was not married – that was enough. He was not even sure what he had to say to her. But this was the moment of his life that he felt he could least easily have dispensed with. There was no triumph, after all, without a girl concerned, and if he did not lay his spoils at her feet he could at least hold them for a passing moment before her eyes.

The house loomed up suddenly beside him, and his first thought was that it had assumed a strange unreality. There was nothing changed – only everything was changed. It was smaller and it seemed shabbier than before – there was no cloud of magic hovering over its roof and issuing from the windows of the upper floor. He rang the doorbell and an unfamiliar coloured maid appeared. Miss Jonquil would be down in a moment. He wet his lips nervously and walked into the sitting room – and the feeling of unreality increased. After all, he saw, this was only a room, and not the enchanted chamber where he had passed those poignant hours. He sat in a chair, amazed to find it a chair, realizing that his imagination had distorted and coloured all these simple familiar things.

Then the door opened and Jonquil came into the room – and it was as though everything in it suddenly blurred before his eyes. He had not remembered how beautiful she was, and he felt his face grow pale and his voice diminish to a poor sigh in his throat.

She was dressed in pale green, and a gold ribbon bound back her dark, straight hair like a crown. The familiar velvet eyes caught his as she came through the door, and a spasm of fright went through him at her beauty's power of inflicting pain.

He said "Hello", and they each took a few steps forward and shook hands. Then they sat in chairs quite far apart and gazed at each other across the room.

"You've come back," she said, and he answered just as tritely: "I wanted to stop in and see you as I came through."

He tried to neutralize the tremor in his voice by looking anywhere but at her face. The obligation to speak was on him but, unless he immediately began to boast, it seemed that there was nothing to say. There had never been anything casual in their previous relations – it didn't seem possible that people in this position would talk about the weather.

"This is ridiculous," he broke out in sudden embarrassment. "I don't know exactly what to do. Does my being here bother you?"

"No." The answer was both reticent and impersonally sad. It depressed him.

"Are you engaged?" he demanded.

"No."

"Are you in love with someone?"

She shook her head.

"Oh." He leant back in his chair. Another subject seemed exhausted – the interview was not taking the course he had intended.

"Jonquil," he began, this time on a softer key, "after all that's happened between us, I wanted to come back and see you. Whatever I do in the future I'll never love another girl as I've loved you."

This was one of the speeches he had rehearsed. On the steamer it had seemed to have just the right note – a reference to the tenderness he would always feel for her combined with a non-committal attitude towards his present state of mind. Here with the past around him, beside him, growing minute by minute more heavy on the air, it seemed theatrical and stale.

She made no comment, sat without moving, her eyes fixed on him with an expression that might have meant everything or nothing.

"You don't love me any more, do you?" he asked her in a level voice.

"No."

When Mrs Cary came in a minute later, and spoke to him about his success – there had been a half-column about him in the local paper – he was a mixture of emotions. He knew now that he still wanted this girl, and he knew that the past sometimes comes back – that was all. For the rest he must be strong and watchful and he would see.

"And now," Mrs Cary was saying, "I want you two to go and see the lady who has the chrysanthemums. She particularly told me she wanted to see you, because she'd read about you in the paper."

They went to see the lady with the chrysanthemums. They walked along the street, and he recognized with a sort of excitement just how her shorter footsteps always fell in between his own. The lady turned out to be nice, and the chrysanthemums were enormous and extraordinarily beautiful. The lady's gardens were full of them, white and pink and yellow, so that to be among them was a trip back into the heart of summer. There were two gardens full, and a gate between them; when they strolled towards the second garden the lady went first through the gate.

And then a curious thing happened. George stepped aside to let Jonquil pass, but instead of going through she stood still and stared at him for a minute. It was not so much the look, which was not a smile, as it was the moment of silence. They saw each other's eyes, and both took a short, faintly accelerated breath, and then they went on into the second garden. That was all.

The afternoon waned. They thanked the lady and walked home slowly, thoughtfully, side by side. Through dinner too they were silent. George told Mr Cary something of what had happened in South America and managed to let it be known that everything would be plain sailing for him in the future.

Then dinner was over, and he and Jonquil were alone in the room which had seen the beginning of their love affair and the end. It seemed to him long ago and inexpressibly sad. On that sofa he had felt agony and grief such as he would never feel again. He would never be so weak or so tired and miserable and poor. Yet he knew that that boy of fifteen months before had had something, a trust, a warmth that was gone for ever. The sensible thing – they had done the sensible thing. He had traded his first youth for strength and carved success out of despair. But with his youth, life had carried away the freshness of his love.

"You won't marry me, will you?" he said quietly.

Jonquil shook her dark head.

"I'm never going to marry," she answered.

He nodded.

"I'm going on to Washington in the morning," he said.

"Oh—"

"I have to go. I've got to be in New York by the first, and meanwhile I want to stop off in Washington."

"Business?"

"No-o," he said as if reluctantly. "There's someone there I must see who was very kind to me when I was so... down and out."

This was invented. There was no one in Washington for him to see – but he was watching Jonquil narrowly, and he was sure that she winced a little, that her eyes closed and then opened wide again.

"But before I go I want to tell you the things that happened to me since I saw you, and, as maybe we won't meet again, I wonder if... if just this once you'd sit in my lap like you used to. I wouldn't ask except since there's no one else – yet – perhaps it doesn't matter."

She nodded, and in a moment was sitting in his lap as she had sat so often in that vanished spring. The feel of her head against his shoulder, of her familiar body, sent a shock of emotion over him. His arms holding her had a tendency to tighten around her, so he leant back and began to talk thoughtfully into the air.

He told her of a despairing two weeks in New York which had terminated with an attractive if not very profitable job in a construction plant in Jersey City. When the Peru business had first

presented itself it had not seemed an extraordinary opportunity.
He was to be third assistant engineer on the expedition, but only
ten of the American party, including eight rodmen and surveyors,
had ever reached Cusco. Ten days later the chief of the expedition
was dead of yellow fever. That had been his chance, a chance for
anybody but a fool, a marvellous chance—

"A chance for anybody but a fool?" she interrupted innocently.

"Even for a fool," he continued. "It was wonderful. Well, I wired
New York—"

"And so," she interrupted again, "they wired that you ought to
take a chance?"

"Ought to!" he exclaimed, still leaning back. "That I *had* to.
There was no time to lose—"

"Not a minute?"

"Not a minute."

"Not even time for..." She paused.

"For what?"

"Look."

He bent his head forward suddenly, and she drew herself to him
in the same moment, her lips half open like a flower.

"Yes," he whispered into her lips. "There's all the time in the
world..."

All the time in the world – his life and hers. But for an instant
as he kissed her he knew that though he search through eternity
he could never recapture those lost April hours. He might press
her close now till the muscles knotted on his arms – she was
something desirable and rare that he had fought for and made his
own – but never again an intangible whisper in the dusk or on the
breeze of night...

Well, let it pass, he thought; April is over, April is over. There
are all kinds of love in the world, but never the same love twice.

Gretchen's Forty Winks

I

T HE SIDEWALKS WERE SCRATCHED with brittle leaves, and the bad little boy next door froze his tongue to the iron mailbox. Snow before night, sure. Autumn was over. This, of course, raised the coal question and the Christmas question; but Roger Halsey, standing on his own front porch, assured the dead suburban sky that he hadn't time for worrying about the weather. Then he let himself hurriedly into the house, and shut the subject out into the cold twilight.

The hall was dark but from above he heard the voices of his wife and the nursemaid and the baby in one of their interminable conversations – which consisted chiefly of "Don't!" and "Look out, Maxy!" and "Oh, there he *goes*!" punctuated by wild threats and vague bumpings and the recurrent sound of small, venturing feet.

Roger turned on the hall light and walked into the living room and turned on the red silk lamp. He put his bulging portfolio on the table, and sitting down rested his intense young face in his hand for a few minutes, shading his eyes carefully from the light. Then he lit a cigarette, squashed it out, and going to the foot of the stairs called for his wife.

"Gretchen!"

"Hello, dear." Her voice was full of laughter. "Come see baby." He swore softly.

"I can't see baby now," he said aloud. "How long 'fore you'll be down?"

There was a mysterious pause and then a succession of "Don'ts" and "Look outs, Maxy" evidently meant to avert some threatened catastrophe.

"How long 'fore you'll be down?" repeated Roger, slightly irritated.

"Oh, I'll be right down."

"How soon?" he shouted.

He had trouble every day at this hour in adapting his voice from the urgent key of the city to the proper casualness for a model home. But tonight he was deliberately impatient. It almost disappointed him when Gretchen came running down the stairs, three at a time, crying "What is it?" in a rather surprised voice.

They kissed – lingered over it some moments. They had been married three years, and they were much more in love than that implies. It was seldom that they hated each other with that violent hate of which only young couples are capable, for Roger was still actively sensitive to her beauty.

"Come in here," he said abruptly. "I want to talk to you."

His wife, a bright-coloured, Titian-haired girl, vivid as a French rag doll, followed him into the living room.

"Listen, Gretchen" – he sat down at the end of the sofa – "beginning with tonight I'm going to... What's the matter?"

"Nothing. I'm just looking for a cigarette. Go on."

She tiptoed breathlessly back to the sofa and settled at the other end.

"Gretchen—" Again he broke off. Her hand, palm upward, was extended towards him. "Well, what is it?" he asked wildly.

"Matches."

"What?"

In his impatience it seemed incredible that she should ask for matches, but he fumbled automatically in his pocket.

"Thank you," she whispered. "I didn't mean to interrupt you. Go on."

"Gretch—"

Scratch! The match flared. They exchanged a tense look.

Her fawn's eyes apologized mutely this time and he laughed. After all she had done no more than light a cigarette; but when he was in this mood her slightest positive action irritated him beyond measure.

"When you've got time to listen," he said crossly, "you might be interested in discussing the poorhouse question with me."

"What poorhouse?" Her eyes were wide, startled; she sat quiet as a mouse.

"That was just to get your attention. But beginning tonight I start on what'll probably be the most important six weeks of my life – the six weeks that'll decide whether we're going on for ever in this rotten little house in this rotten little suburban town."

Boredom replaced alarm in Gretchen's black eyes. She was a southern girl, and any question that had to do with getting ahead in the world always tended to give her a headache.

"Six months ago I left the New York Lithographic Company," announced Roger, "and went in the advertising business for myself."

"I know," interrupted Gretchen resentfully, "and now instead of getting six hundred a month sure, we're living on a risky five hundred."

"Gretchen," said Roger sharply, "if you'll just believe in me as hard as you can for six weeks more, we'll be rich. I've got a chance now to get some of the biggest accounts in the country." He hesitated. "And for these six weeks we won't go out at all, and we won't have anyone here. I'm going to bring home work every night, and we'll pull down all the blinds and if anyone rings the doorbell we won't answer."

He smiled airily as if it were a new game they were going to play. Then, as Gretchen was silent, his smile faded, and he looked at her uncertainly.

"Well, what's the matter?" she broke out finally. "Do you expect me to jump up and sing? You do enough work as it is. If you try to do any more you'll end up with a nervous breakdown. I read about a—"

"Don't worry about me," he interrupted. "I'm all right. But you're going to be bored to death sitting here every evening."

"No, I won't," she said without conviction – "except tonight."

"What about tonight?"

"George Tompkins asked us to dinner."

"Did you accept?"

"Of course I did," she said impatiently. "Why not? You're always talking about what a terrible neighbourhood this is, and I thought maybe you'd like to go to a nicer one for a change."

"When I go to a nicer neighbourhood I want to go for good," he said grimly.

"Well, can we go?"

"I suppose we'll have to if you've accepted."

Somewhat to his annoyance the conversation abruptly ended. Gretchen jumped up and kissed him sketchily and rushed into the kitchen to light the hot water for a bath. With a sigh he carefully deposited his portfolio behind the bookcase – it contained only sketches and layouts for display advertising, but it seemed to him the first thing a burglar would look for. Then he went abstractedly upstairs, dropped into the baby's room for a casual moist kiss and began dressing for dinner.

They had no automobile, so George Tompkins called for them at six thirty. Tompkins was a successful interior decorator, a broad, rosy man with a handsome moustache and a strong odour of jasmine. He and Roger had once roomed side by side in a boarding house in New York, but they had met only intermittently in the past five years.

"We ought to see each other more," he told Roger tonight. "You ought to go out more often, old boy. Cocktail?"

"No thanks."

"No? Well, your fair wife will – won't you, Gretchen?"

"I love this house," she exclaimed, taking the glass and looking admiringly at ship models, colonial whiskey bottles and other fashionable debris of 1925.

"*I* like it," said Tompkins with satisfaction. "I did it to please myself, and I succeeded."

Roger stared moodily around the stiff, plain room, wondering if they could have blundered into the kitchen by mistake.

"You look like the devil, Roger," said his host. "Have a cocktail and cheer up."

"Have one," urged Gretchen.

"What?" Roger turned around absently. "Oh, no thanks. I've got to work after I get home."

"Work!" Tompkins smiled. "Listen, Roger, you'll kill yourself with work. Why don't you bring a little balance into your life – work a little, then play a little?"

"That's what I tell him," said Gretchen.

"Do you know an average business man's day?" demanded Tompkins as they went in to dinner. "Coffee in the morning, eight hours' work interrupted by a bolted luncheon, and then home again with dyspepsia and a bad temper to give the wife a pleasant evening."

Roger laughed shortly.

"You've been going to the movies too much," he said drily.

"What?" Tompkins looked at him with some irritation. "Movies? I've hardly ever been to the movies in my life. I think the movies are atrocious. My opinions on life are drawn from my own observations. I believe in a balanced life."

"What's that?" demanded Roger.

"Well" – he hesitated – "probably the best way to tell you would be to describe my own day. Would that seem horribly egotistic?"

"Oh, no!" Gretchen looked at him with interest. "I'd love to hear about it."

"Well, in the morning I get up and go through a series of exercises. I've got one room fitted up as a little gymnasium, and I punch the bag and do shadow-boxing and weight-pulling for an hour. Then after a cold bath – there's a thing now! Do you take a daily cold bath?"

"No," admitted Roger, "I take a hot bath in the evening three or four times a week."

A horrified silence fell. Tompkins and Gretchen exchanged a glance as if something obscene had been said.

"What's the matter?" broke out Roger, glancing from one to the other in some irritation. "You know I don't take a bath every day – I haven't got the time."

Tompkins gave a prolonged sigh.

"After my bath," he continued, drawing a merciful veil of silence over the matter, "I have breakfast and drive to my office in New York, where I work until four. Then I lay off, and if it's summer I hurry out here for nine holes of golf, or if it's winter I play squash for an hour at my club. Then a good snappy game of bridge until dinner. Dinner is liable to have something to do with business – but in a pleasant way. Perhaps I've just finished a house for some customer, and he wants me to be on hand for his first party to see that the lighting is soft enough and all that sort of thing. Or maybe I sit down with a good book of poetry and spend the evening alone. At any rate I do something every night to get me out of myself."

"It must be wonderful," said Gretchen enthusiastically. "I wish we lived like that."

Tompkins bent forward earnestly over the table.

"You can," he said impressively. "There's no reason why you shouldn't. Look here, if Roger'll play nine holes of golf every day it'll do wonders for him. He won't know himself. He'll do his work better, never get that tired nervous feeling – what's the matter?"

He broke off. Roger had perceptibly yawned.

"Roger," cried Gretchen sharply, "there's no need to be so rude. If you did what George said, you'd be a lot better off." She turned indignantly to their host. "The latest is that he's going to work at *night* for the next six weeks. He says he's going to pull down the blinds and shut us up like hermits in a cave. He's been doing it every Sunday for the last year; now he's going to do it *every night* for *six weeks*."

Tompkins shook his head sadly.

"At the end of six weeks," he remarked, "he'll be starting for the sanitarium. Let me tell you, every private hospital in New York is full of cases like yours. You just strain the human nervous system a little too far, and *bang!* – you've broken something. And in order to save sixty hours you're laid up sixty weeks for repairs." He broke off, changed his tone and turned to Gretchen with a smile. "Not to mention what happens to you. It seems to me it's the wife rather than the husband who bears the brunt of these insane periods of overwork."

"I don't mind," protested Gretchen loyally.

"Yes, she does," said Roger grimly. "She minds like the devil. She's a short-sighted little egg, and she thinks it's going to be for ever until I get started and she can have some new clothes. But it can't be helped. The saddest thing about women is that, after all, their best trick is to sit down and fold their hands."

"Your ideas on women are about twenty years out of date," said Tompkins pityingly. "Women won't sit down and wait any more."

"Then they'd better marry men of forty," insisted Roger stubbornly. "If a girl marries a young man for love she ought to be willing to make any sacrifice within reason, so long as her husband keeps going ahead."

"Let's not talk about it," said Gretchen impatiently. "Please, Roger, let's have a good time just this once."

When Tompkins dropped them in front of their house at eleven Roger and Gretchen stood for a moment on the sidewalk looking at the winter moon. There was a fine damp dusty snow in the air, and Roger drew a long breath of it and put his arm around Gretchen exultantly.

"I can make more money than he can," he said tensely. "And I'll be doing it in just forty days."

"Forty days," she sighed. "It seems such a long time – when everybody else is always having fun. If I could only sleep for forty days."

"Why don't you, honey? Just take forty winks, and when you wake up everything'll be fine."

She was silent for a moment.

"Roger," she asked thoughtfully, "do you think George meant what he said about taking me horseback riding on Sunday?"

Roger frowned.

"I don't know. Probably not – I hope to Heaven he didn't." He hesitated. "As a matter of fact, he made me sort of sore tonight – all that junk about his cold bath."

With their arms about each other they started up the walk to the house.

"I'll bet he doesn't take a cold bath every morning," continued Roger ruminatively, "or three times a week either." He fumbled in his pocket for the key and inserted it in the lock with savage precision. Then he turned around defiantly. "I'll bet he hasn't had a bath for a month."

II

A FTER A FORTNIGHT OF INTENSIVE WORK, Roger Halsey's days blurred into each other and passed by in blocks of twos and threes and fours. From eight until five thirty he was in his office. Then a half-hour on the commuting train, where he scrawled notes on the backs of envelopes under the dull yellow light. By seven thirty his crayons, shears and sheets of white cardboard were spread over the living-room table, and he laboured there with much grunting and sighing until midnight, while Gretchen lay on the sofa with a book, and the doorbell tinkled occasionally behind the drawn blinds. At twelve there was always an argument as to whether he would come to bed. He would agree to come after he had cleared up everything; but as he was invariably sidetracked by half a dozen new ideas, he usually found Gretchen sound asleep when he tiptoed upstairs.

Sometimes it was three o'clock before Roger squashed his last cigarette into the overloaded ashtray, and he would undress in the darkness, disembodied with fatigue, but with a sense of triumph that he had lasted out another day.

Christmas came and went and he scarcely noticed that it was gone. He remembered it afterwards as the day he completed the window cards for Garrod's shoes. This was one of the eight large accounts for which he was pointing in January – if he got half of them he was assured a quarter of a million dollars' worth of business during the year.

But the world outside his business became a chaotic dream. He was aware that on two cool December Sundays George Tompkins had taken Gretchen horseback riding, and that another time she had gone out with him in his automobile to spend the afternoon skiing on the country-club hill. A picture of Tompkins, in an expensive frame, had appeared one morning on their bedroom wall. And one night he was shocked into a startled protest when Gretchen went to the theatre with Tompkins in town.

But his work was almost done. Daily now his layouts arrived from the printers until seven of them were piled and docketed in his office safe. He knew how good they were. Money alone couldn't buy such work; more than he realized himself, it had been a labour of love.

December tumbled like a dead leaf from the calendar. There was an agonizing week when he had to give up coffee because it made his heart pound so. If he could hold on now for four days – three days...

On Thursday afternoon H.G. Garrod was to arrive in New York. On Wednesday evening Roger came home at seven to find Gretchen poring over the December bills with a strange expression in her eyes.

"What's the matter?"

She nodded at the bills. He ran through them, his brow wrinkling in a frown.

"Gosh!"

"I can't help it," she burst out suddenly. "They're terrible."

"Well, I didn't marry you because you were a wonderful house-keeper. I'll manage about the bills some way. Don't worry your little head over it."

She regarded him coldly.

"You talk as if I were a child."

"I have to," he said with sudden irritation.

"Well, at least I'm not a piece of bric-a-brac that you can just put somewhere and forget."

He knelt down by her quickly and took her arms in his hands.

"Gretchen, listen!" he said breathlessly. "For God's sake don't go to pieces now! We're both all stored up with malice and reproach, and if we had a quarrel it'd be terrible. I love you, Gretchen. Say you love me – quick!"

"You know I love you."

The quarrel was averted, but there was an unnatural tenseness all through dinner. It came to a climax afterwards when he began to spread his working materials on the table.

"Oh, Roger," she protested, "I thought you didn't have to work tonight."

"I didn't think I'd have to, but something came up."

"I've invited George Tompkins over."

"Oh, gosh!" he exclaimed. "Well, I'm sorry, honey, but you'll have to phone him not to come."

"He's left," she said. "He's coming straight from town. He'll be here any minute now."

Roger groaned. It occurred to him to send them both to the movies, but somehow the suggestion stuck on his lips. He did not want her at the movies – he wanted her here, where he could look up and know she was by his side.

George Tompkins arrived breezily at eight o'clock.

"Aha!" he cried reprovingly, coming into the room. "Still at it."

Roger agreed coolly that he was.

"Better quit – better quit before you have to." He sat down with a long sigh of physical comfort and lit a cigarette. "Take it from a fellow who's looked into the question scientifically. We can stand so much, and then – bang!"

"If you'll excuse me" – Roger made his voice as polite as possible – "I'm going upstairs and finish this work."

"Just as you like, Roger." George waved his hand carelessly. "It isn't that *I* mind. I'm the friend of the family and I'd just as soon see the Missus as the Mister." He smiled playfully. "But if I were you, old boy, I'd put away my work and get a good night's sleep."

When Roger had spread out his materials on the bed upstairs he found that he could still hear the rumble and murmur of their voices through the thin floor. He began wondering what they found to talk about. As he plunged deeper into his work his mind had a tendency to revert sharply to his question, and several times he arose and paced nervously up and down the room.

The bed was ill adapted to his work. Several times the paper slipped from the board on which it rested and the pencil punched through. Everything was wrong tonight. Letters and figures blurred before his eyes, and as an accompaniment to the beating of his temples came those persistent murmuring voices.

At ten he realized that he had done nothing for more than an hour, and with a sudden exclamation he gathered together his papers, replaced them in his portfolio and went downstairs. They were sitting together on the sofa when he came in.

"Oh, hello!" cried Gretchen, rather unnecessarily, he thought. "We were just discussing you."

"Thank you," he answered ironically. "What particular part of my anatomy was under the scalpel?"

"Your health," said Tompkins jovially.

"My health's all right," answered Roger shortly.

"But you look at it so selfishly, old fella," cried Tompkins. "You only consider yourself in the matter. Don't you think Gretchen has any rights? If you were working on a wonderful sonnet or a... a portrait of some madonna or something" – he glanced at Gretchen's Titian hair – "why, then I'd say go ahead. But you're not. It's just some silly advertisement about how to sell Nobald's hair tonic, and if all the hair tonic ever made was dumped into the ocean tomorrow the world wouldn't be one bit the worse for it."

"Wait a minute," said Roger angrily. "That's not quite fair. I'm not kidding myself about the importance of my work – it's just as useless as the stuff you do. But to Gretchen and me it's just about the most important thing in the world."

"Are you implying that *my* work is useless?" demanded Tompkins incredulously.

"No. Not if it brings happiness to some poor sucker of a pants manufacturer who doesn't know how to spend his money."

Tompkins and Gretchen exchanged a glance.

"Oh-h-h!" exclaimed Tompkins ironically. "I didn't realize that all these years I've just been wasting my time."

"You're a loafer," said Roger rudely.

"Me?" cried Tompkins angrily. "You call me a loafer because I have a little balance in my life and find time to do interesting things? Because I play hard as well as work hard and don't let myself get to be a dull, tiresome drudge?"

Both men were angry now and their voices had risen, though on Tompkins's face there still remained the semblance of a smile.

"What I object to," said Roger steadily, "is that for the last six weeks you seem to have done all your playing around here."

"Roger!" cried Gretchen. "What do you mean by talking like that?"

"Just what I said."

"You've just lost your temper." Tompkins lit a cigarette with ostentatious coolness. "You're so nervous from overwork you don't know what you're saying. You're on the verge of a nervous break—"

"You get out of here!" cried Roger fiercely. "You get out of here right now – before I throw you out!"

Tompkins got angrily to his feet.

"You – *you* throw me out?" he cried incredulously.

They were actually moving towards each other when Gretchen stepped between them and, grabbing Tompkins's, arm urged him towards the door.

"He's acting like a fool, George, but you better get out," she cried, groping in the hall for his hat.

"He insulted me!" shouted Tompkins. "He threatened to throw me out!"

"Never mind, George," pleaded Gretchen. "He doesn't know what he's saying. Please go! I'll see you at ten o'clock tomorrow."

She opened the door.

"You won't see him at ten o'clock tomorrow," said Roger steadily. "He's not coming to this house any more."

Tompkins turned to Gretchen.

"It's his house," he suggested. "Perhaps we'd better meet at mine."

Then he was gone and Gretchen had shut the door behind him. Her eyes were full of angry tears.

"See what you've done!" she sobbed. "The only friend I had, the only person in the world who liked me enough to treat me decently, is insulted by my husband in my own house."

She threw herself on the sofa and began to cry passionately into the pillows.

"He brought it on himself," said Roger stubbornly. "I've stood as much as my self-respect will allow. I don't want you going out with him any more."

"I will go out with him!" cried Gretchen wildly. "I'll go out with him all I want! Do you think it's any fun living here with you?"

"Gretchen," he said coldly, "get up and put on your hat and coat and go out that door and never come back!"

Her mouth fell slightly ajar.

"But I don't want to get out," she said dazedly.

"Well then, behave yourself." And he added in a gentler voice: "I thought you were going to sleep for this forty days."

"Oh yes," she cried bitterly, "easy enough to say! But I'm tired of sleeping." She got up, faced him defiantly. "And what's more I'm going riding with George Tompkins tomorrow."

"You won't go out with him if I have to take you to New York and sit you down in my office until I get through."

She looked at him with rage in her eyes.

"I hate you," she said slowly. "And I'd like to take all the work you've done and tear it up and throw it in the fire. And just to give you something to worry about tomorrow, I probably won't be here when you get back."

She got up from the sofa and very deliberately looked at her flushed, tear-stained face in the mirror. Then she ran upstairs and slammed herself into the bedroom.

Automatically Roger spread out his work on the living-room table. The bright colours of the designs, the vivid ladies – Gretchen had posed for one of them – holding orange ginger ale or glistening silk hosiery, dazzled his mind into a sort of coma. His restless crayon moved here and there over the pictures, shifting a block of letters half an inch to the right, trying a dozen blues for a cool blue, and eliminating the word that made a phrase anaemic and pale. Half an hour passed – he was deep in the work now; there was no sound in the room but the velvety scratch of the crayon over the glossy board.

After a long while he looked at his watch – it was after three. The wind had come up outside and was rushing by the house corners in loud alarming swoops, like a heavy body falling through space. He stopped his work and listened. He was not tired now, but his head felt as if it was covered with bulging veins like those pictures that hang in doctors' offices showing a body stripped of decent skin. He put his hands to his head and felt it all over. It seemed to him that on his temple the veins were knotty and brittle around an old scar.

Suddenly he began to be afraid. A hundred warnings he had heard swept into his mind. People did wreck themselves with overwork, and his body and brain were of the same vulnerable and perishable stuff. For the first time he found himself envying George Tompkins's calm nerves and healthy routine. He arose and began pacing the room in a panic.

"I've got to sleep," he whispered to himself tensely. "Otherwise I'm going crazy."

He rubbed his hand over his eyes and returned to the table to put up his work, but his fingers were shaking so that he could scarcely grasp the board. The sway of a bare branch against the window made him start and cry out. He sat down on the sofa and tried to think.

"Stop! Stop! Stop!" the clock said: "Stop! Stop! Stop!"

"I can't stop," he answered aloud. "I can't afford to stop."

Listen! Why, there was the wolf at the door now! He could hear its sharp claws scrape along the varnished woodwork. He jumped up, and running to the front door flung it open – then started back with a ghastly cry. An enormous wolf was standing on the porch, glaring at him with red, malignant eyes. As he watched it the hair bristled on its neck; it gave a low growl and disappeared in the darkness. Then Roger realized with a silent, mirthless laugh that it was the police dog from over the way.

Dragging his limbs wearily into the kitchen, he brought the alarm clock into the living room and set it for seven. Then he wrapped himself in his overcoat, lay down on the sofa and fell immediately into a heavy, dreamless sleep.

When he awoke the light was still shining feebly, but the room was the grey colour of a winter morning. He got up and, looking anxiously at his hands, found to his relief that they no longer trembled. He felt much better. Then he began to remember in detail the events of the night before, and his brow drew up again in three shallow wrinkles. There was work ahead of him, twenty-four hours of work – and Gretchen, whether she wanted to or not, must sleep for one more day.

Roger's mind glowed suddenly as if he had just thought of a new advertising idea. A few minutes later he was hurrying through the sharp morning air to Kingsley's drug store.

"Is Mr Kingsley down yet?"

The druggist's head appeared around the corner of the prescription room.

"I wonder if I can talk to you alone."

At seven thirty, back home again, Roger walked into his own kitchen. The general-housework girl had just arrived and was taking off her hat.

"Bébé" – he was not on familiar terms with her; this was her name – "I want you to cook Mrs Halsey's breakfast right away. I'll take it up myself."

It struck Bebé that this was an unusual service for so busy a man to render his wife, but if she had seen his conduct when he had carried the tray from the kitchen she would have been even more surprised. For he set it down on the dining-room table and put into the coffee half a teaspoonful of a white substance that was *not* powdered sugar. Then he mounted the stairs and opened the door of the bedroom.

Gretchen woke up with a start, glanced at the twin bed which had not been slept in and bent on Roger a glance of astonishment – which changed to contempt when she saw the breakfast in his hand. She thought he was bringing it as a capitulation.

"I don't want any breakfast," she said coldly, and his heart sank, "except some coffee."

"No breakfast?" Roger's voice expressed disappointment.

"I said I'd take some coffee."

Roger discreetly deposited the tray on a table beside the bed and returned quickly to the kitchen.

"We're going away until tomorrow afternoon," he told Bebé, "and I want to close up the house right now. So you just put on your hat and go home."

He looked at his watch. It was ten minutes to eight and he wanted to catch the eight-ten train. He waited five minutes and then tiptoed softly upstairs and into Gretchen's room. She was sound asleep.

The coffee cup was empty save for black dregs and a film of thin brown paste on the bottom. He looked at her rather anxiously, but her breathing was regular and clear.

From the closet he took a suitcase and very quickly began filling it with her shoes – street shoes, evening slippers, rubber-soled Oxfords – he had not realized that she owned so many pairs. When he closed the suitcase it was bulging.

He hesitated a minute, took a pair of sewing scissors from a box and, following the telephone wire until it went out of sight behind the dresser, severed it in one neat clip. He jumped as there was a soft knock at the door. It was the nursemaid. He had forgotten her existence.

"Mrs Halsey and I are going up to the city till tomorrow," he said glibly. "Take Maxy to the beach and have lunch there. Stay all day."

Back in the room, a wave of pity passed over him. Gretchen seemed suddenly lovely and helpless, sleeping there. It was somehow terrible to rob her young life of a day. He touched her hair with his fingers, and as she murmured something in her dream he leant over and kissed her bright cheek. Then he picked up the suitcase full of shoes, locked the door and ran briskly down the stairs.

III

B Y FIVE O'CLOCK THAT AFTERNOON the last package of cards for Garrod's shoes had been sent by messenger to H.G. Garrod at the Biltmore Hotel. He was to give a decision next morning. At five thirty Roger's stenographer tapped him on the shoulder.

"Mr Golden, the superintendent of the building, to see you."

Roger turned around dazedly.

"Oh, how do?"

Mr Golden came directly to the point. If Mr Halsey intended to keep the office any longer, the little oversight about the rent had better be remedied right away.

"Mr Golden," said Roger wearily, "everything'll be all right tomorrow. If you worry me now maybe you'll never get your money. After tomorrow nothing'll matter."

Mr Golden looked at the tenant uneasily. Young men sometimes did away with themselves when business went wrong. Then his eye fell unpleasantly on the initialled suitcase beside the desk.

"Going on a trip?" he asked pointedly.

"What? Oh, no. That's just some clothes."

"Clothes, eh? Well, Mr Halsey, just to prove that you mean what you say, suppose you let me keep that suitcase until tomorrow noon."

"Help yourself."

Mr Golden picked it up with a deprecatory gesture.

"Just a matter of form," he remarked.

"I understand," said Roger, swinging around to his desk. "Good afternoon."

Mr Golden seemed to feel that the conversation should close on a softer key.

"And don't work too hard, Mr Halsey. You don't want to have a nervous break—"

"No," shouted Roger, "I don't. But I will if you don't leave me alone!"

As the door closed behind Mr Golden, Roger's stenographer turned sympathetically around.

"You shouldn't have let him get away with that," she said. "What's in there? Clothes?"

"No," answered Roger absently. "Just all my wife's shoes."

He slept in the office that night on a sofa beside his desk. At dawn he awoke with a nervous start, rushed out into the street for coffee and returned in ten minutes in a panic – afraid that he might have missed Mr Garrod's telephone call. It was then six thirty.

By eight o'clock his whole body seemed to be on fire. When his two artists arrived he was stretched on the couch in almost physical pain. The phone rang imperatively at nine thirty, and he picked up the receiver with trembling hands.

"Hello."

"Is this the Halsey agency?"

"Yes, this is Mr Halsey speaking."

"This is Mr H.G. Garrod."

Roger's heart stopped beating.

"I called up, young fellow, to say that this is wonderful work you've given us here. We want all of it and as much more as your office can do."

"Oh God!" cried Roger into the transmitter.

"What?" Mr H.G. Garrod was considerably startled. "Say, wait a minute there!"

But he was talking to nobody. The phone had clattered to the floor, and Roger, stretched full length on the couch, was sobbing as if his heart would break.

IV

THREE HOURS LATER, his face somewhat pale but his eyes calm as a child's, Roger opened the door of his wife's bedroom with the morning paper under his arm. At the sound of his footsteps she started awake.

"What time is it?" she demanded.

He looked at his watch.

"Twelve o'clock."

Suddenly she began to cry.

"Roger," she said brokenly, "I'm sorry I was so bad last night."

He nodded coolly.

"Everything's all right now," he answered. Then, after a pause: "I've got the account – the biggest one."

She turned towards him quickly.

"You have?" Then, after a minute's silence: "Can I get a new dress?"

"Dress?" He laughed shortly. "You can get a dozen. This account alone will bring us in forty thousand a year. It's one of the biggest in the West."

She looked at him, startled.

"Forty thousand a year!"

"Yes."

"Gosh" – and then faintly – "I didn't know it'd really be anything like that." Again she thought a minute. "We can have a house like George Tompkins's."

"I don't want an interior-decoration shop."

"Forty thousand a year!" she repeated again, and then added softly: "Oh, Roger..."

"Yes?"

"I'm not going out with George Tompkins."

"I wouldn't let you, even if you wanted to," he said shortly.

She made a show of indignation.

"Why, I've had a date with him for this Thursday for weeks."

"It isn't Thursday."

"It is."

"It's Friday."

"Why, Roger, you must be crazy! Don't you think I know what day it is?"

"It isn't Thursday," he said stubbornly. "Look!" And he held out the morning paper.

"Friday!" she exclaimed. "Why, this is a mistake! This must be last week's paper. Today's Thursday."

She closed her eyes and thought for a moment.

"Yesterday was Wednesday," she said decisively. "The laundress came yesterday. I guess I *know*."

"Well," he said smugly, "look at the paper. There isn't any question about it."

With a bewildered look on her face she got out of bed and began searching for her clothes. Roger went into the bathroom to shave. A minute later he heard the springs creak again. Gretchen was getting back into bed.

"What's the matter?" he enquired, putting his head around the corner of the bathroom.

"I'm scared," she said in a trembling voice. "I think my nerves are giving away. I can't find any of my shoes."

"Your shoes? Why, the closet's full of them."

"I know, but I can't see one." Her face was pale with fear. "Oh, Roger!"

Roger came to her bedside and put his arm around her.

"Oh, Roger," she cried, "what's the matter with me? First that newspaper and now all my shoes. Take care of me, Roger."

"I'll get the doctor," he said.

He walked remorselessly to the telephone and took up the receiver.

"Phone seems to be out of order," he remarked after a minute. "I'll send Bebé."

The doctor arrived in ten minutes.

"I think I'm on the verge of a collapse," Gretchen told him in a strained voice.

Doctor Gregory sat down on the edge of the bed and took her wrist in his hand.

"It seems to be in the air this morning."

"I got up," said Gretchen in an awed voice, "and I found that I'd lost a whole day. I had an engagement to go riding with George Tompkins—"

"What?" exclaimed the doctor in surprise. Then he laughed.

"George Tompkins won't go riding with anyone for many days to come."

"Has he gone away?" asked Gretchen curiously.

"He's going west."

"Why?" demanded Roger. "Is he running away with somebody's wife?"

"No," said Doctor Gregory. "He's had a nervous breakdown."

"What?" they exclaimed in unison.

"He just collapsed like an opera hat in his cold shower."

"But he was always talking about his… his balanced life," gasped Gretchen. "He had it on his mind."

"I know," said the doctor. "He's been babbling about it all morning. I think it's driven him a little mad. He worked pretty hard at it, you know.

"At what?" demanded Roger in bewilderment.

"At keeping his life balanced." He turned to Gretchen. "Now all I'll prescribe for this lady here is a good rest. If she'll just stay around the house for a few days and take forty winks of sleep she'll be as fit as ever. She's been under some strain."

"Doctor," exclaimed Roger hoarsely, "don't you think I'd better have a rest or something? I've been working pretty hard lately."

"You!" Doctor Gregory laughed, slapped him violently on the back. "My boy, I never saw you looking better in your life."

Roger turned away quickly to conceal his smile – winked forty times, or almost forty times, at the autographed picture of Mr George Tompkins, which hung slightly askew on the bedroom wall.

Note on the Text

The text in the present edition is based on the first edition of *All the Sad Young Men* (1926). The spelling and punctuation have been anglicized, standardized, modernized and made consistent throughout.

Notes

p. 6, *'I'm Sorry, Dear'*: A reference to the popular 1916 song 'I'm Sorry I Made You Cry', composed by N.J. Clesi with lyrics by Harry Tobias.

p. 14, *Rose of Washington Square... In basement air*: From the popular 1920 song 'Rose of Washington Square', composed by James F. Hanley with lyrics by Ballard MacDonald.

p. 17, *Junior League... Assembly*: Charitable organizations, run mainly by upper-class women, aimed at helping the poor.

p. 24, *Celliniesque*: A reference to the Italian Renaissance figure Benvenuto Cellini (1500–71), whose talents included sculpture, painting, music and writing and who recounted his exploits in great detail in his famous autobiography.

p. 49, *'Chin-Chin' and The Count of Luxembourg and The Chocolate Soldier*: 'Chin Chin Chinaman' is a song from the 1896 musical *The Geisha* by Sidney Jones. *The Count of Luxembourg* was a 1909 operetta by Franz Lehár, with a libretto by Basil Hood and Adrian Ross. *The Chocolate Soldier* was a 1908 operetta by Oscar Straus, based on George Bernard Shaw's 1894 play *Arms and the Man*.

p. 85, *the Empire Builder, James J. Hill*: James J. Hill (1838–1916), often referred to as the "Empire Builder", was a successful businessman who oversaw the Great Northern Railway lines.

p. 86, *Alger*: Horatio Alger Jr (1832–99) was a prolific American author of young-adult novels.

p. 90, *Domine, non sum dignus... anima mea*: "Lord, I am not worthy that You should enter under my roof, but only say the word and my soul will be healed" (Latin), from the Ordinary of the Roman Catholic Mass.

p. 91, *Corpus Domini... in vitam æternam*: "May the Body of Our Lord Jesus Christ preserve my soul unto life everlasting" (Latin), also from the Ordinary of the Roman Catholic Mass.

p. 91, *Sagitta volante in die*: "The arrow that flieth by day" (Latin). From Psalms 91:5: "Thou shalt not be afraid for the terror by night; nor for the arrow that flieth by day."

p. 96, *Gloria Swanson... Graustark*: Gloria Swanson (1899–1983) was a famous film star of the 1920s. Graustark was the name of a fictional Eastern European principality in a series of novels by George Barr McCutcheon (1866–1928).

p. 112, *earrings*: Handcuffs.

p. 114, *Guelf*: A Germanic royal dynasty, from which the current Windsor royal family of the United Kingdom is descended.

p. 118, *Hausfrau*: "Housewife" (German).

p. 140, *Bessemer*: A type of steel made by blowing air through molten iron.

Extra Material

on

F. Scott Fitzgerald's

All the Sad Young Men

F. Scott Fitzgerald's Life

Francis Scott Key Fitzgerald was born on 24th September 1896 at 481 Laurel Avenue in St Paul, Minnesota. Fitzgerald, who would always be known as "Scott", was named after Francis Scott Key, the author of 'The Star-Spangled Banner' and his father's second cousin three times removed. His mother, Mary "Mollie" McQuillan, was born in 1860 in one of St Paul's wealthier streets, and would come into a modest inheritance at the death of her father in 1877. His father, Edward Fitzgerald, was born in 1853 near Rockville, Maryland. A wicker-furniture manufacturer at the time of Fitzgerald's birth, his business would collapse in 1898 and he would then take to the road as a wholesale grocery salesman for Procter & Gamble. This change of job necessitated various moves of home and the family initially shifted east to Buffalo, New York, in 1898, and then on to Syracuse, New York, in 1901. By 1903 they were back in Buffalo and in March 1908 they were in St Paul again after Edward lost his job at Procter & Gamble. The *déclassé* Fitzgeralds would initially live with the McQuillans and then moved into a series of rented houses, settling down at 599 Summit Avenue.

This itinerancy would disrupt Fitzgerald's early schooling, isolating him and making it difficult to make many friends at his various schools in Buffalo, Syracuse and St Paul. The first one at which Fitzgerald would settle for a prolonged period was the St Paul Academy, which he entered in September 1908. It was here that Fitzgerald would achieve his first appearance in print, 'The Mystery of the Raymond Mortgage', which appeared in the St Paul Academy school magazine *Now and Then* in October 1909. 'Reade, Substitute Right Half' and 'A Debt of Honor' would follow in the February and March 1910 numbers, and 'The Room with the Green Blinds' in the June 1911 number. His reading at this time was dominated by adventure stories and the other typical literary interests of a turn-of-the-century American teen, with the novels of G.A. Henty, Walter Scott's *Ivanhoe* and Jane Porter's *The Scottish Chiefs* among his favourites; their influence was apparent in the floridly melodramatic tone of his early pieces, though themes that would recur throughout

Fitzgerald's mature fiction, such as the social difficulties of the outsider, would be introduced in these stories. An interest in the theatre also surfaced at this time, with Fitzgerald writing and taking the lead role in *The Girl from Lazy J*, a play that would be performed with a local amateur-dramatic group, the Elizabethan Drama Club, in August 1911. The group would also produce *The Captured Shadow* in 1912, *The Coward* in 1913 and *Assorted Spirits* in 1914.

At the end of the summer of 1911, Fitzgerald was once again uprooted (in response to poor academic achievements) and moved to the Newman School, a private Catholic school in Hackensack, New Jersey. He was singularly unpopular with the other boys, who considered him aloof and overbearing. This period as a social pariah at Newman was a defining time for Fitzgerald, one that would be echoed repeatedly in his fiction, most straightforwardly in the "Basil" stories, the most famous of which, 'The Freshest Boy', would appear in *The Saturday Evening Post* in July 1928 and is clearly autobiographical in its depiction of a boastful schoolboy's social exclusion.

Hackensack had, however, the advantage of proximity to New York City, and Fitzgerald began to get to know Manhattan, visiting a series of shows, including *The Quaker Girl* and *Little Boy Blue*. His first publication in Newman's school magazine, *The Newman News*, was 'Football', a poem written in an attempt to appease his peers following a traumatic incident on the football field that led to widespread accusation of cowardice, compounding the young writer's isolation. In his last year at Newman he would publish three stories in *The Newman News*.

Father Fay and the Catholic Influence

Also in that last academic year Fitzgerald would encounter the prominent Catholic priest Father Cyril Sigourney Webster Fay, a lasting and formative connection that would influence the author's character, oeuvre and career. Father Fay introduced Fitzgerald to such figures as Henry Adams and encouraged the young writer towards the aesthetic and moral understanding that underpins all of his work. In spite of the licence and debauchery for which Fitzgerald's life and work are often read, a strong moral sense informs all of his fiction – a sense that can be readily traced to Fay and the author's Catholic schooling at Newman. Fay would later appear in thinly disguised form as Amory Blaine's spiritual mentor, and man of the world, Monsignor Darcy, in *This Side of Paradise*.

Princeton

Fitzgerald's academic performance was little improved at Newman, and he would fail four courses in his two years there. In spite of this, in May 1913 Fitzgerald took the entrance exams for Princeton, the preferred destination for Catholic undergraduates in New Jersey. He would go up in September 1913, his fees paid for through a legacy left by his grandmother Louisa McQuillan, who had died in August.

At Princeton Fitzgerald would begin to work in earnest on the process of turning himself into an author: in his first year he met confrères and future collaborators John Peale Bishop and Edmund Wilson. During his freshman year Fitzgerald won a competition to write the book and lyrics for the 1914–15 Triangle Club (the Princeton dramatic society) production *Fie! Fie! Fi-Fi!* He would also co-author, with Wilson, the 1915–16 production, *The Evil Eye*, and the lyrics for *Safety First*, the 1916–17 offering. He also quickly began to contribute to the Princeton humour magazine *The Princeton Tiger*, while his reading tastes had moved on to the social concerns of George Bernard Shaw, Compton Mackenzie and H.G. Wells. His social progress at Princeton also seemed assured as Fitzgerald was approached by the Cottage Club (one of Princeton's exclusive eating clubs) and prominence in the Triangle Club seemed inevitable.

September 1914 and the beginning of Fitzgerald's sophomore year would mark the great calamity of his Princeton education, causing a trauma that Fitzgerald would approach variously in his writing (notably in *This Side of Paradise* and Gatsby's abortive "Oxford" career in *The Great Gatsby*). Poor academic performance meant that Fitzgerald was barred from extra-curricular activities; he was therefore unable to perform in *Fie! Fie! Fi-Fi!*, and took to the road with the production in an attendant capacity. Fitzgerald's progress at the Triangle and Cottage clubs stagnated (he made Secretary at Triangle nonetheless, but did not reach the heights he had imagined for himself), and his hopes of social dominance on campus were dashed.

The second half of the 1914–15 academic year saw a brief improvement and subsequent slipping of Fitzgerald's performance in classes, perhaps in response to a budding romance with Ginevra King, a sixteen-year-old socialite from Lake Forest, Illinois. Their courtship would continue until January 1917. King would become the model for a series of Fitzgerald's characters, including Judy Jones in the 1922 short story 'Winter Dreams', Isabelle Borgé in *This Side of Paradise* and, most famously, Daisy Miller in *The Great Gatsby*. In November 1915 Fitzgerald's academic career was once again held up when he was diagnosed with malaria (though it is likely that this was in fact the first appearance of the tuberculosis that would sporadically disrupt his health for the rest of his life) and left Princeton for the rest of the semester to recuperate. At the same time as all of this disruption, however, Fitzgerald was building a head of steam in terms of his literary production. Publications during this period included stories, reviews and poems for Princeton's *Nassau Literary Magazine*.

Ginevra King and Ill Health

Army
Commission

The USA entered the Great War in May 1917 and a week later Fitzgerald joined up, at least partly motivated by the fact that his uncompleted courses at Princeton would automatically receive credits as he signed up. Three weeks of intensive training and the infantry commission exam soon followed, though a commission itself did not immediately materialize. Through the summer he stayed in St Paul, undertaking important readings in William James, Henri Bergson and others, and in the autumn he returned to Princeton (though not to study) and took lodgings with John Biggs Jr, the editor of the *Tiger*. More contributions appeared in both the *Nassau Literary Magazine* and the *Tiger*, but the commission finally came and in November Fitzgerald was off to Fort Leavenworth, Kansas, where he was to report as a second lieutenant in the infantry. Convinced that he would die in the war, Fitzgerald began intense work on his first novel, *The Romantic Egoist*, the first draft of which would be finished while on leave from Kansas in February 1918. The publishing house Charles Scribner's Sons, despite offering an encouraging appreciation of the novel, rejected successive drafts in August and October 1918.

Zelda Sayre

As his military training progressed and the army readied Fitzgerald and his men for the fighting in Europe, he was relocated, first to Camp Gordon in Georgia, and then on to Camp Sheridan, near Montgomery, Alabama. There, at a dance at the Montgomery Country Club in July, he met Zelda Sayre, a beautiful eighteen-year-old socialite and daughter of a justice of the Alabama Supreme Court. An intense courtship began and Fitzgerald soon proposed marriage, though Zelda was nervous about marrying a man with so few apparent prospects.

As the armistice that ended the Great War was signed on 11th November 1918, Fitzgerald was waiting to embark for Europe, and had already been issued with his overseas uniform. The closeness by which he avoided action in the Great War stayed with Fitzgerald, and gave him another trope for his fiction, with many of his characters, Amory Blaine from *This Side of Paradise* and Jay Gatsby among them, attributed with abortive or ambiguous military careers. Father Fay, who had been involved, and had tried to involve Fitzgerald, in a series of mysterious intelligence operations during the war, died in January 1919, leaving Fitzgerald without a moral guide just as he entered the world free from the restrictions of Princeton and the army. Fay would be the dedicatee of *This Side of Paradise*.

Literary
Endeavours

Fitzgerald's first move after the war was to secure gainful employment at Barron Collier, an advertising agency, producing copy for trolley-car advertisements. At night he continued to work hard at his fiction, collecting 112 rejection slips over this period. Relief was close at hand, however, with *The Smart Set* printing a revised version of 'Babes in the Wood' (a short story that had previous appeared in *Nassau Literary Magazine* and that would soon be cannibalized for *This Side of Paradise*) in their September 1919 issue. *The Smart Set*, edited by this time by H.L. Mencken and George Jean Nathan, who would both become firm supporters of Fitzgerald's talent, was a respected literary magazine, but not a high payer; Fitzgerald received $30 for this first appearance. Buoyed by this, and frustrated by his job, Fitzgerald elected to leave work and New York and return to his parents' house in St Paul, where he would make a concerted effort to finish his novel. As none of the early drafts of *The Romantic Egoist* survive, it is impossible to say with complete certainty how much of that project was preserved in the draft of *This Side of Paradise* that emerged at St Paul. It was, at any rate, more attractive to Scribner in its new form, and the editor Maxwell Perkins, who would come to act as both editor and personal banker for Fitzgerald, wrote on 16th September to say that the novel had been accepted. Soon after he would hire Harold Ober to act as his agent, an arrangement that would continue throughout the greatest years of Fitzgerald's output and that would benefit the author greatly, despite sometimes causing Ober a great deal of difficulty and anxiety. Though Fitzgerald would consider his novels the artistically important part of his work, it would be his short stories, administered by Ober, which would provide the bulk of his income. Throughout his career a regular supply of short stories appeared between his novels, a supply that became more essential and more difficult to maintain as the author grew older.

Newly confident after the acceptance of *This Side of Paradise*, Fitzgerald set about revising a series of his previous stories, securing another four publications in *The Smart Set*, one in *Scribner's Magazine* and one in *The Saturday Evening Post*, an organ that would prove to be one of the author's most dependable sources of income for many years to come. By the end of 1919 Fitzgerald had made $879 from writing: not yet a living, but a start. His receipts would quickly increase. Thanks to Ober's skilful assistance *The Saturday Evening Post* had taken another six stories by February 1920, at $400 each. In March *This Side of Paradise* was published and proved to be a surprising success, selling 3,000 in its first three days and making instant celebrities of Fitzgerald and Zelda, who would marry the author on 3rd April, her earlier concerns about her suitor's solvency apparently eased by his sudden literary success. During the whirl of 1920, the couple's *annus mirabilis*, other miraculous portents of a future of plenty included the sale of a story, 'Head and

Success

Shoulders', to Metro Films for $2,500, the sale of four stories to *Metropolitan Magazine* for $900 each and the rapid appearance of *Flappers and Philosophers*, a volume of stories, published by Scribner in September. By the end of the year Fitzgerald, still in his mid-twenties, had moved into an apartment on New York's West 59th Street and was hard at work on his second novel.

Zelda discovered she was pregnant in February 1921, and in May the couple headed to Europe where they visited various heroes and attractions, including John Galsworthy. They returned in July to St Paul, where a daughter, Scottie, was born on 26th October. Fitzgerald was working consistently and well at this time, producing a prodigious amount of high-quality material. *The Beautiful and Damned*, his second novel, was soon ready and began to appear as a serialization in *Metropolitan Magazine* from September. Its publication in book form would have to wait until March 1922, at which point it received mixed reviews, though Scribner managed to sell 40,000 copies of it in its first year of publication. Once again it would be followed within a few months by a short-story collection, *Tales of the Jazz Age*, which contained such classics of twentieth-century American literature as 'May Day', 'The Diamond as Big as the Ritz' and 'The Curious Case of Benjamin Button'.

1923 saw continued successes and a first failure. Receipts were growing rapidly: the Hearst organization bought first option in Fitzgerald's stories for $1,500, he sold the film rights for *This Side of Paradise* for $10,000 and he began selling stories to *The Saturday Evening Post* for $1,250 each. *The Vegetable*, on the other hand, a play that he had been working on for some time, opened in Atlantic City and closed almost immediately following poor reviews, losing Fitzgerald money. By the end of the year his income had shot up to $28,759.78, but he had spent more than that on the play and fast living, and found himself in debt as a result.

The Fitzgeralds' high living was coming at an even higher price. In an attempt to finish his new project Fitzgerald set out for Europe with Zelda and landed up on the French Riviera, a situation that provided the author with the space and time to make some real progress on his novel. While there, however, Zelda met Édouard Jozan, a French pilot, and began a romantic entanglement that put a heavy strain on her marriage. This scenario has been read by some as influencing the final drafting of *The Great Gatsby*, notably Gatsby's disillusionment with Daisy. It would also provide one of the central threads of *Tender Is the Night*, while Gerald and Sara Murphy, two friends they made on the Riviera, would be models for that novel's central characters. Throughout 1924 their relations became more difficult, their volatility was expressed through increasingly erratic behaviour and by the end of the year Fitzgerald's drinking was developing into alcoholism.

Some progress was made on the novel, however, and a draft was sent to Scribner in October. A period of extensive and crucial revisions followed through January and February 1925, with the novel already at the galley-proof stage. After extensive negotiations with Max Perkins, the new novel also received its final title at about this time. Previous titles had included *Trimalchio* and *Trimalchio in West Egg*, both of which Scribner found too obscure for a mass readership, despite Fitzgerald's preference for them, while *Gold-Hatted Gatsby*, *On the Road to West Egg*, *The High-Bouncing Lover* and *Among Ash Heaps and Millionaires* were also suggestions. Shortly before the novel was due to be published, Fitzgerald telegrammed Scribner with the possible title *Under the Red, White and Blue*, but it was too late, and the work was published as *The Great Gatsby* on 10th April. The reception for the new work was impressive, and it quickly garnered some of Fitzgerald's most enthusiastic reviews, but its sales did not reach the best-seller levels the author and Scribner had hoped for.

Fitzgerald was keen to get on with his work and, rather mis- *Paris*
guidedly, set off to Paris with Zelda to begin his next novel. Paris at the heart of the Roaring Twenties was not a locale conducive to careful concentration, and little progress was made on the new project. There was much socializing, however, and Fitzgerald invested quite a lot of his time in cementing his reputation as one of the more prominent drunks of American letters. The couple's time was spent mostly with the American expatriate community, and among those he got to know there were Edith Wharton, Gertrude Stein, Robert McAlmon and Sylvia Beach of Shakespeare & Company. Perhaps the most significant relationship with another writer from this period was with Ernest Hemingway, with whom Fitzgerald spent much time (sparking jealousy in Zelda), and for whom he would become an important early supporter, helping to encourage Scribner to publish *The Torrents of Spring* and *The Sun Also Rises*, for which he also gave extensive editorial advice. The summer of 1925 was again spent on the Riviera, but this time with a rowdier crowd (which included John Dos Passos, Archibald MacLeish and Rudolph Valentino) and little progress was made on the new book. February 1926 saw publication of the inevitable follow-up short-story collection, this time *All the Sad Young Men*, of which the most significant pieces were 'The Rich Boy', 'Winter Dreams' and 'Absolution'. All three are closely associated with *The Great Gatsby*, and can be read as alternative routes into the Gatsby story.

Hollywood   With the new novel still effectively stalled, Fitzgerald decamped to Hollywood at the beginning of 1927, where he was engaged by United Artists to write a flapper comedy that was never produced in the end. These false starts were not, however, adversely affecting Fitzgerald's earnings, and 1927 would represent the highest annual earnings the author had achieved so far: $29,757.87, largely from short-story sales. While in California Fitzgerald began a dalliance with Lois Moran, a seventeen-year-old aspiring actress – putting further strain on his relationship with Zelda. After the couple moved back east (to Delaware) Zelda began taking ballet lessons in an attempt to carve a niche for herself that might offer her a role beyond that of the wife of a famous author. She would also make various attempts to become an author in her own right. The lessons would continue under the tutelage of Lubov Egorova when the Fitzgeralds moved to Paris in the summer of 1928, with Zelda's obsessive commitment to dance practice worrying those around her and offering the signs of the mental illness that was soon to envelop her.

Looking for a steady income stream (in spite of very high earnings expenditure was still outstripping them), Fitzgerald set to work on the "Basil" stories in 1928, earning $31,500 for nine that appeared in *The Saturday Evening Post*, forcing novel-writing into the background. The next year his *Post* fee would rise to $4,000 a story. Throughout the next few years he would move between the USA and Europe, desperate to resuscitate that project, but make little inroads.

Zelda's Mental   By 1930 Zelda's behaviour was becoming more and more
Illness   erratic, and on 23rd April she was checked into the Malmaison clinic near Paris for rest and assistance with her mental problems. Deeply obsessed with her dancing lessons, and infatuated with Egorova, she discharged herself from the clinic on 11th May and attempted suicide a few days later. After this she was admitted to the care of Dr Oscar Forel in Switzerland, who diagnosed her as schizophrenic. Such care was expensive and placed a new financial strain on Fitzgerald, who responded by selling another series of stories to the *Post* and earning $32,000 for the year. The most significant story of this period was 'Babylon Revisited'. Zelda improved and moved back to Montgomery, Alabama, and the care of the Sayre family in September 1931. That autumn Fitzgerald would make another abortive attempt to break into Hollywood screenwriting.

At the beginning of 1932 Zelda suffered a relapse during a trip to Florida and was admitted to the Henry Phipps Psychiatric Clinic in Baltimore. While there she would finish work on a novel, *Save Me the Waltz*, that covered some of the same material her husband was using in his novel about the Riviera. Upon completion she sent the manuscript to Perkins at Scribner, without passing it to her husband, which caused much distress. Fitzgerald helped her to edit the book nonetheless, removing much of the material he intended to use, and Scribner accepted it and published it on 7th October. It received poor reviews and did not sell. Finally accepting that she had missed her chance to become a professional dancer, Zelda now poured her energies into painting. Fitzgerald would organize a show of these in New York in 1934, and a play, *Scandalabra*, that would be performed by the Junior Vagabonds, an amateur Baltimore drama group, in the spring of 1933.

His own health now beginning to fail, Fitzgerald returned to his own novel and rewrote extensively through 1933, finally submitting it in October. *Tender Is the Night* would appear in serialized form in *Scribner's Magazine* from January to April 1934 and would then be published, in amended form, on 12th April. It was generally received positively and sold well, though again not to the blockbusting extent that Fitzgerald had hoped for. This would be Fitzgerald's final completed novel. He was thirty-seven.

Final Novel

With the receipts for *Tender Is the Night* lower than had been hoped for and Zelda still erratic and requiring expensive medical supervision, Fitzgerald's finances were tight. From this point on he found it increasingly difficult to produce the kind of high-quality, extended pieces that could earn thousands of dollars in glossies like *The Saturday Evening Post*. From 1934 many of his stories were shorter and brought less money, while some of them were simply sub-standard. Of the outlets for this new kind of work, *Esquire* proved the most reliable, though it only paid $250 a piece, a large drop from his salad days at the *Post*.

Financial Problems and Artistic Decline

March 1935 saw the publication of *Taps at Reveille*, another collection of short stories from Scribner. It was a patchy collection, but included the important 'Babylon Revisited', while 'Crazy Sunday' saw his first sustained attempt at writing about Hollywood, a prediction of the tendency of much of his work to come. His next significant writing came, however, with three articles that appeared in the February, March and April 1936 numbers of *Esquire*: 'The Crack-up', 'Pasting It Together' and 'Handle with Care'. These essays were brutally confessional, and irritated many of those around Fitzgerald, who felt that he was airing his dirty laundry in public. His agent Harold Ober was concerned that by publicizing his own battles with depression and alcoholism he would give the high-paying glossies the impression that he was unreliable, making future magazine work harder to come by. The pieces have, however, come to be regarded as Fitzgerald's greatest non-fiction work and are an essential document in both the construction of his own legend and in the mythologizing of the Jazz Age.

Suicide Attempt and Worsening Health

Later in 1936, on the author's fortieth birthday in September, he gave an interview in *The New York Post* to Michael Mok. The article was a sensationalist hatchet job entitled 'Scott Fitzgerald, 40, Engulfed in Despair' and showed him as a depressed dipsomaniac. The publication of the article wounded Fitzgerald further and he tried to take his own life through an overdose of morphine. After this his health continued to deteriorate and various spates in institutions followed, for influenza, for tuberculosis and, repeatedly, in attempts to treat his alcoholism.

His inability to rely on his own physical and literary powers meant a significant drop in his earning capabilities; by 1937 his debts exceeded $40,000, much of which was owed to his agent Ober and his editor Perkins, while Fitzgerald still had to pay Zelda's medical fees and support his daughter and himself. A solution to this desperate situation appeared in July: MGM would hire him as a screenwriter at $1,000 a week for six months. He went west, hired an apartment and set about his work. He contributed to various films, usually in collaboration with other writers, a system that irked him. Among these were *A Yank at Oxford* and various stillborn projects, including *Infidelity*, which was to have starred Joan Crawford, and an adaptation of 'Babylon Revisited'. He only received one screen credit from this time, for an adaptation of Erich Maria Remarque's novel *Three Comrades*, produced by Joseph Mankiewicz. His work on this picture led to a renewal of his contract, but no more credits followed.

Sheila Graham

While in Hollywood Fitzgerald met Sheila Graham, a twenty-eight-year-old English gossip columnist, with whom he began an affair. Graham, who initially attracted Fitzgerald because of her physical similarity to the youthful Zelda, became Fitzgerald's partner during the last years of his life, cohabiting with the author quite openly in Los Angeles. It seems unlikely that Zelda, still in medical care, ever knew about her. Graham had risen up from a rather murky background in England and Fitzgerald set about improving her with his "College of One", aiming to introduce her to his favoured writers and thinkers. She would be the model for Kathleen Moore in *The Last Tycoon*.

Among the film projects he worked on at this time were *Madame Curie* and *Gone with the Wind*, neither of which earned him a credit. The contract with MGM was terminated in 1939 and Fitzgerald became a freelance screenwriter. While engaged on the screenplay for *Winter Carnival* for United

Artists, Fitzgerald went on a drinking spree at Dartmouth College, resulting in his getting fired. A final period of alcoholic excess followed, marring a trip to Cuba with Zelda in April and worsening his financial straits. At this time Ober finally pulled the plug and refused to lend Fitzgerald any more money, though he would continue to support Scottie, Fitzgerald's daughter, whom the Obers had effectively brought up. The writer, now his own agent, began working on a Hollywood novel based on the life of the famous Hollywood producer Irving Thalberg. Hollywood would also be the theme of the last fiction Fitzgerald would see published; the Pat Hobby stories. These appeared in *Esquire* beginning in January 1940 and continued till after the author's death, ending in July 1941 and appearing in each monthly number between those dates.

In November 1940 Fitzgerald suffered a heart attack and was told to rest, which he did at Graham's apartment. On 21st December he had another heart attack and died, aged just forty-four. Permission was refused to bury him in St Mary's Church in Rockville, Maryland, where his father had been buried, because Fitzgerald was not a practising Catholic. Instead he was buried at Rockville Union Cemetery on 27th December 1940. In 1975 Scottie Fitzgerald would successfully petition to have her mother and father moved to the family plot at St Mary's. *Death*

Following Fitzgerald's death his old college friend Edmund Wilson would edit Fitzgerald's incomplete final novel, shaping his drafts and notes into *The Last Tycoon*, which was published in 1941 by Scribner. Wilson also collected Fitzgerald's confessional *Esquire* pieces and published them with a selection of related short stories and essays as *The Crack-up and Other Pieces and Stories* in 1945.

Zelda lived on until 1948, in and out of mental hospitals. After reading *The Last Tycoon* she began work on *Caesar's Things*, a novel that was not finished when the Highland hospital caught fire and she died, locked in her room in preparation for electro-shock therapy.

F. Scott Fitzgerald's Works

Fitzgerald's first novel, *This Side of Paradise*, set the tone for his later classic works. The novel was published in 1920 and was a remarkable success, impressing critics and readers alike. Amory Blaine, the directionless and guilelessly dissolute protagonist, is an artistically semi-engaged innocent, and perilously, though charmingly unconsciously, déclassé. His long drift towards destruction (and implicit reincarnation as Fitzgerald himself) *This Side of Paradise* sees Blaine's various arrogances challenged one by one as he moves from a well-heeled life in the Midwest through private school and middling social successes at Princeton towards a life of vague and unrewarding artistic involvement. Beneath Fitzgerald's precise observations of American high society in the late 1910s can be witnessed the creation of a wholly new American type, and Blaine would become a somewhat seedy role model for his generation. Fast-living and nihilist tendencies would become the character traits of Fitzgerald's set and the Lost Generation more generally. Indeed, by the novel's end, it has become clear that Blaine's experiences of lost love, a hostile society and the deaths of his mother and friends have imparted important life lessons upon him. Blaine, having returned to a Princeton that he has outgrown and poised before an unknowable future, ends the novel with his Jazz Age *cogito*: "'I know myself,' he cried, 'but that is all.'"

Flappers and Philosophers

Fitzgerald's next publication would continue this disquisition on his era and peers: *Flappers and Philosophers* (1920) is a collection of short stories, including such famous pieces as 'Bernice Bobs Her Hair' and 'The Ice Palace'. The first of these tells the tale of Bernice, who visits her cousin Marjorie only to find herself rejected for being a stop on Marjorie's social activities. Realizing that she can't rid herself of Bernice, Marjorie decides to coach her to become a young femme fatale like herself – and Bernice is quickly a hit with the town boys. Too much of a hit though, and Marjorie takes her revenge by persuading Bernice that it would be to her social advantage to bob her hair. It turns out not to be and Bernice leaves the town embarrassed, but not before cutting off Marjorie's pigtails in her sleep and taking them with her to the station.

The Beautiful and Damned

The Beautiful and Damned (1922) would follow, another novel that featured a thinly disguised portrait of Fitzgerald in the figure of the main character, Anthony Patch. He was joined by a fictionalized version of Fitzgerald's new wife Zelda, whom the author married as *This Side of Paradise* went to press. The couple are here depicted on a rapidly downward course that both mirrored and predicted the Fitzgeralds' own trajectory. Patch is the heir apparent of his reforming grandfather's sizable fortune but lives a life of dissolution in the city, promising that he'll find gainful employment. He marries Gloria Gilbert, a great but turbulent beauty, and they gradually descend into alcoholism, wasting what little capital Anthony has on high living and escapades. When his grandfather walks in on a scene of debauchery, Anthony is disinherited and the Patches' decline quickens. When the grandfather dies, Anthony embarks on a legal case to reclaim the money from the good causes to which it has been donated and wins their case, although not before Anthony has lost his mind and Gloria her beauty.

Another volume of short stories, *Tales of the Jazz Age*, was published later in the same year, in accordance with Scribner's policy of quickly following successful novels with moneymaking collections of short stories. Throughout this period Fitzgerald was gaining for himself a reputation as America's premier short-story writer, producing fiction for a selection of high-profile "glossy" magazines and earning unparalleled fees for his efforts. The opportunities and the pressures of this commercial work, coupled with Fitzgerald's continued profligacy, led to a certain unevenness in his short fiction. This unevenness is clearly present in *Tales of the Jazz Age*, with some of Fitzgerald's very best work appearing beside some fairly average pieces. Among the great works were 'The Diamond as Big as the Ritz' and the novella 'May Day'. The first of these tells the story of the Washingtons, a family that live in seclusion in the wilds of Montana on top of a mountain made of solid diamond. The necessity of keeping the source of their wealth hidden from all makes the Washingtons' lives a singular mixture of great privilege and isolation; friends that visit the children are briefly treated to luxury beyond their imagining and are then executed to secure the secrecy of the Washington diamond. When young Percy's friend John T. Unger makes a visit during the summer vacation their unusual lifestyle and their diamond are lost for ever.

Tales of the Jazz Age

The novella 'May Day' is very different in style and execution, but deals with some of the same issues, in particular the exigencies of American capitalism in the aftermath of the Great War. It offers a panorama of Manhattan's post-war social order as the anti-communist May Day Riots of 1919 unfold. A group of privileged Yale alumni enjoy the May Day ball and bicker about their love interests, while ex-soldiers drift around the edges of their world.

In spite of the apparent success that Fitzgerald was experiencing by this time, his next novel came with greater difficulty than his first four volumes. *The Great Gatsby* is the story of Jay Gatsby, born poor as James Gatz, an *arriviste* of mysterious origins who sets himself up in high style on Long Island's north shore only to find disappointment and his demise there. Like Fitzgerald, and some of his other characters, including Anthony Patch, Gatsby falls in love during the war, this time with Daisy Miller. Following Gatsby's departure, however, Daisy marries the greatly wealthy Tom Buchanan, which convinces Gatsby that he lost her only because of his penuriousness.

The Great Gatsby

Following this, Gatsby builds himself a fortune comparable to Buchanan's through mysterious and proscribed means and, five years after Daisy broke off their relations, uses his new-found wealth to throw a series of parties from an enormous house across the water from Buchanan's Long Island pile. His intention is to impress his near neighbour Daisy with the lavishness of his entertainments, but he miscalculates and the "old money" Buchanans stay away, not attracted by Gatsby's *parvenu* antics. Instead Gatsby approaches Nick Carraway, the novel's narrator (who took that role in one of the masterstrokes of the late stages of the novel's revision), Daisy's cousin and Gatsby's neighbour. Daisy is initially affected by Gatsby's devotion, to the extent that she agrees to leave Buchanan, but once Buchanan reveals Gatsby's criminal source of income she has second thoughts. Daisy, shocked by this revelation, accidentally kills Buchanan's mistress Myrtle in a hit-and-run accident with Gatsby in the car and returns to Buchanan, leaving Gatsby waiting for her answer. Buchanan then lets Myrtle's husband believe that Gatsby was driving the car and the husband shoots him, leaving him floating in the unused swimming pool of his great estate.

All the Sad Young Men

Of *All the Sad Young Men* (1926) the most well-known pieces are 'The Rich Boy', 'Winter Dreams' and 'Absolution'. All three have much in common with *The Great Gatsby*, in terms of the themes dealt with and the characters developed. 'The Rich Boy' centres on the rich young bachelor Anson Hunter, who has romantic dalliances with women, but never marries and grows increasingly lonely. 'Winter Dreams' tells the tale of Dexter Green and Judy Jones, similar characters to Jay Gatsby and Daisy Miller. Much like Gatsby, Green raises himself from nothing with the intention of winning Jones's affections. And, like Gatsby, he finds the past lost. 'Absolution' is a rejected false start on *The Great Gatsby* and deals with a young boy's difficulties around the confessional and an encounter with a deranged priest.

The lesser-known pieces are also of merit and develop ideas that have found their way into Fitzgerald's longer fiction. 'The Baby Party', 'The Adjuster', 'Hot and Cold Blood' and 'Gretchen's Forty Winks' all deal with problems faced by young, surburban, middle-class married couples, '"The Sensible Thing"' with the transience of love and the difficulty of reconciling it with professional ambition, and 'Rags Martin-Jones and the Pr-nce of W–les' depicts a successful but world-weary society belle.

'Babylon Revisited' is probably the greatest and most read story of the apparently fallow period between *The Great Gatsby* and *Tender Is the Night*. It deals with Charlie Wales, an American businessman who enacts some of Fitzgerald's guilt for his apparent abandonment of his daughter Scottie and wife Zelda. Wales returns to a Paris unknown to him since he gave up drinking. There he fights his dead wife's family for custody of his daughter, only to find that friends from his past undo his careful efforts.

The next, and last completed, novel came even harder, and it would not be until 1934 that *Tender Is the Night* would appear. This novel was met by mixed reviews and low, but not disastrous sales. It has remained controversial among readers of Fitzgerald and is hailed by some as his masterpiece and others as an aesthetic failure. The plotting is less finely wrought than the far leaner *The Great Gatsby*, and apparent chronological inconsistencies and longueurs have put off some readers. The unremitting detail of Dick Diver's descent, however, is unmatched in Fitzgerald's oeuvre. *Tender Is the Night*

It begins with an impressive set-piece description of life on the Riviera during the summer of 1925. There Rosemary Hoyt, modelled on the real-life actress Lois Moran, meets Dick and Nicole Driver, and becomes infatuated with Dick. It is then revealed that Dick had been a successful psychiatrist and had met Nicole when she was his patient, being treated in the aftermath of being raped by her father. Now Dick is finding it difficult to maintain his research interests in the social whirl that Nicole's money has thrust him into. Dick is forced out of a Swiss clinic for his unreliability and incipient alcoholism. Later Dick consummates his relationship with Rosemary on a trip to Rome, and gets beaten by police after drunkenly involving himself in a fight. When the Divers return to the Riviera Dick drinks more and Nicole leaves him for Tommy Barban, a French-American mercenary soldier (based on Zelda's Riviera beau Édouard Jozan). Dick returns to America, where he becomes a provincial doctor and disappears.

The "Pat Hobby" stories are the most remarkable product of Fitzgerald's time in Hollywood to see publication during the author's lifetime. Seventeen stories appeared in all, in consecutive issues of *Esquire* through 1940 and 1941. Hobby is a squalid Hollywood hack fallen upon hard times and with the days of his great success, measured by on-screen credits, some years behind him. He is a generally unsympathetic character and most of the stories depict him in unflattering situations, saving his own skin at the expense of those around him. It speaks to the hardiness of Fitzgerald's talent that even at this late stage he was able to make a character as amoral as Hobby vivid and engaging on the page. The Hobby stories are all short, evidencing Fitzgerald's skill in his later career at compressing storylines that would previously have been extrapolated far further. *Pat Hobby Stories*

*The Last
Tycoon*   Fitzgerald's final project was *The Last Tycoon*, a work which, in the partial and provisional version that was published after the author's death, has all the hallmarks of a quite remarkable work. The written portion of the novel, which it seems likely would have been rewritten extensively before publication (in accordance with Fitzgerald's previous practice), is a classic conjuring of the golden age of Hollywood through an ambiguous and suspenseful story of love and money. The notes that follow the completed portion of *The Last Tycoon* suggest that the story would have developed in a much more melodramatic direction, with Stahr embarking on transcontinental business trips, losing his edge, ordering a series of murders and dying in an aeroplane crash. If the rewrites around *Tender Is the Night* are anything to go by, it seems likely that Fitzgerald would have toned down Stahr's adventures before finishing the story: in the earlier novel stories of matricide and other violent moments had survived a number of early drafts, only to be cut before the book took its final form.

– Richard Parker

Select Bibliography

Standard Edition:
The Cambridge University Press edition (2007) of *All the Sad Young Men*, with extensive annotations, variants and background material, is the most authoritative edition to date.

Biographies:
Bruccoli, Matthew J., *Some Sort of Epic Grandeur: The Life of F. Scott Fitzgerald*, 2nd edn. (Columbia, SC: University of South Carolina Press, 2002)
Mizener, Arthur, *The Far Side of Paradise: A Biography of F. Scott Fitzgerald*, (Boston, MS: Houghton Mifflin, 1951)
Turnbull, Andrew, *Scott Fitzgerald* (Harmondsworth: Penguin, 1970)

Additional Recommended Background Material:
Curnutt, Kirk, ed., *A Historical Guide to F. Scott Fitzgerald* (Oxford: Oxford University Press, 2004)
Prigozy, Ruth, ed., *The Cambridge Companion to F. Scott Fitzgerald* (Cambridge: Cambridge University Press, 2002)

ALMA CLASSICS

ALMA CLASSICS aims to publish mainstream and lesser-known European classics in an innovative and striking way, while employing the highest editorial and production standards. By way of a unique approach the range offers much more, both visually and textually, than readers have come to expect from contemporary classics publishing.

～

To order any of our titles and for up-to-date information about our current and forthcoming publications, please visit our website at:

www.almaclassics.com